Darkness
Falling

A Novel *of* the Great Famine

Darkness Falling

PATRICK MACDONALD

Dedication

For Mum

'Love looks not with the eyes, but with the mind.'

(Shakespeare, *A Midsummer Night's Dream* Act 1, Scene 1)

CHAPTER ONE

Hunger consumed him, driving out all thought other than the urgent need to fill his belly which ached as though a rat was trying to chew its way out. The previous evening, Michael McGuinness had given his two sons the last of a small sack of oatmeal. He had not eaten himself for two days now and nor had his wife Sorcha. Their priority was their two sons and they could not afford to let them starve.

He felt lightheaded and knew he was in no condition to do this, but he had no choice. Michael stood staring up at the cliff face, searching for the areas where most of the gulls' nests seemed to be sited. He spotted a ledge about halfway up on which sat at least a dozen nests and searched for the best route to reach it. Much of the cliff face had already been stripped of nests. Men would be lowered down on ropes to reach the more accessible nests so what was left was either beyond the reach of a rope or too difficult to climb up to. McGuinness was determined though, and twice previously had managed to scale a section of the cliff to reach some of the unclaimed nests. This was the third time; the route would again be new and require all his skill and nerve to climb. He took a deep breath and started to climb.

As he hauled himself level with the nest, he felt a heavy blow to his neck which almost dislodged him. A different angle would have sent him spinning earthwards. Blood trickled down his neck and back, which were already soaked with sweat despite the cold. He knew the seagull would return for another attack, but there was nothing he could do to defend himself. Gripping an outcrop of rock with his left hand, he reached down into the nest with his right and lifted the first egg which he pushed down into a canvas sack tied around his waist.

He glanced round; gulls weaved and danced around him, dipping their black-tipped wings, their angry cries sawing the air. Turning to look at them was a mistake. He felt another blow to his head and a piercing pain just above his right eye. One of the gulls had used its sharp talons to open a deep wound in his forehead. Blood spilled down into his eye, obscuring his vision. He blinked to try and clear it, using the heel of his right hand to try and wipe the blood away from the eye socket. His heart beating furiously and, still half-blinded, he reached down for another egg, hurriedly stuffing it into the sack while using his hand as a buffer to make sure he didn't damage the first egg. He was now being pelted by shit from the gulls wheeling above him. He collected the remaining two eggs.

There was a second nest on a nearby ledge but to reach it he would have to trust his weight to a thin slab of rock less than half the width of his boot. He eased himself across, hugging the cliff face as tightly as he could. As the ledge took his full weight, he felt it shift beneath him. There was a thin rattle of stones and soil as the slab suddenly tilted downwards. His adrenaline surging, he lunged upwards and grabbed onto another shelf of rock immediately above his head. With a loud roar, the slab beneath him broke away and tumbled to the rocks hundreds of feet below. His grip held for the brief moment it took for his feet to find fresh purchase on the rock face. Relief coursed through him.

He released one of his arms to bring it slowly to his side where he had spotted a fissure in the rock. He used this to provide a more secure handhold, wedging his hand deep into the crack. His legs were trembling. He anxiously searched the cliff face near him for a hand or foothold which would both allow him to move closer to the other nest and to feel more secure. The nest itself was level with his hip. He calculated that if he could shuffle across a little, he might be able to stretch over and reach the eggs. Gazing down, he saw a narrow nub of rock which he thought might serve as a foothold and, more importantly, bear his weight. He very slowly eased out his right hand from the fissure and replaced it with his left hand. He groped with his right hand again for a handhold just above the nest and swung his right foot across onto the nub of rock, hauling himself across, so the nest was now directly in front of him, wedged against his belly. Switching his grip on the rock face to his left hand, he reached into the nest with his right and quickly emptied it into his sack. He now had seven eggs, enough to feed his family for that evening at least. There was still the small matter of getting safely off the cliff face. He gazed up. The top of the cliff was roughly forty feet above him. Angry gulls were still diving and swooping at his back. Slowly, he started to haul himself up.

At the top of the cliff, he lay on his back and stared up at the sky which was a leaden grey. He felt oddly exhilarated but also very tired. Shutting his eyes for a brief second, he felt a wave of exhaustion and almost drifted off. He stood and gazed back down the cliff face. Far below, the sea boiled and roared against the rocks at the base of the cliff. He could just pick out a figure making his way over the sandy beach towards some rocks close to the sea edge. He was carrying a wooden bucket and every now and then, fell to his knees scrambling in the sand and then throwing what he found up into the bucket. There was a glitter from the interior of the bucket which meant it had been half-filled with seawater to keep the shellfish alive and fresh until it could be eaten. He smiled to himself. Whoever it was down there was taking a hell of a risk. It was on Clifton's land and his bailiff, Moran, regularly patrolled the shoreline to keep intruders at bay. If they stumbled across anyone, they fired on them – usually just enough to frighten them off, but once Moran had seriously wounded a man who finally died from his injuries two days later. Still, men were desperate enough to risk it. They were even desperate enough to try and venture out to see to if they could catch some fish using small currachs. These were built with a lattice of timber over which was stretched tarmacked canvas to waterproof it. There was no keel and so steering relied solely on paddles. Two men usually occupied these, but they had little success finding fish as a source of food because on most days both the weather and the dangerous cove the boats were launched from meant only the bravest or most foolhardy ventured out.

He sighed and turned his attention to the sack, opening it to examine the precious eggs that had been so hard won. Fortunately, none had been damaged. They were slightly larger than a hen's egg and were mottled with green and brown markings. Sorcha would be delighted, he thought. He hadn't told her he intended to collect some eggs. He had simply muttered something about seeing if he could get a bit of seaweed down on the shore to make up a broth, knowing how frightened and worried she would have been if he had told her the truth. He would ask his sister Mary to join them for supper as well.

A shaft of light pierced the clouds and he watched as the shadows on the mountains across the bay slowly rolled across the landscape. The mountains were patched with a luminous green which shimmered for a few seconds before dissolving into darkness again. It was magical and he never tired of seeing it. The landscape itself was a bleak affair. He had once heard a soldier remark to his companions that there were no trees to hang a man and scarcely enough soil to bury one either. This was the truth. The land was dominated by the Ox mountains to the north. In the south lay the town of Sligo and the flat slab of Benbulben. To the west and east, a featureless landscape of marsh land, granite rock, and dark scars where the peat had been sliced away for turf fires. Much of the land was riven with streams and bogs, the bogs themselves bordered by black-tipped grasses and thick spikes of sedge. There were bog cottons too, which in the early summer produced a meadow of white tufts shimmering in the breeze.

As cruel as the land was, he also loved it, and if the land was cruel, then so too were people and they were the same wherever you went. The ports were crammed with them fleeing Ireland, desperate to get away and make new lives elsewhere, but Michael knew he would never leave. The sun vanished and darkness fell again. Turning away from the cliff and peering into the gloom he could just make out the dim outline of the white-washed church far in the distance. Sunday would be hard he knew, and he would need to summon up all his courage to face down the priest. He frowned and, leaning forward into the wind, pushed for home.

CHAPTER TWO

Mary woke with a start, gasping for breath. It was still dark but there was a very faint glimmer of light around the edges of the sheepskin hung across the window. She could also hear the first tentative sounds of birdsong welcoming the dawn. It was so cold that if she chose to breathe through her mouth, thick clouds of vapour immediately swirled up into the air above her head. When she had been young, she had found this entrancing and magical; now, she just felt despair.

Like those of her neighbours, her house was of rough unmortared stone, with a roof of crudely laid sheaves of hay, held in place with a lattice of staves. There was a front and rear entrance and one small window. She was luckier than many of her neighbours; her husband had taken care to add a chimney to vent the open fire and had included a second room to serve as their bedroom to give them at least some privacy. Several of the houses around her were more crudely built with a single room and sods of earth for a roof covering rather than hay.

Others were not even of stone but had been built using sods of clay; these were no more than hovels, which seemed to shrink down and merge with the landscape even as you gazed on them. The smoke from their fires emerged from a hole in the thatched roof or, in some cases, was simply vented through an unglazed window.

She was haunted by the same vision or half-dream, one which kept recurring and was at its most powerful when she had just woken up, the remnants of sleep still fogging her mind. She had a vision of walking across the boggier parts of the land near her cottage and struggling not to sink lower and lower into the earth. As she sank calf-deep into the wet clinging mud, a hand would suddenly reach up through the soil and grab her lower leg, pulling her irresistibly down into the ground. Other hands then joined the first one, grabbing her ankles, her legs, and her clothes, the hands and arms sliding over each other like snakes, gripping more and more fiercely. When the wet mud had reached her waist and then finally her shoulders and she could no longer halt her descent, the hands finally released their grip, slithering down into the depths, accompanied by a soft hissing sibilance. There's something about this land, she thought, there's a malevolence there, something evil, something which wants to destroy us all.

The first real failure of the potato crop had been the previous year. She remembered one fine warm autumn day, walking with her husband, Owen, up into the fields to see how the crops were doing and whether now was the time to begin lifting them. It was the smell which struck them first, a horrible smell of rot and decay filling their nostrils and immediately making them gag and retch. The smell had drifted towards them on the breeze and they were yet to have sight of the crops, but they already knew what had happened. A feeling of dread seized them both; they had caught their first glimpse of the fields and had stared in horror at what confronted them. The leaves and stalks of the plants were black and limp, hanging earthwards. Owen had hurriedly dug down with a spade under the roots of the first plant he came to, lifting it into the air and anxiously studying it to see whether the potatoes themselves were unscathed and healthy. They could both see though that they were spoilt, black and pulpy looking. He lifted another plant and this time the tubers appeared to be sound; the potatoes were of a good size and looked firm and plump. He pulled one from the plant and held it in his hand but as he squeezed, it collapsed immediately into pulp. It was the blight. They had seen it before in previous years but never on this scale. As far as they could see, the fields were a blackened mess of decay.

Some of their neighbours appeared to have fared better and their crops seemed sound; they dug up the plump tubers and laid them down in deep pits for storage, covering the potatoes with rushes and clay. When they came to lift them, though, weeks later, almost invariably the entire crop had rotted. That was the start of it. Some potatoes remained from the summer crops, which had already been lifted and stored, but these soon ran out and families were quickly reduced to foraging in the hedgerows and fields for nettles and berries, anything remotely edible to try and stave off the savage pangs of hunger they were now feeling.

A scientific commission set up by the Government in England to investigate why the crop had failed decided the problem was caused by "wet rot." Elaborate instructions were drawn up on how best to combat the problem and circulated through pamphlets and newspapers. Priests were also used, explaining to their congregations the measures that should be adopted; Father McNamara had devoted several sermons to the issue. People were urged to dry the potatoes in the sun, dig new storage pits, and cover and pack the potatoes with a mixture of lime, sand, turf, and sawdust. Rods were also supposed to be inserted to ventilate the pits. Despite all this, the potatoes still rotted. Farmers would take the few potatoes they managed to salvage from their crops and store them in pits in exactly the way instructed to do so by the commission. When the pits were uncovered again, they would then discover that the potatoes had still turned to a black festering mass in the ground.

The scientists also solemnly declared that potatoes, even if partially rotted, were still edible if certain cooking instructions were followed. So, once again, people carefully separated out those potatoes which seemed salvageable, cut out the black spots, grated the potatoes into a tub, and washed and strained the gratings twice. The gratings were then squeezed through cloth and the pulp dried on a griddle over a fire. It was finally mixed with the water used to wash the potatoes and used to make a kind of bread. The bread caused bloody diarrhoea and cramps; some children were so weakened as a result of this that they died.

People suffered cruelly during the first year of the famine. To avoid starvation, many of those with smaller plots of land were reduced to eating the seed potatoes which should have been saved for the spring harvest the following year. Consequently, the yields for both the spring and autumn harvest were only a fraction of what they should have been, and starvation worsened. It was the following year that the real horror started. In early August, the weather turned; every day it rained. The plants which appeared to be flourishing, their small lilac flowers held up to the sun, now sank lower to the earth, beaten down by the heavy, relentless rainfall. Virtually overnight, it seemed entire crops became black and wilted, the stench of their decay drifting on the wind until it seemed all-enveloping.

Everyone had sold all they possessed in a frantic attempt to obtain money to feed their families. Now fever and disease set in.

One morning, Owen was too weak to stir from the bed. He was shivering and complained of a severe headache. Mary laid her hand gently on his brow and it burned beneath her touch. She could already see a faint red mottling on his skin and a terrible fear gripped her. She had seen two of her neighbours with the same symptoms and both had died within a fortnight. Róisín's son Donal had just turned fourteen when he succumbed. Róisín said that when she saw the black between the toes, her heart had stopped; she knew immediately that he had the black fever. Poor Donal had become delirious, tossing and turning without rest in his bed, ranting nonsense, the black haemorrhaging of the blood vessels beneath his skin spreading quickly up his calves and then his thighs. Once the other neighbours found out, the family had been shunned; everyone feared the black fever, and with good reason – very few survived. Róisín had stayed on her own to look after her son, her husband and three other children moving out to take refuge with a cousin in another village. She had died herself within a month of her son's death. Now, it seemed Owen was to suffer the same fate and Mary might herself also succumb. Owen knew he had the black fever and begged Mary to leave him and save herself, but she refused. She bathed him with cool water from the well, cleaned up his vomit, and held him close, hugging him and murmuring softly how much she loved him. Like Donal, Owen lapsed into delirium; several times he tried to struggle to his feet. *Da wants me to go to the market with him*, he would mutter, *I need to get up. We're to take the two pigs with us…they should fetch a fair price and your man needs his rent money. Let me up…I need to get up…*

Owen died a horrible death, but Mary survived. At first, she wished she had died with him, couldn't understand how she had failed to fall sick herself. Soon, she started to feel nauseous; she had little food in any case but what little she did eat she couldn't keep down. She spent days dry heaving, stumbling outside to be sick. It must be the fever, she thought. When her symptoms failed to worsen, she finally realised the truth; she was pregnant.

CHAPTER THREE

I t was on her second visit that Mary finally found the courage to enter the church hall next to the Protestant church. The church itself was an imposing building with grey stonework and a slate roof. Even though it had been built less than a decade ago, it already had an air of permanence. It was so different, she thought, to the village Catholic church with its rough whitewashed walls and badly thatched roof and she had loathed it on sight. It was an arrogant display of wealth. Together with some of the other village children, she had been schooled by the local priest. He had led them here one day and quivering with anger, had pointed at it.

"The same people who built that," he said, "drove out Catholic landowners from the fertile lands in the east of Ireland, and forced them to resettle in the west. The people who built that forced my ancestors to go into hiding to escape execution. That church is built of stone; the English would only allow Catholics to build their churches from wood."

Mary had been just seven years old at the time and she

had smiled shyly at one of the other girls. She could see the priest was angry, but it was lost on her; adults always seemed to be in a permanent lather about something or other. It was just their nature and they couldn't help themselves. Now, she thought back to that day. I can't remember when I last smiled, she thought. I just can't remember.

The hall was at the rear of the church; it was constructed of the same careful neat stonework, topped with a slate roof, but its design was less ornate, a simple box-like shape with two large square windows on each side and a studded oak door with a large iron hoop for a handle. It was as welcoming as the church itself was forbidding but, despite this, Mary hesitated. Father McNamara had warned them all at Mass what the Protestants were about, that they were fishing for souls and the bait was soup; make the mistake of taking it and you would be reeled in and forever lost to the one true faith. Only Catholics would be welcomed in Heaven; all the other false sects would be spurned. To become a Protestant was to risk your immortal soul. Mary had no intention of becoming a Protestant; what she wanted was to save the child in her womb. If she had to dissemble a little to achieve this, surely God would understand? And yet she was frightened.

The first time she had walked over to the church, which was two miles from her cottage, her steps had become slower and slower as she neared it, so that when she was barely fifty feet away, she had suddenly stopped. She stood paralysed, unable to move forward, incapable of turning back. She stared at the ground, her eyes blank and unseeing. Her thoughts spun in an unceasing loop in her head; should I go on? Should I go back? If I don't do this, my baby will perish; if I do it, perhaps I risk both my own soul and the baby's? But this is Owen's child; I owe it to him to try and save this baby, to bring it into the world.

Finally, she had slowly turned and walked away, the permanent ache of hunger in her belly replaced for the moment with a terrible nausea as though her own hands had somehow been plunged into her stomach where they fluttered and swooped like trapped birds.

The following day, she tried again and this time, she forced herself to quicken her pace as she neared the hall, her head down, ignoring both the renewed roiling in her stomach and the fierce wind which leapt around her, pulling at her clothes, tugging her backwards. In the end, she almost fell through the door, wrenching the hooped handle upwards and pushing the heavy door inwards with her arm.

It was the smell that first struck her. She could see a large black cauldron set up on a trestle table at the far end. The smell was rich and sweet and seemed to fill the room; her mouth watered and for a moment she stood transfixed, gazing at it and the long, ragged line of men and women patiently queuing.

"Are you alright Miss?"

Mary looked up, startled. To her side stood a young man, much taller than her and far better dressed than most of the other inhabitants of the hall, many of whom were barefoot, their clothes patched and torn. He was wearing corduroy breeches over grey woollen stockings with polished brogue shoes. He had the sort of face that, once seen, was soon forgotten but his features were transformed when he smiled. He was smiling now as he gazed at her.

"It's just you looked as though you were…would you like me to get you something to eat?"

"Yes…I would…are you sure – shouldn't I queue?"

He smiled.

"You look as though you wouldn't last out the queue…look, sit yourself down, and I'll bring you something."

He gestured to another trestle table close by, a few hinged wooden chairs arranged around it. Most of the seats were full already but there were a couple of vacant places towards the middle and he now gently guided her to one. He pushed back through the crowd and, shortly after, returned with a serving of soup in a tin bowl and a thick hunk of dark bread, which he carefully set in front of her. The soup was delicious, and she fell upon it greedily. It was only after she had gulped down several spoonfuls that she suddenly felt embarrassed and looked up at him.

"I'm sorry – what must you think of me – I…"

"I think you're hungry, is what I think. I'm Simon Mayhew, by the way – I'm one of the volunteers here. And you are?"

"Mary – Mary Hogan. I'm very pleased to make your acquaintance, Simon."

She smiled awkwardly up at him.

"And I yours, Mary."

He hesitated for a second.

"Hopefully, I'll see you again," he said and, nodding briefly, he turned and walked away.

She finished her soup and bread and slowly got up to leave. Apart from Simon, no-one else had approached her. She had thought she might have been set upon by the Reverend or his acolytes, anxious to persuade her to abandon her faith and become a Protestant, but this hadn't happened, and nor had she noticed anyone else being approached either. Perhaps this was purely humanitarian; they were simply good people who were not prepared to stand by whilst others starved.

The following day, she came back, and, this time, stood patiently in the queue. She came back a third day and a fourth and still she was left alone. She was oddly terrified she might spot one of her neighbours there, although if this had been the case, then they would surely have been as embarrassed to see her. There had been a lot of dark mutterings in the village about those who had taken the soup, a particular contempt reserved for them. She still felt ashamed, but, at the same time, she could also feel her strength slowly returning and she was convinced her baby had, once again, started to thrive. She felt well, better able to cope.

On the fifth day, just as she was about to take a seat to eat her soup, she felt a presence behind her. She turned. At her shoulder stood a small, plump man who gazed down at her with a genial smile. He was very red in the face, as though his white collar was somehow choking him.

"It's Mary, isn't it? Simon pointed you out to me when you first came to us. I'm Jeremy…Jeremy Spence."

Mary got awkwardly to her feet and held out her hand, which Spence shook. She noticed, with a little shudder of revulsion, that his handshake was a limp affair and his hand left a smear of sweat on her own. She suppressed the instinct to wipe her hand on her dress.

"I'm very pleased to meet you, sir…what you're doing here is wonderful – I –"

"It's not much but we do what we can – there's a service on Sunday and I was wondering whether you might like to join us? We're always keen to welcome new people into the church –"

"That's very kind of you but I'm not sure I can – I'm Catholic, you see –"

"Yes, I understand…but we do welcome all faiths and creeds – ours is a broad church – we all believe in the same God, after all."

"Yes…yes, of course…but –"

"Look, the service starts at ten – we'd love to see you there but don't worry if you can't make it – perhaps another time."

He smiled and turned away. At the same time, she suddenly became aware that Simon was staring at her from across the hall. She smiled shyly at him and he walked across to her.

"How are you?" he said.

"I'm fine. And, how are you?"

"I'm well – Jeremy didn't upset you, I hope?"

"No, no – he was charm itself."

Simon raised an eyebrow.

"I doubt that – he can be a little…pushy. Look, I know he's asked you to attend the Sunday service but don't feel you have to – it's really not a problem."

"That's very kind of you."

She hesitated and then spoke again.

"It's not that I'm not grateful…it's just that I'm worried – really, I shouldn't be here at all."

"Of course you should…you're hungry…we have food – what could be simpler?"

She looked at the ground.

"If only it were that simple."

"Ah, but it is – it really is."

"In your eyes, perhaps – but not everyone sees it that way."

"Well, I hope you'll come again anyway because I, for one, would be sorry not to see you again."

Mary looked up at him and saw he was blushing. He had obviously said more than he intended to. She blushed herself.

"That's very kind of you – I have to go –"

He stood back a little to allow her to pass and with her head down, she strode out of the hall. She knew he was following her with his eyes, but she was determined not to glance back. So, there it was – not one but two reasons she couldn't go again. First, the damned priest or reverend or whatever he styled himself as, and then this Simon character making eyes at her. And what did she need with another man in her life when she was still in mourning for her husband and pregnant with his child? God give me strength, she thought. Are all men so soft in the head that they have to go around making moon eyes at every woman that so much as smiles at them? Damn them. Damn the pair of them. Both eejits together. What the hell am I supposed to do?

Mary lay awake much of that night trying to decide what was for the best. In the end, she realised she had no choice; what was important was the life of her child, not whether she felt personally uncomfortable with the situation. She would have to make the best of it, perhaps even attending a church service if Spence wouldn't let it go – it didn't mean she had forsaken her faith; it was just a service after all. What harm could there be? As for Simon, well, she was used to dealing with the unwanted attentions of men and she was sure she could manage him without too much trouble.

The following day she went back. To her dismay she saw Simon standing speaking to another man when she entered the hall. He was stood at the far end, but he noticed her immediately and came across.

"Mary…I'm so pleased to see you. I was worried we might have frightened you off."

"Do I look like someone who frightens easily?"

She had spoken more sharply than she intended, and Simon reeled back as though he had been slapped.

"No… no…of course not. I'm sorry – everything I say to you seems to come out wrong. I didn't mean to offend you."

Mary softened.

"It's fine – I'm not offended…and I was a little worried about coming."

"Great…I mean 'Great' you're not offended, not 'Great' you were worried…Before I make an even bigger fool of myself, let me get you some soup. Sit down and I'll bring it over."

He hurried away and Mary smiled to herself. He seemed nice enough and in different circumstances she might well have been interested. She needed to warn him off though and she had decided whilst lying awake exactly how she might manage that.

She stayed standing until he returned. He carefully set the bowl of soup and bread down at a table near her and pulled back a chair so she could sit down. She moved next to him and dropped her voice so no-one near them could hear.

"Thanks Simon, I'm very grateful. I'm not really doing this for myself, you understand – I'm with child."

She blushed as she said it.

"Ah…yes…I see. When is the baby due?"

"Well…it's a while yet…next April, it should be."

"And your husband must be pleased?"

She frowned.

"My husband is dead."

"My God – that's awful – how did he die?"

"Black fever," she said flatly, and stared defiantly at him.

"I'm so sorry…if there's anything I can do…."

"No, there isn't…I'm fine"

She saw Spence out of the corner of her eye quietly observing them. I didn't see him earlier, she thought – he must have just come in. An idea suddenly came to her.

"Simon, would you mind telling the Reverend Spence for me…no-one else, mind, just him. I'd like him to know."

"Yes, yes, of course I will."

"Thank you. He's just come in, I think, so you could tell him now."

She touched him lightly on his shoulder with her hand and then turned and sat down to eat, dismissing him.

Mary felt uneasy. She hoped the news of her pregnancy might deter Simon as a potential suitor and persuade Spence to ease up on her, unless the prospect of capturing two souls rather than one made her an even more desirable prize. She had not meant, though, to reveal she was a widow and she was intensely aware that, far from putting Simon off, it had given him hope that she might be available. She also noticed that when she had stood so close to Simon, she had sensed not only his obvious desire for her, but an answering flicker in her own being, faint but unmistakable. Something had passed between them. When he had stood behind her, she was acutely aware of the length of time he spent staring at her, even though she could not see him; she had felt her scalp prickling with the intensity of his gaze and, as he moved away, the sensation had also disappeared. She made no attempt to try and look at him again or to search out where he was in the room. She kept her head down, finished her soup and bread and left.

She was barely a mile from her cottage when she saw it. It

looked like a bundle of rags abandoned in a ditch at first, but as she got closer, she saw to her horror that it was a corpse. It appeared to be a woman. The skin was stretched tightly over the skull and had a waxy, jaundiced look. Her eyes were still open, a claw of a hand stretched up, her bare arm skeletal and white. Mary shuddered, wondering how she had come to this.

It was not the first body she had seen in the open. So many were dying now that there were no coffins to bury them. The previous week, she had come across an entire family. It had been in a rough shelter, a scalp, not far from their village and it was the smell that alerted her as she came close, a stench of decaying flesh. She had gagged and, pushing her shawl up over her nose in a forlorn attempt to block the smell, had carefully stepped down into the ditch to peer in. Branches had been laid over it and above these lay some thin sods of yellowing turf. In the hollow underneath, she had found three bodies; those of a man and two small children. The body of the man lay across those of the children, his last gift to them the warmth of his own dying body. Strangely, the man's hair and beard appeared to be moving. Mary realised his head was covered with a thick, pulsating mat of flies. The smell had been so intense, it was like a physical assault; she could taste it on her tongue and at the back of her mouth. She had staggered back and vomited. When she recovered herself, she pulled the branches, so they collapsed around the bodies, flies rising in angry clouds around her head.

The following day, Simon wasn't there. The Reverend

Spence also made an announcement. He told everyone that the soup kitchen would be closed on the Saturday but would re-open immediately after the service on Sunday. It was a neat trick, virtually guaranteed to ensure most of those there would feel compelled to attend the service. Could she brazen it out? Perhaps she could survive without for two days and just go back on the Monday? No, she would have to endure the Sunday service and hope no-one found out about it – there would be Father McNamara to reckon with. Damn them. Damn them all. Very gently she rested her hands on her belly. Soon the baby would start to move. She had been surrounded by death but now there would be a new life, a spark of light in the darkness, and with it, a renewal of hope.

"A Coroner's Inquest was held on the lands of Redwood, in the Parish of Lorha, on yesterday, the 24th, on the body of Daniel Hayes, who for several days subsisted almost entirely on the refuse of vegetables, and went out on Friday morning in quest of something in the shape of food, but he had not gone far when he was obliged to lie down, and, melancholy to relate, was found dead some time afterward."

Tipperary Vindicator.

Posting in the Cork examiner, 30 October 1846

CHAPTER FOUR

The priest stared at his parishioners. In the first pew was the brother of the woman he was about to excommunicate. Michael McGuinness stood with his wife and two young sons, staring coldly back at him. He knew what was about to happen; nothing else had been talked about in their small village for the last week. The church was packed and several people had been forced to stand at the rear, their backs jammed against the rough whitewashed wall. There was a smell of damp in the air but it had been raining steadily for days now and with the onset of winter, all of their houses emitted the same sour smell; it was within the walls of their poor hovels, in the air they breathed, and in their clothes. The only thing that masked and contained it was the smoked earth smell of their peat fires.

Father McNamara was a tall man, and in his youth, there were a number of women who had mourned his loss to the church. For a moment, he hesitated. He looked briefly at the ground and then looked again at his congregation. He had to protect the faith – Bishop Brennan had urged him. The Protestants are out to destroy Catholicism in this country – to save the souls of our people, we must stop them. Father McNamara breathed deeply and spoke, throwing his arms wide.

"Close up the shutters!"

Those closest to the windows immediately took hold of the heavy wooden shutters and banged them shut. The church was plunged into darkness, the only light coming from a tall fat candle placed on a wooden column close to the priest.

"I have today to pronounce an Anathema! There is a woman in this church, Mary Hogan, who has turned her back on her faith and is attending a Protestant Church, a woman who has taken the soup and is more concerned with feeding her belly than saving her immortal soul! I know you are starving…but none of you have done this; you all know this is a veil of tears through which we must pass before ascending to our true home in Heaven. We must suffer here before experiencing the everlasting joy of God's presence. But she has turned her face against God and in His name I now curse her – I curse every part of her wretched sinful body, from the hair on her head to the very tips of her feet, every inch of her carcass, including everything that would spring from her!"

At this, there was a gasp from his audience. Everyone there knew Mary was pregnant. His heart in his mouth, Michael moved to the end of his pew and stepped into the aisle facing the priest.

"No! This is wrong, Father – you cannot do this. This is

wrong…she's taken bread to save her unborn child – you can't do this! Sorcha, come on – we're leaving."

He gestured to his wife, who nervously stepped out beside him, followed by their two small sons. He then strode out of the Church, leaving the door deliberately open so that light now streamed in. Sorcha followed slowly, dragging her right foot, the legacy of polio as a child. She could feel everyone's eyes on her as she limped down the Church, her two sons walking ahead. Sunlight blinded them as they passed through.

"Shut that door!" screamed the priest and a man at the back rushed to close it, plunging the church once more into darkness.

Father McNamara leaned over his lectern and studied the Latin text in the Bible propped against it. His hands were trembling as he clutched the sides of the lectern and he hoped that in the deep gloom no-one would notice. What he couldn't hide was the nervousness in his voice when he started to speak again. It cracked with emotion and he stopped for a moment to steady himself. He started the text again and as he found his rhythm, his voice became steadily more powerful and assured. He ended with the words, "…*tradentes eum satanae in interitum carnis, ut spriritus ejus fiat in die judici.*" Gazing out over the hushed congregation, he decided to also give them the Gaelic translation.

"We deliver her to Satan to mortify her body that her soul may be saved on the Day of Judgement."

There was a small silver-plated bell sat at the front of the lectern and he now rang this, snapped the Bible shut, and savagely swept the candle and its stand to the floor with his arm. There was a crash as the stand fell against the stone floor and the candle went out. The church was now in complete darkness and silence fell. As their eyes adjusted to the gloom, the congregation realised that the priest had left; he must have walked out through the small door to the rear. Still, no-one dared speak or even move. Finally, one of the men standing at the back turned and pushed open the door and, without looking back, hurriedly made his exit. This broke the spell and nervously people left their pews, genuflecting quickly on their knees as they did so. Still, no-one spoke and it was only as they burst into the weak sunlight of a cold, damp autumn day that they seemed to recover themselves. Even then, they spoke to each other in shocked low voices.

Michael urged his wife to take herself and the children home, telling her he was going to see his sister. He broke into a run. He wanted to get to Mary before anyone else did. She would be devastated when she heard what had happened. Her house was not far from the church but sat a lot higher than its neighbours and by the time he had struggled up the steep incline to it, he was already out of breath.

A loop of rope secured the front door and he first unfastened this before pushing through and into the dimly lit interior. He saw at once that Mary was lying prone on a straw-covered bench in the corner of the room.

"Mary – are you alright?"

She sat up and turned towards him. His heart ached as he looked at her. There had been six children in their family and Mary was the youngest, a good ten years younger than Michael, who had been the first born. Michael had brought her up, watched out for her, scolded her when she misbehaved, praised her after a hard day's work in the fields. Bookended between Michael and Mary there had been another three boys and a girl, Maisie, who had died of consumption at the age of five. Maisie's long, painful illness still haunted him; he remembered how pale and thin she had become, the ever-present quiet struggle for breath, her final sigh when she died, and then the awful stillness in the room. Following her death, his mother had simply given up; she would lie for days at a time in her bed refusing to get up. His father was worse; Michael had always thought he was too gentle a soul for this world. When Maisie died, he had gone into himself, seldom speaking and was often drunk on poteen. It was left to Michael, as the eldest, to look out for his younger siblings, to harry them to fetch water from the well, and help him with digging peat or planting or lifting potatoes, sowing grain, and getting their meagre harvest in.

Mary's voice,, when she spoke was low and her words came very slowly, as though each word required an enormous effort.

"Yes, just a bit tired…thought I'd lie down for a bit."

"That bastard went through with it – I wanted to choke the breath out of him, the fucking bastard –"

Mary felt a chill enter her heart. She knew there had been

gossip in the village that the priest had been told by Bishop Brennan to make an example of her. She hadn't been able to bring herself to believe it. Father McNamara was a good priest and had been kind to her on several occasions when she was growing up.

"Michael – don't."

"It's not right – it's just not right – after all you've been through –"

Tears pricked his eyes and he turned away to hide them from her.

Her mind raced. She felt a dizzying terror at what had been done; by his actions the priest had imperilled her soul and cast her into darkness. Yet she had to hide her feelings from her brother. She couldn't reveal what she felt without him being impelled to seek revenge in some way, a revenge which could only make things worse.

"Michael…it's fine. Please don't worry about me."

She stood up and, crossing the room, pulled him to her and hugged him, burying her head against his shoulder. His jacket smelt of peat and rain but, above all, it also smelt of him, a mixture of sweat and body odour which to her was as rich in fragrance as lavender or wild roses. She inhaled deeply. Michael was tall and well-built with large hands roughened from labouring in the fields. No-one would describe him as handsome, but he exuded an effortless charisma; when he entered a room, all eyes would naturally turn to him. Mary adored him and was endlessly entertained by the number of her friends who nursed a secret and hopeless passion for him.

"How could I not worry about you – you've spent half your life getting into trouble with me having to rescue you," he said.

Despite herself she laughed. "Ah yes, but it was yourself that usually led me into trouble in the first place."

"You didn't need much encouragement –"

"No – that's true"

"What's to become of us? I'm scared, Mary. I never felt like this before, but now…"

Mary stared at him.

"Michael, you've never been scared of anything and don't you start now either. I need you – we all need you."

"Everyone thinks I'm strong, but the things I've seen over the last year – my children are starving, and I struggle to find food for them. We go hungry ourselves, but they have to have food – I couldn't bear to lose them."

"It will be alright – God is good. It will work out. Pray, Michael, pray – we must all pray."

Michael's laugh was bitter and short.

"The only thing I'll pray for is a painful death for that bastard priest."

"Michael – don't, please don't – that's blasphemy. You mustn't blame Father McNamara. He's a good man – he's scared too. He's frightened others will take the soup, and with good reason –"

"Mary – do you know what he's done? He's cursed you,

barred you from Heaven itself. No-one will talk to you – you'll be shunned by everyone."

"Well, if that's the case, why are you talking to me? There's some as won't talk to me but I never cared for the likes of them anyway, so where's the loss? My real friends will stand by me and the rest can go feck themselves!"

Michael smiled ruefully.

"What am I going to do with you? Well, if you are going to hell I might as well join you. I'm sure the entertainment will be better there anyway."

Mary smiled back at him.

"I think there's already a place reserved for you."

Michael gently rubbed his hand across her stomach.

"How's the baby?"

"It seems fine."

"If it's a boy, what will you call it?"

"Owen."

"Well, I might have guessed…"

"And if it's a girl?"

"Maisie."

Michael had been gazing into Mary's eyes but at this, he looked away.

"I still miss her, you know."

"So, do I, Michael, so do I."

"Well, if it's Maisie you're calling her, I'll hope for a girl."

He kissed her softly on her forehead.

"I have to go, Mary. Sorcha will be getting anxious."

"She will too – go then. Don't worry about me – I'll be fine."

Mary stood at the door to watch him leave. It had already fallen dark and she watched until he disappeared from sight, slowly swallowed up by the gloom.

CHAPTER FIVE

Mary sighed as she lifted the lid of the barrel and realised that only a spoonful of water remained. She would need to go to the well again, a task she struggled with even when she was in the best of health, but which now, in her weakened state, seemed too formidable to even attempt. The well stood a short distance from the cottage but she needed the pony and cart to carry the barrel and harnessing the pony took all her strength and determination. Once at the well, she lowered the barrel into the water and, her arms aching with the strain, clumsily lifted it first against her hip, and then high enough to clear the raised side of the cart. Water slopped from the barrel and drenched her dress. As she neared her home again, her neighbour Peter Furey rushed to help her, carefully setting the barrel down in the corner of the main room of the two-bedroomed cottage.

"Thanks, Peter – I just seem so weak lately..."

Peter looked at her. He hesitated for a moment and then spoke.

"The priest…he went too far…he's a good man but –"

"Do you know how other people feel about it?"

"There was a lot of muttering afterwards. Bridie Kelly and Ann Murphy – best stay away from them. They've both got poisonous tongues in their head. I was talking to Cathal though; he's of the same opinion as myself. Don't worry, Mary – let them talk. They'll soon find something else to mither about."

"It's hard though…what with everything else."

"I know – you have to stay strong Mary. Michael will look after you and you know I'm always here for you."

"You're a good man, Peter. Maggie was a lucky woman."

Tears filled Peter's eyes and to hide them, he turned away.

"It was me that was lucky – next time you need some water, give me a shout. Don't go trying to do it yourself now."

It was after Peter had gone that she had suddenly noticed the spots of blood around her feet and felt a warm, trickling stickiness down her thighs. She rushed out of the cottage and made her way into some densely growing blackthorn bushes close by where she knew she would not be seen by anyone. Lifting her rough cotton shift to her thighs, she glanced down. She already knew what she would find but was still horrified by the volume of blood which now coursed down her legs. She collapsed onto her back and lay there for a while. Tears pricked her eyes. For a moment, she fought them, and gave in as grief took hold, starting to sob. She had just begun to show. Her husband, Owen, had been dead for just six weeks.

She felt a wave of pain sweep through her, followed almost

within seconds by an even stronger gripping pain. Contractions. Someone had told her the labour pains suffered during a miscarriage were even worse than those of a normal labour. She forced herself to look down; thick almost black gobbets of blood clung to her thighs. Then as she stared, she saw, to her horror, lying draped on the ground and against her inner thigh, what appeared to be a translucent film of skin. Underneath, and no longer than the length of one of her fingers, she could just make out the shape of a head and, most horrifying of all, a hand with its own perfectly formed, tiny, curled fingers. She gave a piercing scream before rousing herself, her body still shaking with racking sobs, and very gingerly picked her way back over the field into her cottage, gazing anxiously around her all the time in fear that she might be seen.

Once inside, she tore off her blood-spattered dress and hurled it into the peat fire. It immediately caught and a coarse black smoke ballooned upwards into the chimney. She put on another grey cotton shift and, snatching up a piece of rough linen, walked back to where she had lain and very delicately lifted up the tiny form and wrapped it in the cloth. She pushed the cloth into her pocket and walked slowly back to the brook which fed the well. Part of the brook was much deeper, and she often used it to swim or wash in. Gazing round to make sure no-one was watching, she quickly threw off the shift and removed her undergarments. She stood shivering for a moment, but, placing the small bundle on the grass beside the brook, she gratefully lowered herself down into its icy cold depths. She found that if she crouched, it was just deep enough to cover her shoulders and she dipped down to make sure the water covered both her shoulders and neck. The cold water both numbed and soothed her. She ducked her head under and held her breath; it was so tempting to carry on holding it, to give up and drown, exhausted, beneath the water's glittering surface. She lay there for a long time, head tilted back, eyes shut. Finally, she sighed, rose, lifted the tiny bundle up again, and made the slow journey back to the cottage, where she immediately fell into a deep and dreamless sleep.

When she awoke, she could just see the pale light of dawn piercing the narrow gaps around the sheepskin draped over the window frame. There was nothing left. First Owen had died and now her baby had perished as well. The priest had cursed both her and the baby and this was the result – God had punished her. Well, she thought bitterly, if the baby is dead, then I must die too. She reached for the cotton shift she had worn the previous day, draped over the foot of the bed. Just as she was about to put it on, she suddenly changed her mind. Walking to a heavy oak chest in the corner of the room, she lifted the lid. It was filled with bed linen and clothes. She had kept Owen's clothes and stored them at the bottom of the trunk and she now lifted out one of his old jumpers and held it to her face. It was heavy and damp, but she could still smell him on it. She inhaled deeply. She sighed and carefully put it back, lifting out her Sunday dress. It was a cream cotton dress, printed with a floral design of roses picked out in a deep yellow, pinched in at the waist, and with a white embroidered collar. It was the dress she had got married in, the happiest day of her life. She put the dress on, picked up the bundle holding her baby's corpse, and walked out of the cottage, leaving the heavy wooden door ajar.

The cliffs overlooking the bay were a good half hour's walk from her cottage. She moved in a trance, oblivious to her surroundings. It started to rain, a soft, persistent drizzle which soaked her through to the skin in minutes. She barely noticed. Once she reached the cliffs, she continued walking until she stood at their very edge, her bare feet only inches from the steep, dizzying fall to the rocks below. She glanced down and felt the familiar sensation of wanting to immediately hurl herself off. She had noticed this before when standing on these cliffs and had often wondered where the desire for self-destruction came from and why it was so powerful. The instinct to throw herself off had also been accompanied by another strange sensation; she had often fantasised that if she had jumped, then seconds before hitting the rocks below, she would somehow save herself, her helpless fall would turn into a triumphant, swooping ascent as she discovered she could suddenly and miraculously fly.

As she stood here now though, she knew there would be no magical transformation, that the fall would be both final and fatal. She edged forward again, her feet slippery on the wet grass. Suicides, she knew, were cursed and they would never enter into the kingdom of heaven to sit in God's presence. They would languish forever in limbo. Nor could they be buried in consecrated ground. But she remembered that her own unbaptised child was similarly exiled and cursed. So, she would join her baby then. She was cursed anyway because of the wretched priest.

Still, she hesitated – even though she was cursed, did she really dare kill herself? An excommunication might be reversed but not a suicide. If she committed suicide, she was cursed beyond any hope of salvation for all eternity. Seagulls wheeled and called in the air in front of her and she could hear the roar of the ocean at the base of the cliffs. The tide was in so the rocks which normally skirted the cliff were hidden by the foaming waves crashing against its base; she knew her body would be instantly smashed against them and then carried away out to sea. A gust of wind suddenly whipped against her and almost swept her over the edge. She felt her heart leap in her chest with fear. Calming herself, she shut her eyes and spread her arms wide as though she might mimic the seagulls diving and soaring around her and take flight herself. I'll let God decide, she thought; the wind would be his agent. It would be his decision, not mine. Trembling, and still with her eyes fast shut, she took another step forward.

"The land in Ireland is infinitely more peopled than in England; and to give full effect to the natural resources of the country, a great part of the population should be swept from the soil."

The Reverend Thomas Malthus (1766 – 1834)

CHAPTER SIX

Hewetson was staying at his town house in Southampton when he received the letter. It bore the seal of the British Treasury. Could this be the answer to his prayers? Rescue at last from the genteel poverty of being a half-pay Commissariat Officer? He tore it open and anxiously read it.

Yes – it was as he had hoped. The letter was from Commissary General, Sir R. Routh. Following the holidays, he was to report to Routh to "superintend arrangements for disposing of the Indian corn and meal shortly expected to arrive from America."

He almost hugged himself with delight. In fact, so pleased was he with himself, that he executed a jig of delight on the spot. Several weeks earlier, he had written an unsolicited letter to Peel urging him to purchase Indian corn to provide relief operations in Ireland. In the letter, he had described himself as an authority on the subject; in practice, he knew little more about it than that there seemed to be an abundance of the stuff and it was remarkably cheap to purchase. No matter, he thought to himself; I'm a quick study and I'm also sure there's not a lot to learn. You grind it and then you eat it – what could be simpler?

Two months later, he found himself wandering down a harbour street in Cork. He realised that he must cut a very strange figure in his top hat, black woollen coat, and gloves, and he was already attracting a number of frank stares and whispers from those he passed. Whenever he caught someone's eye, he stared boldly back, preening himself in the knowledge that they were all his social and intellectual inferiors. He was a proud member of a nation whose empire stretched to the furthest reaches of the earth. They were the simple-minded members of one of the empire's many colonies and one of the more inferior ones at that.

Hewetson was searching for a mill. He had been told there was one in Hawker's Lane, but when he finally stumbled upon it, he could see through the darkened and cobweb encrusted windows that it must have fallen into disuse many years earlier. The purchase of the maize by Peel was still a secret so he had been unable to reveal the reason for his interest in acquiring a mill. When asked directly, he would simply tap the side of his nose, smile, and say the matter was commercially sensitive and discretion was his watchword.

It was becoming dark when he finally stumbled across what he needed. He was making his way down a narrow lane where the houses on each side seemed to lean in towards him with almost malevolent intent. The gas lamps had yet to be lit and the sky above him was a gun-metal grey. Although it was still only four in the afternoon, he could clearly see the moon hanging snared in the dark beard of the clouds. Ahead of him, the lane widened out a little and against a wall he noticed an array of barrels. He came closer. Just beyond the barrels, there was an opening into a courtyard. He turned into it. In front of him stood two huge doors, large enough to admit a dray and horses. More promising still, he could see to the left of one of the doors a discarded millstone which had been propped against the wall. The doors themselves weren't completely shut and by turning sideways he was just able to slide through. There was a gruff shout.

"And who might you be?"

A man stood in front of a large trestle table which was littered with bundles of paper.

"William Hewetson – I'm attached to the Commissariat."

"Are you now? And what's that to me and what are you doing in my yard?"

"I've been commissioned to find and rent a mill and you, sir, appear to be in charge of one. How many millstones do you have and how many barrels can you store here?"

The man stared shrewdly at him.

"Fifteen granite millstones and enough space to house eighteen thousand barrels. If you want to use the mill though, it will be £600 a month, one month's cash up front."

"The government will pay £500 a month – that's as high as I've been authorised to go. Do we have a deal?"

The mill owner gave a brief snort of disgust.

"£600 a month – take it or leave it. I don't much care either way."

"I'll take it."

*

Correspondence as between Charles Trevelyan and William Hewetson

Mr Charles Trevelyan
Assistant Secretary to HM Treasury
3rd November 1845
Dear Charles
As you know we have a serious problem with a shortage of mills, both in this country and abroad. Warehouses are fully stocked with unground corn but, of course, in this state it's worse than useless and certainly can't be issued to the general populace.

I have been speaking to a colleague of mine, a Captain Percival, who has had the marvellous idea of soaking the corn in cold water for twelve hours and then boiling it the following day for three and a half hours. If this is done, then he thinks the corn will be fine for eating. What do you think? Is this worth pursuing?

I look forward to receiving your reply.
Yours sincerely
William Hewetson
Commissariat Superintendent

*

William Hewetson
Commissariat Superintendent
6th November 1845
Dear William

Captain Percival has clearly spent a lot of time dwelling on the problem, almost as much, I imagine, as the fifteen and a half hours his recipe will take to steep and boil the corn. I do believe the first day of fighting at Waterloo took less time than this.

I have also been pondering the problem. I've been wondering whether some form of hand mill might suffice. This can then be used by people to grind their own corn. I've written to Mr Byham at the Board of Ordinance and I also have enquiries out with a Mr Traill in Scotland and a Mr Melvill, who is a director at India House. I hope to have some good news for you shortly.

Yours sincerely
Mr Charles Trevelyan
Assistant Secretary to HM Treasury

*

William Hewetson
Commissariat Superintendent
2nd January 1846
Dear William

Unfortunately, things have not worked out as I hoped. I was sent a coffee grinder by My Byham's office and Mr Traill sent me a hand mill which failed to grind any corn but did cause a serious

first for not coming back to you on this issue more quickly. It was indeed under my instructions that Mr Hewetson has been asked to only submit the corn to a single grinding. I do not agree with you that as a result of this, the corn is indigestible or indeed leads to stomach ailments of the type described by you.

The government has been extraordinarily generous in providing these supplies of maize, but the grinding process is an expensive business. Moreover, we must not aim at making the provision of the corn too comfortable a process. It would do permanent harm to make dependence on charity an agreeable mode of life. The supply of corn is a temporary measure and the Irish must learn to stand on their own two feet. Her Majesty's government cannot be expected to continue its supply indefinitely. Even were it the case that a single grinding did lead to indigestion problems this will also help to ensure that the Irish do not become too reliant on it.

Yours sincerely
Charles Trevelyan
Assistant Secretary to HM Treasury

*

Mr William Hewetson
Commissariat Superintendent
15th February 1846
Dear William
I have just come out of a meeting with Mr Trevelyan. We had what could be described as a fairly robust debate on the issue but,

at length, it was agreed that the Indian corn should be ground twice and I would be grateful if you could make immediate arrangements for this. This should hopefully make the maize less indigestible and therefore ensure its recipients no longer suffer some of the stomach ailments reported to date.

I would also like a new method to be adopted with the mixing of three parts of cornmeal with one part of oats. This should make the maize more palatable. Finally, I would like you to send the depots copies of the booklet of corn recipes which has been produced for circulation amongst the population. This includes the splendid recipe for corn biscuits produced by the Dublin Baker, O'Brien, which I have tasted myself and found exceedingly good.

Yours sincerely
Sir Randolph Routh
Irish Relief Commission

*

Sir Randolph Routh
Irish Relief Commission
4th March 1846
Dear Sir Randolph

There have been complaints by the commercial importers of cornmeal that Government supplies are undercutting the market and forcing them to lower their own prices. It is extremely important that we don't undermine the local economy in this way, and I must therefore insist that the price of the corn sold at the depots is raised to suppress demand and allow the mercantile trade to make good the shortage at more profitable levels.

This measure must be implemented immediately, and I have also taken steps to stop the further import of meal as scarcity will further assist the mercantile trade in this matter. No steps whatever must be taken to replace the meal in depots which run short of supplies.

Yours sincerely

Charles Trevelyan

Assistant Secretary to HM Treasury

*

Mr Charles Trevelyan

Assistant Secretary to HM Treasury

7th March 1846

Dear Charles

I implore you to reconsider your stance on this and allow the import of meal for the local depots. All Donegal and County Mayo are crying out for supplies and parts of the country appear to be approaching the final extremity. In Kilkenny, the locals are staggering through the streets with hunger. Starvation and suffering are now a common currency and the number of deaths increases daily. Such is the demand for coffins that in some areas the dead are being buried wrapped in newspaper and string or left unburied by the wayside to be preyed upon by dogs and crows.

I have been told too that you reprimanded Sir James Dobrain for ordering an immediate dispatch of corn to the Killeries; never was a town more aptly named. *This situation cannot be allowed to continue.*

I await your response.

Yours sincerely

Sir Randolph Routh

Irish Relief Commission

*

Sir Randolph Routh

Irish Relief Commission

11th March 1846

Dear Sir Randolph

You have ignored my very clear instructions as set out in my letter of 4th March to immediately raise the price of cornmeal to the same level set by commercial merchants. I think my gift for clarity of expression must be deserting me for I cannot see any other reason for you behaving in this way.

An unduly low price prematurely exhausts our depots by bringing the whole country down upon them; surely you must see this? No addition we can make to our stock can stand a demand arising from such a cause.

Please raise the price as originally demanded of you and confirm to me that this has been done.

Yours sincerely

Charles Trevelyan

Assistant Secretary to HM Treasury

*

Mr Charles Trevelyan

Assistant Secretary to HM Treasury

14th March 1846

Dear Mr Trevelyan

I am quite certain I have not erred in fixing the price. An increase would produce a strong expression of feeling in the country and I have no intention of allowing this. You will be pleased to learn as well that you have not lost your gift for clarity of expression. I understood only too well the instructions given in your letter of 4th March and I have no intention of following them. If you feel you must now take this up with the Prime Minister, then have at it; I will not do as you ask.

Yours sincerely

Sir Randolph Routh

Irish Relief Commission

*

Sir Randolph Routh

Irish Relief Commission

17th March 1946

Dear Sir Randolph

I must ask you yet again for an early revision of prices. I have no need to seek further guidance on this from the Prime Minister; his wishes in this matter are more than clear and as I have responsibility for implementing Her Majesty's policies in Ireland, I insist you do precisely as I ask.

Yours sincerely
Charles Trevelyan
Assistant Secretary to HM Treasury

*

Mr Charles Trevelyan
Assistant Secretary to HM Treasury
23rd March 1846
Dear Charles
Thank you for your letter of 17th March.
The country cannot, by any possible means, bear a higher price.

I cannot write more as I am an invalid today.
Yours sincerely
Sir Randolph Routh
Irish Relief Commission

*

Sir Randolph Routh
Irish Relief Commission
19th March 1846
Dear Sir Randolph
We have no time to be ill.
Yours sincerely
Charles Trevelyan
Assistant Secretary to HM Treasury

CHAPTER SEVEN

Clifton had decided to accompany the bailiffs and soldiers during the evictions. He had heard from other landlords that evicted tenants often stayed near their houses, erecting scalps of wooden poles covered over with the thatch or sods of earth from their tumbled dwellings and placed either against the house walls or built nearby over ditches. It was very important these people were not just evicted but pushed off the land; he also did not want them taking thatch or trying to remove any of the stones from their houses which might be useful in building temporary shelters elsewhere.

It was a bitterly cold day and he had wrapped a scarf around his face to keep out the worst of the chill wind. As he mounted his horse, he looked anxiously at the darkening sky. The wind was becoming stronger and threatening to become a fierce gale and the air was already spattered with rain drops. He needed to get this done as quickly as possible if they were to avoid getting soaked. He thought it was also possible it might even snow later as it grew still colder. He gave a brisk nod to Captain Lambert, who was already mounted. There had been increasing levels of resistance by tenant farmers in the county and it had been agreed that a small contingent of troops should accompany all future evictions. Lambert had, though, tried to persuade Clifton to delay these until the Spring, or, at the least, until Christmas had passed, but he was unmoved. He needed the land for grazing sheep and cattle which he had calculated would prove far more profitable. All he was achieving keeping these wretched tenants was mounting debts; they couldn't afford to pay their rents but he was still expected to find the money to pay the poor rates. It was easy to pretend to have a conscience when it wasn't your wealth that was being destroyed. He knew the presence of the military was purely ceremonial; the real work would be done by the bailiff and his men and he eyed the crowbars they carried with approval. These would prove far more useful for the task in hand than the swords worn by Lambert and his men. Clifton gazed with contempt at their scarlet uniforms and tall black hats and, savagely digging his heels into the flanks of his horse, urged it forward. Clifton owned land in three villages, Mullangar (which was the smaller of the three), Tyrone, and Inishcrone. He would deal with Mullangar first.

The bailiff's men used their crowbars to knock on the door of the first cottage they came to. The door was opened by a young woman in her twenties, who immediately realised why they were there.

"Oh God, no – there are sick people here – for the love of God, leave us alone!"

The bailiff, a thick-set bull of a man, pushed to the front of his men.

"You're in arrears with the rent and we have a notice for your eviction – all of youse are to leave now or we'll take the house down around you."

He lunged forward and, grabbing her arm, pulled her out of the cottage. Two men beside him immediately made their way into the cottage. In the gloom inside, they could see two small children, a boy and a girl, cowering in one corner and, on straw matting, a man who was painfully trying to lift himself on one elbow.

"I have the fever," he gasped, "– have pity, will ye."

The men looked at each other. With starvation and weakened immune systems, disease was rife. Cholera and typhus both raged through the county. It was black fever, though, which frightened people the most. Peering down at him, they could see the man's legs were already as black as the soot on the wall behind the fire. There was a stench of gangrene. They did not dare touch him and hurriedly made their way back outside again.

"There's one of them with the black fever – we're not going near him."

The bailiff turned to the woman.

"Fetch him out or we'll burn your hut over the top of you!"

"Please – you can't – he'll die!"

Lambert, who had been watching the dismal scene with mounting dismay, edged his horse closer to Clifton's own horse and spoke to him in a low, urgent voice – loud enough for Clifton to hear but not so loud that his own men or the bailiff's men might overhear their conversation. He had struggled to understand the Gaelic spoken between the bailiff and the couple, but he had no need of the language to understand what was happening in front of him.

"Clifton! Let them stay – this is not right!"

Clifton glared at him and deliberately raised his own voice so his own men and the soldiers closest to him could hear. Clifton, too, had no knowledge of Gaelic and despised the language, so his words were in English.

"If he's the black fever, they'll all be dead in days anyway – it makes no difference whether they die in that hut or out on the moor. Moran – take down that roof and get these people out of there!"

Three of the bailiff's men moved forward with short wooden ladders which they leaned against the wall of the cottage and scrambled up. Using crowbars, they quickly levered out the wooden staves supporting the thatched roof, which slid down to the ground in huge untidy mounds. The fierce wind lifted the thatch as it fell and loose strands of hay swirled in the air around both horses and men. Moran grabbed the woman roughly by one hand and pulled her round so she faced back into the cottage. He pushed her forward with the flat of his hand against her back.

"Get them out!"

The two small children, both barefoot and in rags, ran

forward and hid themselves in the folds of their mother's dress. She was now wracked with sobs and the children, seeing her so distraught, also burst into tears.

"My husband's too ill to move and I can't shift him –"

Moran turned to the group of villagers standing closest to him.

"Two of you – get that man out and put him in a cart."

No-one moved. Scanning them to pick out the weakest, Moran strode across and punched him hard in the stomach. The man groaned and doubled over. Moran lifted his club and struck him again with a savage blow to the back of his head. The man collapsed and lay crumpled on the floor. A woman from the crowd of villagers ran forward, kneeling over him and screaming. Blood seeped from the blow to his head, mixed with an oozing grey matter. Seeing this, she continued to scream, a terrible high-pitched wail which unnerved many of those around her.

Moran moved closer to the crowd; lifting his club again, he quickly picked out two of the men with it, pointing the club menacingly at them.

"Ye two – you'll do nicely. Fetch him out."

The two men moved nervously to the door of the cottage, averting their eyes from the prone corpse of their neighbour, his wife still keening over him. They lifted the diseased man and laid him carefully in a cart, the donkey hitched to the cart shifting a little as it adjusted to the weight. Whilst this was happening, the bailiff's men had also entered the hut and were throwing the family's meagre possessions into the yard. Two of them had tears in their eyes. A blackened cooking pot, shovels, wicker baskets, tin plates, and straw bedding were heaped up outside, together with a mound of clothes carelessly dumped into a pool of muddy water.

Moran pointed towards the men who had lifted the woman's husband into the cart and gestured at the untidy heap of belongings.

"Get those in the cart as well."

The hut itself was now just bare standing walls, grey smoke still billowing from the fire through the few remaining roof staves.

Clifton pointed across at the next nearest hut.

"That one next! I want all these cottages cleared before it's dark. If you find any cattle or pigs, take those as well; they can pay off some of the rent arrears owed."

He turned to Lambert.

"I've seen enough. Your men can assist the bailiff's men on the other evictions and ensure everything happens in an orderly fashion."

This was said with a sneer. Lambert felt a wave of anger sweep up through him and, for a moment, was close to striking Clifton across the face.

"My instructions are to protect your men whilst they clear these cottages and to ensure there is no outbreak of disorder – no more, no less. It's clear to me these poor villagers will not be able to resist you and your men so there's nothing more for me to do here."

With this, Lambert wheeled his horse away and shouted across the yard to his men, none of whom had so far dismounted.

"We're leaving – follow me!"

Clifton looked in disbelief as Lambert and his troop of soldiers turned away and within seconds had disappeared, the sound of their clattering hoof beats swallowed up by the wind in an instant, as though they had never existed.

Moran's men looked both anxious and dismayed; they were clearly worried that without the restraining presence of the soldiers, the villagers might become violent. Moran had only a dozen men alongside him; a crowd of thirty or more villagers stood around them and more were joining them even as he tried to estimate their chances of controlling them. However, all the villagers could lay their hands on were sticks or shovels and perhaps the odd knife. Five of his men were armed with shotguns and he knew they wouldn't hesitate to use them. At the front of the crowd, stood a particularly tall and well-built man armed with a long-handled scythe, which he now lifted and held out in front of him.

Without taking his eyes off the villager, Moran motioned with a hand towards one of his men standing to the rear of him.

"O"Brien!" Moran growled.

A man stepped forward with a shotgun coolly levelled in the direction of the villager armed with the scythe.

"Put that down," said Moran, "or my friend here will put a hole in you large enough for us all to walk through."

Slowly the villager lowered his scythe to the ground.

"Listen all of you," said Moran, "We are legally empowered to carry out these evictions and if you resist or get in our way, you will be shot. Leave your weapons on the ground now and move back or my men will start firing."

There was a clattering sound as tools and weapons fell to the ground and Moran watched with satisfaction as the crowd began to retreat backwards.

"Good, very sensible of youse all. I'm much obliged."

He motioned again to the men behind him.

"Keily and O'Hearne, pick up all of this rubbish and put it in a pile against that wall there. O'Brien and Conway, keep your guns trained on these people – if there's so much as a breath out of any of them, shoot them! The rest of you, follow me – we've got work to do."

Moran walked down to the next cottage. He rapped loudly on the door with his fist, although he already knew the occupants must have slipped out earlier to join the crowd at his back and wasn't expecting a response. When none came, he stood back.

"OK men – off with the roof."

Immediately, two of his men sprang forward with their ladders and, scrambling up them, started to crowbar out the roof supports.

Moran was very aware that during all of this, his employer, Clifton, had sat grimly on his horse, uttering not a single word. Like all bullies, Clifton was a coward at heart, Moran thought. Still, that in itself was useful to find out and he might be able to use it to his advantage at some point in the future. As the roof of the second cottage tumbled to the ground, Clifton at last stirred, nudging his horse nearer to where Moran stood.

"You seem to have everything under control here so I'm going to go back."

"That's fine, sir – we'll have this lot out on the road and the houses tumbled by the end of the day for you. It's a pity about the soldiers but they were only for show anyway."

"I'll be speaking to Lambert's colonel tomorrow about all of this – the man's a disgrace to his uniform. He should be court-martialled for his behaviour."

"True enough – whether that will happen though, is another matter."

Clifton was momentarily taken aback by his bailiff's over-familiarity and insouciance. The man lacked respect, he thought, and needed to be taught a lesson in manners; however, that was probably best kept for another time. At the moment, he needed him.

"Can you ask one of your men to accompany me back… preferably one that is armed?"

So, he was definitely lily-livered, Moran thought.

"Conway!" he shouted, "Escort Mr Clifton back. Then return here again – I've still work for ye".

Moran watched as Clifton and Conway cantered away from the village. It was a great pity the fool wouldn't stumble into a bog on his way back and drown, he thought – no man would miss him, that was sure.

There were thirty houses in the village. By nightfall, all that remained of them were their supporting walls; even there, some of the more poorly built huts had partly collapsed, the unmortared stones lying in heaps on the ground. The families had been driven into the deepening dusk; one or two had donkeys and carts they could use to carry their belongings, but most carried their meagre possessions in their arms or hoisted on their shoulders. The wind had not let up and a heavy rain had started to fall. Moran was well aware that some of the elderly and sicker villagers might not survive even the first night in the open. He wasn't happy about it, but he had a family himself that needed feeding; these were hard times, he thought, and if he didn't harden his own heart, then his wife and children would very quickly be reduced to begging themselves.

Next time would be worse still because he had instructions to evict most of the tenants in the village of Tyrone and these would include families close to the cottage of someone he had once considered a friend, Michael McGuinness. They had grown up together, gone fishing for trout and salmon in the local rivers, competed for the same girls at dances, and played in the same hurling team; ironically, Clifton himself had established this a number of years ago and they had often played fierce matches against the teams of other landowners. He also knew that Michael was a force to be reckoned with. Someone, he was sure, would already have alerted him as to what had happened at Mullangar and if today had proved difficult, much worse was to come. Still, tomorrow could take care of itself, he thought, tonight, he would feast on pork from Clifton's estate. A pig had been slaughtered the previous day with a promise from Clifton that if the evictions went well, all the bailiff's men would have their share. Moran couldn't remember when he had last enjoyed meat and his mouth salivated just thinking about it. So, pork, a well-fed family and then perhaps a tumble with the wife. That would ease the ache in his shoulders, he was sure.

CHAPTER EIGHT

"We have to bring Peel down," said Disraeli, pacing up and down in his growing excitement.

Russell looked up. He had been staring at the floor. He was in despair; he despised Peel as a person but hated his wretched attempts to force through the repeal of the Corn Laws even more. They had been enacted to levy tariffs on imported grain and the legislation protected the price of home-grown corn, but in Peel's view, it also prevented the free import of grain to Ireland to mitigate the effects of the famine. The proposal to repeal them had divided the country and had split both the opposition and his own party into angry factions. Worst still, the repeal was a Whig proposal and Russell bitterly resented Peel's attempt to now present it as a Tory measure. Russell had convened a meeting with Disraeli and his erstwhile enemy Lord George Bentinck. Russell led the Whigs in Parliament and Bentick was a key figure in the opposing Tory party, as was Disraeli. Russell had decided they needed to join forces to defeat Peel and they were now ensconced in the library at Russell's house.

Disraeli was still pacing; he was a Jew and Russell had a personal antipathy towards him, but Disraeli was also very shrewd and if anybody could find a way through, then he was the man to do it.

"And how precisely might we do that?" Disraeli asked, his interest piqued.

"We cannot fight him on the Corn Laws because we would almost certainly lose the vote but there is another way – the Irish Coercion Bill."

Bentinck looked mystified.

"I don't understand," he said. "The Coercion Bill is supposed to quell civil unrest in Ireland. How might that help us?"

"The Bill comes before Parliament next Tuesday; our job is to make sure it's defeated and with its defeat, Peel will be forced to resign. It will bring down the government."

Bentinck winced. He hated the Corn Laws, as did his other protectionist colleagues, but to conspire to bring down the government and usher in the Whigs could destroy his own party. Still, he thought, what choice do we have?

Although he didn't like him, Russell felt a grudging respect for Peel. The man had already resigned once over the issue but Russell himself had been unable to overcome the tensions in his own party and been forced to admit that he would be unable to form a new administration. Peel was duly summoned by the Queen again and graciously informed that he must withdraw his resignation as Prime Minister and once more take up the mantle of office. Peel felt enormously satisfied; he said he felt like a man restored to life after his funeral service had been preached.

He was no fool either. He had no great love of the Irish, but he wasn't prepared to let them starve. Behind his own cabinet's back, and some weeks before his resignation and the miracle of his resurrection from the grave, he had ordered £100,000 of Indian corn from the United States for import into Ireland. This ingeniously overcame the barrier of the Corn Laws because there was no trade in Indian corn, and nor did it interfere with private enterprise. Instead of attempting to climb the wall, Peel had simply walked around it.

Now, though, he was attempting to walk through the wall and his enemies were waiting on the other side.

*

The Speaker rose solemnly to his feet. There was a hushed silence. Members had already seen a messenger enter the chamber, his face flushed, his demeanour that of someone who could hardly contain his excitement. There had been a rapid exchange with the Speaker before the man hurried away.

"I have an announcement to make," said the Speaker. He was a small pompous man who had been referred to by one member of Parliament as a sanctimonious dwarf. He also had a wife who was a good six inches taller than him, which had prompted a number of ribald comments to the effect that he clearly had talents in the bed department entirely lacking in his taller colleagues.

Even so, small as he was, he towered over Russell, who had the added disadvantage of a disproportionately large head, which his body seemed scarcely able to support.

"The Lords have agreed to the Bill repealing the Corn Laws." The Speaker paused, enjoying the drama of the moment. "Without amendment."

There was a hushed silence and then uproar.

"Silence," growled the Speaker. "I would remind members that discourse in this House should be conducted with dignity. Honourable members must show each other respect; shouting at each other is not – in my estimation – a sign of respect."

The House fell silent, but it wasn't long before there was a subdued and resentful muttering.

Peel rose to his feet.

"I congratulate the House of Lords for their wisdom in allowing this Bill to pass. As you all know, I have long been an advocate – "

There was a ripple of contemptuous laughter.

"Order. Order," shouted the Speaker. "The Prime Minister must be allowed to speak."

"I have long been an advocate of reform. The taxes on imported grain are for the benefit of the few but have meant intolerably high prices for those poor men and women who toil in mill and factory throughout this great land of ours. This is indeed a momentous day in Parliament, and I welcome the repeal."

As he sat down, there was a heavy hammering of the benches by those in favour of repeal and an equally loud chorus of dissent from those who had opposed it.

Peel looked appealingly at the Speaker, but the Speaker merely shrugged as though to say, what can you expect in the face of such controversial legislation?

Finally, the cacophony ceased, and the Speaker again rose to his feet.

"We turn now to the matter of the Coercion Bill and I invite the Prime Minister to open the debate."

Peel stood. He felt elated at the passage of the Corn Laws Bill and was confident the Coercion Bill would have a much smoother passage. It was uncontroversial, recommending the implementation of measures to suppress the civil unrest which now existed in Ireland as a consequence of the famine. He described the measures contained in the Bill: the imposition of curfews and the granting of exceptional powers to magistrates allowing them to convict offenders to seven years transportation.

He sat down and the Speaker waited expectantly for those who opposed the Bill to now stand and respond. Nobody stood and, after a moment, the Speaker called for a vote. Members then left the chamber, moving quickly to the lobbies to record their votes. These having been counted, the Speaker rose again.

"The ayes to the left," he said, "one hundred and forty-three votes. The noes to the right, two hundred and sixteen. The noes have it, the noes have it. Unlock!"

Peel looked stunned. Within the space of an hour, he had gone from elation to utter despair. The government had lost by seventy-three votes and he immediately knew the scale of the defeat meant he would have to resign. Russell, his own elevation to Prime Minister now within touching distance, smiled triumphantly, and to Peel's disbelief, Bentinck was grinning broadly as well.

*

Lieutenant-Colonel Harry Jones sat impatiently in an outer office within the Whitehall complex of buildings. At a desk in the same office, a secretary sat, quill pen in hand, copying text from a large ledger propped in front of him. The scratching sound made by the quill was beginning to irritate Jones; as the Chairman of the Board of Works in Ireland, he wasn't used to being kept waiting.

"Trevelyan does know I'm here?"

The clerk looked up, as though startled to find that Jones was still in the room with him.

"Ah, yes, Colonel – I informed him the moment you arrived."

"Well, would you mind telling him that I have another meeting to go to at twelve and it's now ten thirty and I thought we had agreed to meet at ten?"

"Sorry, Colonel – I'll do that now."

The clerk scrambled to his feet. Crossing the room, he knocked at an oak panelled door and, without waiting for a response, pushed the door ajar and entered.

He closed the door behind him, and Jones strained to hear what was being said inside the room. A moment later, the door opened again.

"He'll see you now, Colonel – please accept my apologies for the wait."

Jones was ushered into a large room with enormous floor-to-ceiling windows facing out onto the street below. At the far end, behind a large desk, sat Trevelyan. What was remarkable about it, and which struck Jones immediately, was the absence of any papers or files; not a single sheet of paper marred the polished walnut surface. It was completely at odds, he thought, with his own desk back in Ireland, which was so burdened with huge files and mountains of paper that to the casual onlooker, it looked as though the desk's occupant was trying to build a wall between him and any visitors he might have. At the front of Trevelyan's desk, in contrast, sat a handsome silver mount with an inkpot and quill – otherwise the desk was quite bare.

It was the first time Jones had met Trevelyan and, for a moment, he simply stood at the end of the room studying him. So, this was the great Trevelyan, Assistant Secretary to the Treasury and the man with the power of life and death over the entire population of Ireland. Although undoubtedly handsome, he had an oddly effeminate look about him with thick sensual lips and dark hair swept to one side across his forehead. The hair sat untidily around his ears in a way that gave him an almost girlish appearance. At the same time though, he had a strong masculine jaw and piercing blue eyes.

Trevelyan stood up and came around the desk to greet him, extending a hand for Jones to shake.

"I apologise, Colonel, for keeping you waiting. I was trying to finish an urgent report for the cabinet, I'm afraid."

"Ah, I see – and have you finished it?"

"Not quite, but I'm told you have another meeting so it will have to wait. I'm delighted to meet you at last. How is it all going over there?"

"I have to confess, not well, and I'm extremely worried. With the failure of the second potato harvest in the summer, much of the population is starving – I have labourers arriving for work so weakened from lack of food that any work I might get out of them is entirely worthless. The first snows have also hit, and I fear the number of deaths from starvation and disease will only increase."

Trevelyan regarded Jones coolly.

"The problem with Ireland, as no doubt you're aware, is that it's vastly over-populated and the land itself is used inefficiently; much of it would be better given over to grazing cattle and sheep than wasted on the production of potatoes. Some might see the blight as a blessing in disguise – sent by Providence, so to speak, although I think the Catholics don't quite subscribe to this view."

Trevelyan gave a thin smile as he finished speaking and looked at Jones to see what effect his words were having.

Jones struggled to contain his rising anger and walked across to one of the windows, pretending to take in the view as he tried to compose himself.

"I'm neither an economist nor a politician – just a simple soldier – but I do believe in God and I don't believe it's God's will that people should be allowed to suffer like this."

"It is unfortunate, yes, but sometimes suffering is necessary in the short term if it serves to deliver a greater good. You're a soldier – you must know this; to protect a cause or way of life, sometimes men have to fight and some of them will die in battle, but their sacrifice is worthwhile because they are the saviours of an entire nation or people."

This was too much, and Jones turned from the window to now look directly at Trevelyan, no longer bothering to hide the anger surging through him.

"War is sometimes necessary – that's why people like me exist – but please don't presume to lecture me on the subject. If you had ever fought, rather than hiding behind a desk, you would know what it is to watch men die in front of you in battle and you would also know what a bloody, messy business it often is. If you have the power to prevent suffering, then you should do it – in fact, you have a duty to do it."

Jones finished speaking and stared directly at Trevelyan. To his surprise, his own anger hadn't prompted a similar anger in Trevelyan. Instead, the man appeared shocked at his outburst and looked as though he was struggling to find the correct way to deal with it.

"Calm yourself, sir," Trevelyan said at last. "The views I've expressed are entertained by both the Prime Minister and a number of others in Parliament. I do understand what you're saying, but I hope, as well, you understand how others feel on this issue. Did you get my last letter?"

"Yes, I did – I've brought it with me to discuss with you."

"And? I suggested that now that the hard weather is upon us and men are unable to work because of it, then they should only receive a proportion of what they would otherwise earn – that seemed only sensible to me. Have you put this in place?"

"No – I haven't and nor will I. In some districts the men are so enfeebled they are unable to earn above four or five pence per diem – even ten pence a day would only provide one meal of corn a day for a family of six; they don't earn enough as it is to keep their families from starving – why would I make it worse?"

Trevelyan looked exasperated.

"The Irish must become self-reliant. I know you think this is a hard medicine, but it is necessary if they're to learn to stand on their own two feet. I'm also struggling to get the relief money I need from some of the landlords in Ireland. Lord Lucan has flat-out refused – he told me to my face barely two weeks ago: '*why should I pay paupers to breed priests?*' I have to balance the books and I'm accountable to Parliament for that – you must try and understand my position."

"I'm now late for my next meeting but you also have to understand my position. These are supposed to be relief works – where is the value of them if the very people they're supposed to help end up dying in the ditches and on the roads anyway? I don't want to be responsible for something where my efforts to help are hamstrung by others who simply refuse to see the reality of what's happening in Ireland."

"I know the reality of what's happening there better than most, Colonel – unlike many of my countrymen, I have taken the liberty of travelling extensively in Ireland and I have made a close study of its people. I'm satisfied the Government's policies are the correct ones. You, I think, take a narrower view."

Jones glared at Trevelyan – the man was insufferable, the worst sort of prig. He had heard some grim tales about him before he travelled but he was even worse than he had imagined.

"I have been appointed Chairman of these works and I won't allow you to interfere. Stay away from me and we'll get along fine!"

With that, Jones turned his back on Trevelyan and strode out of the room, leaving the door wide open as he exited.

Trevelyan sat down again at his desk. They've clearly made the wrong appointment, he thought – he would bring this up with Russell next time they were together and see what he could do about having the fool removed from his post.

"*The Government provided work for a people who love it not. It made this the absolute condition of relief. It knew that the people would all times rather be idle than toil.*"

Times Newspaper, 22 September 1846

CHAPTER NINE

Simon Mayhew found the door of Mary's cottage ajar. He hesitated for a moment outside and resting his hand against the door to push it open still wider, softly called her name. There was no answer so he walked in. A singed mass of cloth or material was draped across the ashes in the hearth; peering closer, he could see that the cloth appeared to be stained with what looked like blood. He felt his heartbeat quicken. Where was she, he wondered, and what has happened here? He walked back outside again and looked around. The nearest cottage stood less than fifty metres away and he now made his way towards this. It was a long time before anyone answered and he had almost turned away when the door suddenly opened. An elderly man peered anxiously out at him. He had grey wisps of hair on his head but heavy, wiry eyebrows which hung in a curtain over his eyes.

"I'm looking for Mary Hogan – I was told she lived in the cottage at the end here, but she doesn't seem to be there."

"And you are?"

Mayhew hesitated.

"A friend –"

The man looked sharply at him.

"A Protestant friend?"

Mayhew sighed.

"I'm worried about her...there's blood on a dress in her cottage. Have you seen her?"

The man stared off into the distance. Then he grunted and looked directly into Mayhew's eyes. He seemed to have decided to trust this stranger.

"I saw her half an hour ago – she was heading up towards the Mullet."

"How did she seem? Was she alright?"

"In truth, she looked awful pale. She also had on her best Sunday dress, which I thought was strange given how I only ever saw her at Mass in it..."

His voice trailed off and he looked down. There was an uncomfortable silence between them then Mayhew spoke again.

"Did she say anything?"

"Well, I was sat outside making a basket and she asked me would I do one for her afterwards."

"Anything else?"

"No, not really, she seemed anxious to get on –"

"Right...I'll go up and see if I can find her. Thank you – you've been very helpful."

Mayhew hurried away. It was a steep climb up to the cliffs

and because the land fell and then rose again in front of him, he didn't have sight of the final bluff and the sea beyond for some time. At last, he came over the brow of a hill and looked down towards the bay beyond. His heart stopped; in the distance, perched on what looked like the very edge of the headland, was a tiny figure. Although the figure was still some distance away, he knew immediately it was Mary. Her arms seemed to be outstretched. He stared for a moment and then quickened his pace, half running, half stumbling through the yellow gorse which tore at his clothing. He had to fight against a fierce gale but although he inwardly cursed, it he also knew it instantly swept away any sound he made and therefore made it possible to make his way to Mary as quickly as possible without alerting her to his presence. He was almost upon her when she must have, at last, heard something because she half turned her head; as she did so, he grabbed her around the waist and they both fell backwards onto the grass, Mary lying on her back on top of him, Mayhew still breathing hard from his exertions. He was sweating, perspiration running down his face, but Mary was pale, and he could feel her body's violent shivering through her thin shift.

"Mary, why are you here? Are you alright?"

"I'm fine, Simon…please let me go."

Reluctantly, he released his grip and slowly, Mary got to her feet.

"I saw you from the top…you looked as though…"

He left the sentence unfinished.

"I'm fine – just out for a walk is all – I often come up here. Why are you here though?"

Mayhew looked anxiously up at her.

"I was worried about you – I came out to find you."

"I told you – I'm fine. You shouldn't be here – if people saw us together…"

"I'm sorry – it's a week since you last came to the church. I was anxious – I thought something must have happened…"

He had risen to his feet. He desperately wanted to hold her again, to pull her towards him but there was something in the way she was holding herself which made it clear this wouldn't be welcomed.

"Please leave me alone. Nothing has happened – or, at least, nothing you can help with anyway."

She had turned her back on him and was staring out to sea. Gulls spun above their heads, calling to each other in harsh keening cries. Then, something strange happened. The sun broke through the clouds and, suddenly, a rainbow appeared. But what was odd about it was that it was a perfect circle, as though two separate rainbows had decided to join hands and dance together. It hung just in front of them, like a portal to another world, so close it was as though a single step would allow you to pass through it.

*

It was an omen, she thought, a sign from God. He still wanted her; she wasn't cursed after all. He was still there for her. She felt a brief surge of hope. Then the thought struck her; if God had sent the rainbow, then he must also have sent Simon. She turned and looked at him.

"The rainbow – have you ever seen one like it before?"

"No…I haven't…it's wonderful."

She smiled at him.

"Yes, it is, it's wonderful."

She hesitated and then seemed to make her mind up.

"Walk me home, Simon."

CHAPTER TEN

Snow had fallen overnight and lay in deep drifts against the sides of the cottages in Tyrone. Some of the drifts were five or six feet high and many people struggled to even get out of their homes, such was the weight of snow against their doors. Most of the houses were no more than mud huts but there were a handful of more substantial houses of unmortared stone. The largest of these belonged to Michael McGuinness and had a slate roof instead of the rough thatch used by his neighbours.

A small group of villagers had made their way from Mullangar the previous night to warn family and relatives living in Tyrone of the evictions which had taken place. Clifton's tenants in Tyrone knew that if they took in any of the families that had been evicted, then they would almost certainly face eviction themselves. Even so, some families had taken that risk; since they were already in arrears with their own rent, their own eviction was almost certain and at least they would be able to offer one night's shelter before they were all forced out.

Michael was not in arrears but then his family enjoyed a much larger plot than many of his neighbours and up until the first failure of the potato crop the previous year, he had also owned some livestock. He also had a twenty-one-year lease which afforded him a measure of security few others enjoyed; most were on tenancies-at-will, which meant they could be evicted on a whim by the landlord. Still others had no land at all. They lived in mud huts on the fringes of the mountains and relied on labouring for their landlords in lieu of rent.

Michael's larger plot allowed him to grow wheat and oats as well as potatoes and he used the grain harvests to pay his rent. The irony was that he was not allowed to harvest these crops for his own use; once reaped by Michael, the grain was thrashed and milled by the Landlord's men and then loaded onto wagons and driven to market, to be sold for export. It was the livestock which had provided his real wealth. Prior to the famine, he had owned a cow, some hens, and a brood of pigs; these had brought him an income and also meant that he had, initially at least, been able to feed his family far better than many of his neighbours. He had kept the cow, but all of the other livestock had long been slaughtered. It was the milk from this and whatever else he managed to forage that had kept his family from completely starving. Michael was a generous man and often went hungry himself to put food on the tables of others, particularly those who were elderly or struck down by illness. Still, there was barely enough to meet the needs of his own family and it had pained him enormously not to be able to do more. During Owen's illness, Sorcha had gone without, hoping in vain that the meagre amount of food they gave him might sufficiently restore his strength to allow him to recover. When the villagers from Mullangar arrived, it wasn't long before one of his neighbours persuaded some of them to make themselves known to Michael and to explain what had happened.

Three men and two women were brought to his cottage by Jamie Gallagher. Jamie was one of seven children in the Gallagher family and the eldest at twenty-three; Michael had always liked him. He was quiet but hard working and big-hearted; he never had a bad word to say about anyone and had a shrewd intelligence. Like Michael, he was one of the very few in the village who could read and write. The two women were dressed in little more than rags with thin shawls draped across their shoulders. They, at least, had shoes. The men's feet were wrapped in rags and Michael could see that one of them already had frostbite, his toes reddened and blistered. All looked starved, and far older than their years, with shrunken gaunt faces and swollen bellies.

"Tell Michael what happened," said Jamie.

The villagers looked at each other and one of the men spoke, his voice little more than a hoarse rasp, which Michael struggled to hear. He told how even the sick had been dragged out of their homes and how not just the thatch had been tumbled from the roofs, but some of the walls had been caved in as well. Only two families and their huts in the entire village had been spared. Michael listened in horror.

"Was Clifton there?"

"He was, although he left soon after the soldiers went."

"And yet he's a man who never goes near his tenants – it was probably the first time he'd ever seen Mullangar," muttered Michael.

"Well, for sure it was the first time any of us had ever seen him," one of the women now said.

"The bailiff – was it Moran?"

Another of the men spoke up.

"It was Moran alright – I remembered him from a hurling game I played two years ago, a nasty gobshite of a man. He deliberately caught me across the back of my hand with his stick and I gave him a fierce dig in his own ribs later on, hard enough to give him trouble breathing for a week anyway."

Michael smiled.

Pleased with the reaction his story had produced, the man felt emboldened to speak again.

"They'll be coming here next, I'm sure of it – all the villages are in arrears."

"Yes, I'm sure you're right," said Michael. He glanced at Jamie.

"Ask your Dad to come and see me tonight and get him to bring Gerard and Ronan with him."

"I will so," said Jamie and he hesitated. "What about…?" He gestured to the villagers.

"They can stay with me tonight – I've got room enough for

them in the barn. There's plenty of hay in there they can use for bedding. They'll need feeding though."

They had been ushered into a back room when they had first entered and, standing, Michael now threw open the door and called through into the kitchen.

"Sorcha – can we rustle up some food for these poor people?"

Sorcha looked at him, one eyebrow raised as much as to say: *"And how do you expect me to perform this miracle?"*

Michael gave a helpless shrug.

"I'll see what I can do," she said. "I might be able to manage some kind of broth or soup, I suppose. It will be poor fare; all I have is some turnips and cabbage. I can feed these but what about the dozens outside?"

"There's nothing we can do for them so. Let's do what we can for these, that's all there is to it."

He smiled at her.

"You're a fine woman – did I ever tell you that?"

"Only when you want something."

"True enough."

He went back into the room where the villagers anxiously stood. He could give them shelter until tomorrow but then they would need to leave. He had scarcely enough food for his own family as it was. He would need to harden his heart even though he knew all they had to look forward to was a long trek to the local workhouse in Mourne and even further to the workhouses in Westport or Ballina. Some of the more fortunate might be able to find board elsewhere with other members of their family or cousins, but many of them would simply perish in the open before they even reached a workhouse. Even if they did make it, he knew they were unlikely to gain entry; in Westport hundreds huddled outside the gates begging to be admitted and the same was true for both Mourne and Ballina. All the workhouses had many times the number of inmates they were supposed to admit.

There's a lot to do, he thought, and not much time in which to do it. It's our own people I need to worry about. The rest can take care of itself.

CHAPTER ELEVEN

Clifton gazed around the room. He was feeling anxious and depressed and this was not what he had anticipated when he had first planned the dinner; it was supposed to be a celebration. He had spent some weeks plotting the series of evictions now being carried out and had invited two other local landowners and their families to the dinner with the express desire of showing them how decisive he could be when it came to the hard business of managing his estate. So, there they all sat: Reith with his dried-up husk of a wife dressed head-to-toe in drab black; Dode McGee, accompanied by his own much prettier wife and two stunningly attractive dark-haired daughters; and his own wife, still attractive but now running to fat. He knew Reith, who sat across from him, had failed to show the same courage, worrying about possible reprisals. Reith was fat-bellied with sagging jowls and heavy pouches under his eyes. The folds of flesh around his eyes were such that it was sometimes difficult to tell whether the man was awake or asleep. He was very much awake now and the greedy fool's face was coated with a sheen of sweat. He looks like a glazed pig's head about to go in the oven, thought Clifton with disgust.

McGee, who owned the estate adjoining Clifton's, was a different proposition. He was a handsome man with sandy hair just beginning to grey around the temples. The only advantage Clifton had over him was one of height; McGee was a good head shorter than Clifton, yet he still managed to somehow carry himself with the air of a much taller man. Clifton himself was undistinguished looking, the only remarkable thing about him was the scattering of pockmarked scars across his cheeks left by the acne that had afflicted him throughout his adolescence. Clifton was acutely aware that it was his money that had bought him his wife; she wouldn't have given him a second glance but for this. McGee spent little time in Ireland, preferring to live mainly on his estate in the Scottish Highlands. His ancestors had come across as part of the enforced settlements in the sixteenth century; Catholic landowners being driven from their lands to be supplanted by English and Scottish Protestants.

The pig's head now spoke.

"Did you hear about poor Haines? Shot dead in his carriage as he was travelling back to his estate."

Clifton hadn't known any of this and wasn't best pleased to be told now, particularly given the look of fear which had suddenly appeared on his wife's face. She would give him hell later, he thought. He swore that as she got fatter, her lips got thinner and meaner looking. She was also showing far too much flesh, leaning forward to show off her breasts to McGee whenever she got the chance and at one point, even pushing her breasts shamelessly into his shoulder as she reached across to refill his wine glass. She had been vehemently opposed to the evictions and had told him he had a duty to try and relieve the sufferings of his tenants, not add to them by driving them out of their homes. Only the previous week, she had taken a carriage and horses down to one of the villages with Sarah, the wretched housekeeper, and stood in the square handing out oatmeal and buttermilk, carrots and cabbages, and God knows what else they could ill afford to give away.

Relishing the dismay on Clifton's face, Reith pressed on.

"It was thought a priest got him killed – he denounced him from the altar saying '*he was worse than Cromwell – and yet he lives.*'"

Reith was delighted to see that his words had had the desired effect; everyone looked both shocked and enthralled, particularly McGee's two younger daughters. All eyes were also now on Clifton to see what he might now say.

"The priests are a pestilence in this country. No-one dares breathe unless he's got his priest's permission first. The man should have been hanged for incitement to murder."

The pig's head laughed but no-one else joined in.

"I heard Lambert's men left you today in the middle of the evictions," Reith said.

"I didn't need him and his toy soldiers," Clifton said. "The bailiff's men were more than a match for any nonsense we might have got from the tenants."

"Why weren't the police there?"

"I asked for the sheriff and a police presence – I was told they had no men to spare; too many laid up, I was told. In any case, I had no need of them; I have no intention of going bankrupt just to keep a roof over these people's heads. I can't afford the poor rates and once the tenants are gone, I can use the land for pasture; the future is in cattle, not bloody potatoes. I want cattle on my land and God knows they'll be much less trouble than those fucking peasants."

Clifton's wife looked sharply at him.

"Please watch your language. There are ladies present."

Some around the table clearly agreed with his sentiments and were none too worried about his choice of words. They had said worse in private themselves. There were some appreciative nods. Reith wasn't finished though.

"I believe you have more evictions planned?" he said smoothly

Clifton was not enjoying being the centre of attention like this and he could see his wife looking more pained with every passing moment. Why didn't that fool Reith shut up?

"I do," Clifton said savagely, "I'll have Tyrone cleared by the end of the week."

"Well no-one could ever accuse you of not being decisive," said Reith with a wry smile.

Clifton shifted uncomfortably in his chair. This was

supposed to be his moment of triumph; so why did he feel as though everyone was secretly laughing at him? They clearly saw him as a stalking horse; happy to see if the fool managed to bring it off and then perhaps, they would have a go themselves.

He felt relieved when his servants had shown out the last of his guests and he was able to retire at last to bed. He pretended to his wife that he had a headache and said he would sleep in one of the guest bedrooms at the rear of the house; in truth he was anxious to avoid a tongue-lashing because he knew she had drunk too much and that was when she was always at her most vicious. *In vino veritas*, he thought bitterly; it was when she was in her cups that her real opinion of him and his schemes emerged. She started to say something as he left the marital bedroom, but he quickened his steps to get away from her and hastened to one of the bedrooms he often used as a bolt hole on occasions like this.

Haines' murder had unsettled him and he struggled to fall asleep. He was worried about the Tyrone evictions and wondered if perhaps he should leave them to his agent and the bailiffs to deal with; he could easily pretend he had other, more pressing, estate business. He settled into a shallow, uneasy sleep; in his dreams, the man with the black fever who had been dragged out and dumped on the ground in front of his cottage suddenly sat up and, with a triumphant and terrible smile, levelled a shot gun at Clifton's chest. Clifton shrank back in horror, raising the reins of the horse in front of him to somehow ward off what was about to happen, but it was too late

– there was a loud deafening roar and he felt himself falling to the ground, one of his feet still snared in the stirrups so that he found himself on his back with one leg still awkwardly caught. So, this is what it feels like to be shot, he thought. It's not as bad as I'd imagined; I thought it would be painful, but I don't seem to feel anything. And yet I'm dying…

He woke with a start and, for a moment, struggled to realise where he was and whether he had been dreaming or really had been shot. His body was soaked in a cold, clammy sweat; he could feel the perspiration running down across his chest and sides and soaking into the sheets. He lay there re-running the dream in his head, trying to make sense of it. Suddenly, he heard a piercing scream; a strange unearthly noise which he doubted could have been made by anything human. In the same instant, he realised to his horror the scream must have come from his wife. He lurched out of bed and strode unsteadily across the landing to their bedroom. The door was still closed and, for a second, he stood outside, afraid to go in, his hand trembling on the cold brass handle. He braced himself and, turning the handle, slowly pushed the door back.

It was a large room with two large sash windows facing onto the grounds at the front of the house. Both windows had heavy green drapes and he struggled to see anything at first. He noticed that one of the sets of curtains seemed to be moving, bowing and then shrinking back, which struck him as odd unless…

The bed was at the far end of the room at a right angle to the door; it was a large, imposing four-poster with an oak frame and an elaborately embroidered yellow silk canopy. He peered cautiously round the edge of the door and his eyes met those of his wife, who was sitting bolt upright, staring at him with a look of complete terror on her face. She seemed transfixed, incapable of movement.

"Emma, are you alright? I thought I heard a noise."

His wife blinked. Her mouth opened but no words came forth. It was as though she had suddenly found herself mute, struck dumb.

He tried again moving closer to the bed so he could see her more clearly.

"My love, what's wrong? Why did you –?"

"There was a…crash," she stammered, "the window…glass breaking –"

He peered again at the bowing curtains and, slowly, realisation dawned. Somehow the window had broken. Very cautiously, he moved forward to the window and slowly moved one of the curtains back with a hand so he could look behind it. Jagged edges of glass around the frame of the window confronted him. There was an icy breeze. Looking down, he could see shards of glass against the dark oak floor and in amongst the shards, there appeared to be something else, something wrapped in paper. He reached down and lifted it up to study it more closely. It was a rock which was about the size of a fist. Wrapped around it was some sort of paper or document.

He carefully unwrapped the rock and looked at the stiff

piece of paper. It had some sort of writing on it but even though it was a clear night with a full moon, he struggled to make out what was on it. He peered out through the shattered window trying to see if whoever had done this might still be lurking outside. At first, he struggled to see anything, then, as his eyes adjusted, he realised with a start that there were footprints in the snow leading up to and then away from the front of the house. The world seemed to have fallen entirely silent. There was a large ornate stone fountain in the immediate courtyard which formed the centre of a large turning circle for carriages. Normally, he would be able to hear the soft splashing sound of water cascading into the central font but in the last two days, it had completely iced over, and large tendrils of ice splayed over the edges of its upper bowl, hanging in lumpy curtains down its edges.

Carrying both the rock and the parchment, he stepped back into the room and moved across to a large walnut dresser set against the wall opposite the bed. He set the rock and document carefully down on the top of the dresser and reached for the oil lamp which sat in the centre. There was a small metal box next to the oil lamp and he removed a match from this, which he struck against a small piece of sandpaper. The phosphorous tip of the match flared briefly, and he used this to light the lamp, the top of which had a stiff cone of silk to amplify the flame. He brought the lamp closer to the parchment. The script was both ragged and untidy, but the words were clear enough and he felt an immediate shaft of fear lance through him.

"What is it Charles? What's on…the paper?"

Clifton slowly turned towards his wife, the hand holding the piece of paper trembling uncontrollably. He started to speak but no words would come. His mouth felt horribly dry and he was struggling to breathe. He could feel his heart racing in his chest.

"What's wrong? Tell me!" his wife shouted.

He tried to speak again but with the same result. Still clasping the piece of paper, he walked out.

CHAPTER TWELVE

Jones stared at McDowell. He felt exhausted after the strenuous boat trip back from London. The ship had docked just before dawn and it had now been two days since he had last slept. A meeting had been arranged for him for the morning of his return with Connor McDowell, the Board of Works Inspector for Donegal. Jones was desperate for sleep and he had audibly groaned when he found out. For a moment, he considered asking for the meeting to be re-arranged for the following day, but he knew how rude this would appear. Now the man stood before him, visibly trembling with anger.

"Roads starting from nowhere and going nowhere," McDowell said. "That's about the height of it. And payment on a piece rate basis for a starving people who struggle to even stand up, never mind lift a shovel or a pick. Do you know, sir, that some of these roads don't even join up properly? A road finishes in one district and the road it's meant to link up with in another district is half a mile away – the districts don't even talk to each other."

McDowell was expressing many of the same sentiments Jones himself held; the problem was he had only met McDowell once before and he was uncertain how much he could trust him. Jones was the Chairman of the Board; it was difficult for him to openly criticise his own organisation, even with his own subordinates. But he instinctively liked McDowell, who had an open, honest look about him and after brooding for a moment, Jones decided to take a risk and share his own feelings.

"When I came back from England," Jones said, "I travelled up by rail to Liverpool in brand new carriages owned by the London and North Western Railway company. This is a company which was formed barely months ago. The Government is spending two hundred million pounds on new rail lines in England and I can't help but compare this with the nonsensical public works we're supposed to oversee in Ireland."

"Exactly," said McDowell. "And we both know why this is as well – the Whigs don't want spending in Ireland to interfere with or get in the way of market forces, which is all well and good, but how can it be sensible to waste public money on digging holes in roads and then asking the poor wretches to fill them in again? It would be more useful to start putting in a railway network over here to match the one in England."

"It would," sighed Jones, "but it's not going to happen."

"I have to be frank with you," said McDowell. "I'm in despair. Trevelyan has kept the wages we pay at barely enough to keep a labourer and his family from starvation. If a man falls sick or dies, then his wife and children take his place. I have never before seen starvation up close but what I have seen in the last few months would make a stone statue cry."

Jones had also been witness to the brutal effects of starvation. When he had first taken up his post, he had made a point of travelling as widely as possible so he could see for himself how works were being administered. This had been a depressing experience. The labourers employed on the schemes were already starving and yet were expected to work ten to twelve hours a day, six days a week, levelling hills, building bridges, and digging drainage ditches. People who were starving became childlike and cringing; their skin stank and had a brown filthy coating to it. Children looked prematurely aged and struggled to either walk or talk, their limbs wasted away and stick-like. Yet for every labourer employed, a hundred more lurked by the roadside, all eager to step forward should someone collapse or prove unable to continue. The children too young to work huddled round small turf fires which their parents hastily assembled before starting their labours in the morning.

Jones looked again at McDowell. He was a much younger man than Jones, probably in his late thirties, with a shock of unruly black hair which many other men might envy at his age. There was something odd about his eyes – the irises seemed to be both brown and green at the same time, something Jones had never seen before. It made McDowell seem strangely charismatic.

"I saw Trevelyan," Jones said, "when I was over in London. Now it's winter, he wants me to cut back wages still further –

he doesn't want us to pay for days when the weather prevents people working."

"You're not going to implement that, I hope?"

"I told him I wouldn't but, at the end of the day, I'm just a functionary. All of this has been agreed with the Lord Lieutenant. However, even with bad weather, I'm sure some work is possible if you take my meaning..."

"Yes, I'm quite sure it is," said McDowell. "If the roads are too bad to work on, would stone breaking be allowable as labour?"

"Yes, I don't see why not. Breaking stones is part of road building, even if some of the stones lie a little to the side of a road...Take care though – we're both taking a risk doing this."

"I know, but I can't stand by and watch people die either."

"No – we have to do the best we can despite the constraints on us."

"I wonder if these politicians were to see with their own eyes some of the things we've seen, whether they might not then relent a little and show some basic humanity," McDowell said.

"Perhaps...perhaps not. It's a complex picture – the Whigs believe in self-reliance and they also believe Ireland is over-populated...that the people are feckless and lazy and so on; they refuse to help themselves so why should we get involved? There's a deeply ingrained prejudice there and also some very ingrained political beliefs. On top of that, there are strong economic reasons for pushing through change, turning the land over to grazing and so on. Put it all together, and perhaps it's not that surprising we are where we are. It doesn't remotely begin to justify it, but it does provide an explanation – of sorts, anyway. So even if you confronted Russell, Wood, Grey, Trevelyan, the whole pack of them, with the reality of what's happening here – made them see it with their own eyes – I'm not sure there would be a change in policy. There might be a lot of hand-wringing and perhaps some tinkering around the edges to ease their consciences, but there wouldn't be fundamental changes – and that's what's needed. As to prejudice against the Irish, have you seen some of the cartoons in *Punch*?"

"No, I haven't had the pleasure, I'm afraid," said McDowell.

"I've kept a copy of the magazine somewhere."

Jones gazed at the untidy pile of papers on this desk and remembered that he had placed the magazine in one of his desk drawers. He opened it and, finding the right page, pushed it across the desk.

"Here, look at this," he said.

McDowell stared at the cartoon. It was a pen and ink drawing of an ape-like creature squatting on the floor. A napkin was draped around its neck, a spoon held to its mouth, whilst the other paw clutched a bowl. This was bad enough but then his eye was drawn to the text below the image. It read: *As we've dared to call the monkeys in the Zoo by Irish names, Erin's sons, in wrath, declare us snobs and flunkies and demand that we withdraw them – nor should we ignore their claims – for its really very hard – upon the monkeys.*

He glanced up at Jones.

"This is disgusting," he said. "How can they...?"

"Very easily, I'm afraid," said Jones, "because there's a ready audience for it. You do that to a people then they become sub-human and if you believe a people aren't remotely the same as you, then it becomes easier to treat them badly – they don't suffer the same, do you see? They're not human after all, so how could they?"

"And you think this is what is happening in Ireland?"

"To an extent, yes – at least it makes it easier to turn a blind eye."

"You paint a bleak picture."

"I'm a soldier – I see things as they are, not as people might want them to be. I've seen enough horrors in my lifetime not to waste time on fantasies. You have to deal with what's in front of you."

Jones pushed his chair back impatiently and stood up. His desk backed onto a window and he now turned and gazed out into the street below, busy with carriages and people scurrying to and fro, picking their way carefully around the piles of horse shit which liberally decorated the road, staining the freshly fallen snow. He now had his back to McDowell and, for a moment, simply stood still, silently contemplating the street scene below. Although Jones had not intended it, McDowell took this as his cue to leave and rose from his own chair.

"I'm sorry – I know you're busy. I must get back in any case. I enjoyed our conversation – I only wish there were more like you."

Jones turned to face him and gave a brief smile.

"And you, McDowell…and you. It was a pleasure seeing you again."

When McDowell had left, Jones looked briefly again around his office. It was a large and elegant room and on one of the dark wood-panelled walls hung a portrait in oils of Arthur Wellesley, the Duke of Wellington. It had an ornate gold frame and showed the Duke in full military regalia, his arms folded, unsmiling. Jones stared at the painting. God, the Duke was a handsome bastard, Jones thought. And what a man.

Jones remembered the tears Wellesley had shed at the siege of Badajoz at the sight of so many British dead piled upon each other at the foot of the walls of the fortress. He also remembered something else. Nearly five thousand men had died in the assault on the Spanish fortress, an assault Jones had also been present at. Blood flowed like rivers in the ditches and trenches; he had seen men blown apart by the crude barrels of gunpowder hurled down on them from the ramparts, mown down by a merciless hail of musket fire by the Spanish troops. Some of the scenes he had seen that day still haunted his sleep, but it was what happened afterwards which had marked him most profoundly. Maddened by the slaughter they had endured and the deaths of so many of their friends and comrades, the soldiers had broken into liquor stores and then gone on a rampage, massacring thousands of civilians, including woman and children. They had even shot some of their own officers who tried to stop them. So yes, he had seen the evil men were capable of and he had no illusions as to the depravity men could sink to. Eventually, order had been restored but, by then, of course, it was too late. How quickly had a well organised and trained army descended into brutality; how thin is the veneer of civilisation? What was happening in Ireland dismayed him but nor was he surprised by it.

He sighed and looked down again at his desk. My job is to do my duty as best I can, he thought; do what I can to mitigate the evil being done and then move on. And in the end, he thought, isn't that all any of us can do?

CHAPTER THIRTEEN

Michael hadn't slept well. He had sat up long into the night with Jamie's Dad, Liam Foley, and Gerard and Ronan Lynch, arguing on what should be done about Clifton. Liam was in his mid-forties but looked much older and there was already a defeated air about him. Michael knew that both he and his wife now frequently went without food themselves so they could at least provide something for their children but with the second failure of the potato crop, there were now often occasions when all of them went hungry. Ronan was closing on fifty but was better preserved; Gerard was his only son, his wife having died in childbirth. Ronan had been so overcome by grief at the time that he wanted nothing to do with the new baby, refusing even to look at it when it was brought to him for the first time. His sister had taken the child in, but despite her urging, he had refused to see his son and for the first few weeks, the child remained without a name. Finally, she decided to call him Gerard; she had two small daughters and had already decided that if her next child was a boy then she would name it Gerard after their grandfather on their mother's side. Since the next pregnancy seemed to be taking its own sweet time, she was happy to use the name instead for her brother's child. She arranged for Father McNamara to baptise him and, being a sensible woman, decided to stop badgering her poor brother and simply wait until he came to his senses.

Gerard was eight months old when his father finally made the two-mile journey to his sister's cottage to see him. Gerard had just discovered the delights of rolling to make his way around, having decided this was infinitely preferable to either crawling or bottom shuffling. He was sat up on the floor of the cramped interior of the cottage when Ronan arrived. His aunt softly called his name. The baby turned and with a smile, rolled across to her, his arms held out straight in front of him like someone about to take their first dive. Ronan gave a spontaneous snort of laughter and immediately fell in love. They agreed she would continue to bring him up since, as a man, Ronan would clearly be hopeless with young children, but that he would come across to see him as often as he could. When the boy turned nine, Ronan brought him back to his own cottage so Gerard could start to help out in the fields. Ronan had never remarried, and Gerard had grown up both headstrong and hot-headed. Gerard was now in his late twenties and had yet to marry himself, although he had had several relationships and was rumoured to be the father of Frances Carey's little girl. Michael had been reluctant to admit him as a member of their group but his father, who was entirely blind to his faults, had insisted. In the intense debate of the previous night, Gerard had shown exactly why Michael had been right to have reservations about him.

"The man needs to be shot! That's the best way to put both a stop to him and any other landlord who might take it into their head to try and evict their tenants."

"Gerard, keep your voice down, for God's sake," said Michael. "My two sons are asleep next door! And don't be preaching murder either – that's not what we're about."

"Haines was shot, wasn't he, and didn't that send a powerful message to all the other landlords? Clifton has turned people out just as the hard weather sets in and many of them will die in ditches whilst he sleeps soundly in his bed!"

Liam was looking increasingly anxious and afraid. He took another sip of the potcheen, from the small shot glass in front of him and then spoke. It was good stuff; a strong spirit made from grain, sugar beet, or potatoes. He didn't know Michael's source, but he made sure he never turned down an offer of it when he came around.

"Killing Clifton will get us killed and I don't want my children to become orphans," Liam murmured.

Michael nodded approval.

"Liam's right, this is a political movement, not a charter for murderers. And in any case, Gerard, who exactly would be doing the shooting? The only thing you've ever shot was a couple of rabbits and I think one of those you missed, and it fell over in fright instead."

The others laughed but Gerard's face flushed red with both embarrassment and anger; Michael was their leader, but Gerard didn't care to be scorned in this way.

"Clifton would be easier to hit than a rabbit! And if you're all too scared to do it, then I'll happily take it on."

"Easy Gerard," said his father. "Calm down. No-one's shooting anybody, not tonight, nor any other time either."

"Look," said Michael, "All we need to do is to send a warning. The threat will be enough. It needs to be done tonight though – tomorrow will be too late."

"So, what did you have in mind, Michael?" asked Liam.

Michael got up from the table and walked across to a heavy oak chest in the corner of the room. He lifted the lid and after rummaging for a moment, returned with a rough scrap of paper and a quill pen. He then retrieved a small pot of ink from a shelf immediately above the fireplace. He set the pot down on the table, smoothed the paper out, and taking the quill, which he first dipped into the ink, carefully started to scratch out some words. None of the others could read or write so they were all fascinated by what he was now doing and leaned closer to peer down at the paper. It was as though he had produced a wand and was about to use it to cast some terrible spell. What none of them realised was that Michael had also deliberately chosen to write with his left hand to disguise his handwriting. The script he produced was therefore both childlike and ragged but still clearly legible. When he had finished, he leaned back in his chair and gave a sigh of satisfaction.

"What have you written Michael?" asked Liam.

Michael grinned at him.

"Enough to keep the man in his bed tomorrow," he said teasingly.

"So, what does it say?" asked Gerard impatiently.

"It says: *'You've destroyed Mullangar and now we'll destroy you'* and I've signed it *'The Molly Maguires.'* I've also added a drawing of a coffin at the bottom."

"But its Young Ireland we support" said Ronan, "not the Molly Maguires – they're just thugs – why have you said that?"

"Because Clifton knows full well what those lads get up to; they probably had a hand in Haines' death. This will hopefully frighten the life out of him and stop any nonsense tomorrow."

"If Clifton finds out, or even suspects, then it's either the gallows or a trip to Botany Bay for all of us," said Liam nervously. "Are you sure about this?"

Michael smiled.

"That's why I've left Tyrone out of it. If I'd mentioned Tyrone, he would have had the police and troops round us all up but too many people lived in Mullangar and they've all now been scattered to the four winds. It will work, trust me, and we're safe enough."

"I'm not sure you're right," said Ronan. "The tenants in Mullangar have already been evicted and the likeliest explanation is that at least a few of those tenants were already members of the Molly Maguires and sought revenge because of the evictions. Is it in Irish or English you've written it?"

"English – that fool doesn't know a word of Irish. He spends most of his time in England, anyway, as do most of the landlords. We know it's common knowledge in the district that evictions were planned for us next. We're also the nearest village to Mullangar. Clifton has another dozen villages on his land, but it stands to reason he'll start with us. In any case, if we succeed in protecting Tyrone, the other villages should benefit as well – the main thing is to avoid suspicion falling directly on us."

"And how will we deliver it?" asked Gerard. "We can hardly walk up to the door with it, can we?"

"I'll deliver it," said Michael, "…on the end of a rock."

He leaned back and grinned again.

"I'll come with you," said Gerard.

"No – it's better I do it on my own. Having two people there just increases the chances of someone hearing and us getting caught."

"Well, I'm happy to go instead of you."

"No, Gerard – this is something I need to do. You'll have your time, don't worry, but this isn't it."

Michael glanced at Ronan and he could see he was relieved. Gerard looked frustrated but at least he appeared sensible enough not to push it.

"Right, that's agreed then. We'll have another drop of potcheen and then call it a night."

Liam smiled.

"Do you remember the time Father McNamara asked for all

the stills to be brought to the church so they could be broken up?"

"I do," said Michael. "It made a change to hear a sermon from him on the evils of drink rather than his usual preaching that we were all going to Hell, apart from himself and the bishop."

"Darragh's wife made him take his still down and when he got there, didn't he notice a much better copper one left on the ground. So, he left his and took that one back instead."

They all laughed.

"I'll bet he didn't show it to his wife," said Ronan.

"He did not! He hid it in a hedge near the house and he's been using it ever since. Well, at least he was up until last year; no-one's had money to pay for barley since the blight struck."

Liam looked across at Michael. "You have your own source, of course." He raised his own glass in a salute and downed what was left with a single swallow. "Good man yourself!"

As they left the cottage, it was already snowing heavily, a silent glistening cascade. Michael stood for a moment in the doorway, looking out at it. He used to love the snow as a boy. The first fall seemed to cleanse the world, draping everything in the softest white, hiding the grim reality which often sat underneath. Then there were snowball fights with his mates and sledging recklessly down the steepest hills they could find. He also remembered the agonies he endured when he returned home as his hands slowly thawed, the knifing pain through his fingers, the shouts of laughter between him and his siblings as they compared their bruises. Now though, he was anxious. How long would those evicted from Mullangar survive in this, he thought? They would either have to sleep in the open or in a ditch or in whatever scalpeen they managed to cobble together. He shivered briefly in his thin clothes. I'll need my coat, he thought, before I ride out in this. The snow was now beginning to settle and was already creeping over the top of his boots. He realised that if he didn't make a start soon, he might have to abandon the trip altogether and then Tyrone would lie at Clifton's mercy in the morning. He sighed and retreated inside to find his coat. In the distance, he could still hear laughter from the other men as they made their way slowly back to their own cottages.

Gerard was still unhappy with the way in which he felt he had been slighted and made little of by Michael and he grumbled noisily to his father as the two of them made their way back to his father's cottage, where Gerard also still lived.

"A piece of paper is not the way to deal with a man like Clifton. Someone needs to take revenge for what's happened at Mullangar."

"Musha, Gerard – leave it alone, will ya? Michael knows what he's doing."

"No, Da, I won't leave it alone. I'm going to give Clifton something else to think about besides a broken window!"

"Careful, son – the last sight I want on this earth is of you hanging from a gallows, and they hang you now for just looking as though you might do something, never mind actually carrying it out."

"Don't worry, Da, I'll be careful enough, but I just can't sit by and do nothing either."

Ronan sighed.

"I can't stop you, Gerard, but I'm still your father and if you bring disgrace on our house, I swear I'll help them hang you myself! It's not just yourself you need to consider – if you do anything stupid, you risk us all being transported, and I can tell you now, I'm far too old to be worked to death with whips in Australia."

Gerard was silent for a moment. He had never heard his father speak so forcefully and with such passion. Still, he was old – what did he know of men like Clifton and how best to deal with them? Gerard decided to humour his father; let him think I've listened, he thought. In the meantime, I'll decide myself what should happen next.

"Calm down, Da – you're right. I'll let Michael handle Clifton. I'm not sure I envy him anyways going out on a night like tonight. I'd rather be in my bed, I'm sure."

His father glanced up at him; his son was a good head taller than he was and much stronger. He seemed to have taken the point, he thought. Let's hope to God he had anyway.

*

Sorcha was waiting for Michael as he turned to go back into the house. She stood in the middle of the room, arms folded and unsmiling.

"Are you coming to bed?"

"I have to go out…there's something I need to do."

"And what possible reason would you have to go out on a night like this?"

"It's important, Sorcha – you don't need to know any more than that."

"Is that right? Well, if it affects me and the children, then I do have a right, so what are you up to?"

"Please, Sorcha – I wouldn't do anything that might hurt you and the boys – if anything, I'm trying to protect us."

"Protect us – how?"

Michael turned away from her, grabbing his coat which hung on a crudely fashioned wooden peg jammed into a crack in the wall.

"I can't tell you – I need to go."

She grabbed him by the shoulder as he went to leave, pulling him roughly back.

"If you go, don't bother coming back."

"Maybe I won't," he said bitterly.

He disappeared into the darkness. For a moment, she stood in the doorway staring miserably out, tears running down her cheeks.

"Michael!"

It was a half scream, half shout of desperation.

Then she heard the sudden clatter of hooves as Michael reappeared briefly from the darkness, mounted on their horse, Róisín, a white mare Sorcha loved to distraction. Horse and rider paused for a moment, caught in the candlelight from the open doorway. Then they were gone.

"Let us strike the culpable, not only in their persons, but in their dearest interests and affections; let not only their cattle be houghed, their houses burned, their land turned up, their harvests destroyed, but let their friends and relations be devoted to death, the wives and daughters to dishonour."

The Molly Maguires Code

CHAPTER FOURTEEN

C lifton also slept badly. The Molly Maguires were notorious and much feared and not only were they prepared to murder the landlords they took against and burn their houses to the ground, but it was even rumoured they had on occasion resorted to the rape of their women folk. He had been too frightened to reveal the content of the message to his wife and fortunately she hadn't tried to go after him when he left the bedroom. Despite his lack of sleep, he was still obliged to get up before dawn because he knew Moran and his men would be shortly arriving for the planned evictions at Tyrone. He had also asked his Agent to join them and it was Johnson who arrived first. Johnson was English and managed both Clifton's English estate in Dorset and the County Mayo estate. He had just turned sixty but still had a full dark head of hair with, as yet, only one or two strands of grey. He also sported a neatly trimmed moustache. Johnson had an easy confidence about him and was also extremely shrewd.

Whilst they waited for the bailiff and his men, they retired to a large living room overlooking the front of the house. This was expensively decorated in the Italian style with elaborately patterned dark blue silk wallpaper set off by heavily upholstered ruby red armchairs and settees. There were a number of smaller oil paintings and prints, but two huge canvases dominated the wall facing the windows depicting naval battle scenes. It was an impressive room and a clear statement of the wealth of the owner of the house.

They settled themselves in two armchairs in front of a large marble fireplace; Johnson was glad of the warmth from the turf fire; his own house was at the far end of Clifton's estate, a good mile distant. He had initially thought he might ride across but had then decided to walk. He liked walking because he often felt he could think more clearly about issues than when sat at a desk; however, he had failed to realise just how bitterly cold it was and despite his heavy wool coat, he was shivering by the time he arrived. Clifton quickly explained what had happened during the night and showed him the rock and the piece of paper which had been wrapped around it. Johnson carefully examined both the rock and paper and then looked at Clifton.

"Very worrying," he said. "However, this might not be the work of the Molly Maguires – whoever sent this might be using their notoriety to try and scare you. It's more likely to have come from some of the tenants at either Mullangar or Tyrone and I'm guessing its Tyrone because I imagine the only thing people evicted from Mullangar were worried about yesterday was finding some form of shelter and avoiding freezing to death in the snow."

"So, who do you think it might be?"

"Well, aside from the priests and gentry, I doubt there's more than a dozen people in the whole of the county who can read and write, so if it comes from Tyrone, then that narrows it down even more – perhaps two or three people at most. Now, the only two I'm aware of are Michael McGuinness, his sister Mary, and perhaps Sorcha, his wife. Michael taught Mary, I believe, and it makes sense that once they were married, he also taught Sorcha her letters."

"And how was McGuiness taught his letters and arithmetic?"

"He was taught by an itinerant armed with a blackboard and chalk. I believe that's quite common in this part of the country. Moran knows McGuiness well too – apparently, they grew up together. I bet he knows Mary too."

"The problem is, it's all very well suspecting somebody – it's different altogether having the evidence to justify an arrest."

Johnson thought for a moment and then smiled. "I've heard that Michael is one of the readers in the village for *The Nation*; you know, the rag produced by the Young Ireland movement. When it's published, they all meet up, apparently, and Michael will read it aloud to everyone. Now, if we could find out when they're next meeting, we might be able to get the sheriff and his men to arrest him – argue he's trying to incite people to sedition and rebellion. Once we've done that, we get Michael to produce a sample of his handwriting, match it to the message you've received, and we've got him."

"What if it wasn't him though – wouldn't we then just have arrested the wrong man and the real villain goes free?"

"Well, everything points to it being him. And even if it wasn't, why do we care? At worst, we'll have got him out of the way whilst we carry out the evictions at Tyrone. At best, we might see the bastard hanged. If it was someone else, it will also send a message."

"Yes, makes sense."

"So, I suggest we leave off the evictions for the moment. When Moran and his men turn up, dismiss them but ask Moran to stay behind. We won't tell them about the incident last night; we'll only tell the sheriff but we'll swear him to secrecy for the time being as well; we'll tell the sheriff you don't want it getting out because you don't want to worry your wife. We'll then say we have our suspicions about who might be responsible, but we need to carry out some discreet investigations of our own first before involving the police. As far as the evictions and Moran are concerned, we'll tell him we need to go back to the Quarter Sessions to get some further warrants before finally going ahead. Then I'll see if I can persuade Moran to try and find out when the next reading is to take place; he'll want to know why I'm interested, I'm sure, but I'll just say that if I can let the judge know of the sort of thing that goes on in Tyrone, then he's more likely to be sympathetic to giving us the warrants. If the judge thinks it's a hotbed of sedition, he'll happily grant what we need to clear the whole village."

"Right – I understand. What do you think of Moran, by the way?"

"Barely competent and not entirely trustworthy either – if I had to score him between one and ten, he would be a four at best."

Clifton smiled.

"You score everyone, don't you, Johnson? Sometimes I wonder how you've scored me."

Johnson regarded him coolly. He thought his employer barely rated a three, but it would obviously not be politic to reveal this.

"Eight," said Johnson finally. "And before you ask, no-one gets a ten – "

"Then, from you, I imagine eight is high praise indeed."

Johnson rose to his feet. "Moran should be here soon – I suggest you explain the evictions are off and I'll deal with the rest, fill him in on the reasons for the cancellation, and then talk to him privately about the next reading."

"Thanks, Johnson – once he's gone, I'll ride over to the sheriff and tell him about last night."

"I could do it for you if you like."

"No, it's fine – it's probably better if I do this."

Johnson grinned. "So, the trap is set then – should be fun. I'm looking forward to this."

"Yes, and I hope the bastard does hang – I always enjoyed a

good hanging; especially if the neck's not broken and you get to see them dance for a bit."

Johnson stared at him. What a very unpleasant man you are, he thought. I wouldn't mind seeing you dance on the end of the rope, never mind McGuinness.

"I've got some accounts to go through," said Johnson. "Could you get one of the servants to let me know once Moran's arrived?"

"Yes, of course."

"Good – I'll see you shortly then. Don't get up – I can let myself out."

Johnson nodded briefly to Clifton and briskly left the room. Clifton had felt supremely confident whilst Johnson was there but, oddly, once he had gone, he started to worry again.

Johnson is clever, he thought, but McGuinness wasn't daft either. If he was arrested but then set free again, he would be a very dangerous adversary. Still, what choice do I have? If I do nothing the Molly Maguires might strike again anyway and next time it could be a lot worse than a rock through the window. I have to trust Johnson knows what he's doing.

He sighed. He didn't usually reach for the port or whisky until after lunch but perhaps today he would make an exception. He needed something to calm his nerves after all.

CHAPTER FIFTEEN

As Michael slid beneath the thin blankets covering their bed, Sorcha, who had been curled up on her side facing him, immediately turned to lie on her other side, presenting him with her back. Cautiously, he placed a hand on her shoulder.

"I'm sorry – I had to do this."

"Had to do what? You haven't told me what you were up to."

"It's better you don't know but it's for all of our sakes anyway."

"Yes – well, we'll see, won't we. What did you do? I've a right to know."

Michael hesitated.

"I…delivered a message…a warning…that's all."

"You'll have to do better than that – what sort of message? What did it say? How did you deliver it?"

"Please don't ask me – I've already told you more than I should have. I'm trying to stop Clifton doing to us what he did at Mullangar."

"All your fool schemes will do is make matters worse. You're a first-class eejit. God knows why I married you. One minute you're in despair, barely able to shift out of the bed, and the next you're tearing around like a lunatic, one mad scheme after another, making my life a complete misery."

Michael was immediately furious.

"For the love of God, will you leave me alone, woman. All I get from you is your poisonous tongue. I'm trying – I really am – to do my best for everyone, for you, for the boys, and all I get back is insults. You're wondering why you married me – well don't you think I feel the same about you?"

"I did once love you...and I still do sometimes...but you frighten me with your moods. I don't know who I've married. I never know which way you're going to jump. If it wasn't for the boys –"

"If it wasn't for the boys...what? You'd leave me? Is that it? Well, do it then. Do it. But if you try and take them with you, you won't get five yards –"

"Keep your bloody voice down – they can hear you."

"Jesus, Mary, and Joseph – will you leave it? Just stop, for Christ's sake."

He threw back the bedclothes and stood up, glaring across at her. Then he abruptly turned. He went to a small oak chest of drawers and snatched the clothes he had left draped across the top. Within moments, he was dressed again. He strode to the door, pulled on his boots, grabbed his coat which still lay on the ground and walked out, the door banging savagely behind him.

Sorcha collapsed back on to the bed and, burying her head

in the pillow, burst into tears. She loved Michael with a fierce passion but in the last two years he had changed. At first, she had barely noticed the difference; he just seemed a little more excitable sometimes with a restless energy. This would last for a few weeks and then he would suddenly plunge into a deep depression. At one point, he had even told her that he no longer wanted to live and that he had seriously thought about ways to kill himself. She remembered how her hands shook then, how the world she thought she knew and over which she felt she had at least some control, suddenly tilted into chaos. Michael had been the one sure thing she could depend on. Now, in an instant, that had gone; he had gone and she was confronted with a stranger.

For days afterwards, she had felt frightened every time he left the house. Had he really gone to work in the fields or was he about to take his own life? She had been particularly terrified when he had announced he was going to see if he could collect some seaweed from the shore. Was that his real intention or did he plan to hurl himself off the cliffs above? Stop, she thought. Stop letting your thoughts run away with themselves. Michael might be a lunatic sometimes, but he wouldn't be daft enough to kill himself. She had to stop dwelling on this. Where had he gone now though? Should she go after him? No, she couldn't leave the boys. He had just gone to cool off somewhere; he would be back soon enough. She had to calm down. Try and get some sleep. Tomorrow could take care of itself. And if he had been up to some new madness? What then? What would become of them? She rolled on to her side. I have to be strong, she thought. Whatever happens, I'll deal with it. Whatever the day brings, I'll cope somehow – even if it has to be on my own.

*

For a moment, Michael stood staring into the darkness. Should I go back, he wondered? No, I need to be on my own for a bit. I was suffocating in there. Why didn't she understand? I need to walk off my anger. Which way? Towards the sea or inland down past Lorcan's place?

He hesitated briefly and then made his mind up, striding quickly down towards the shore. The grass lay thick and matted beneath his feet. He brushed mindlessly past some nettles and immediately felt a stinging sensation in his hand and wrist. He wandered past large clumps of yellow irises growing wild in the hedgerows. In the pre-dawn light, the flowers were grey but in full sunlight the yellow sang, and it was a sight he had always loved. As he neared the shore, he was assailed by the sour sulphurous smell of rotting seaweed. He could just make out the dim phosphorus glow of the waves as they broke on the sand. There also seemed to be some sort of shadow about fifty yards ahead of him. Driftwood, he thought. A boat of some sort? Then it moved. He peered more closely. It was a man walking slowly down into the shallows. What was he doing?

It was a bitterly cold night and the sea itself would be freezing. No-one in their right mind would venture into the sea on a night like this. Michael quickened his stride. The man was still moving and was now up to his waist in the water. To Michael's amazement, the man leant forward and started to swim: an unsteady breaststroke, only his head now visible. Michael knew there was a strong riptide and he could see the man had now stopped swimming and was being swept helplessly out to sea. He had to try and save him. He plunged in. The water was icy cold and, for a moment, he struggled to breathe or move, his body in shock. He knew it would be a mistake to try and fight the riptide. He needed to let it take him out and hope that at the point its force was spent, he would still be close enough to rescue this lunatic.

Michael put his head back and let the tide carry him, fighting all the time to control the fear welling up in him that he might be swept too far from shore and drown himself. He kept glancing anxiously over his shoulder trying to catch sight of the other man. He would glimpse him and then moments later he was gone again. Finally, the surging water around Michael seemed to ease. He twisted round frantically trying to see where the man now was. There was a dark mass floating motionless in the water quite close to where he swam, and he lunged towards it. The man was floating face down. Michael grabbed him by his shirt collar and pulled him closer, keeping his face and upper torso free of the waves. Kicking hard Michael made for the shore. He was close to exhaustion.

When he had finally dragged the man onto the beach, he sat for a moment, breathing hard. Using both hands, he started to pump the man's chest. There was no response; the body lay inert beneath him. He felt for a pulse in the man's neck but there was nothing; he was dead. Michael gazed at him, the man's sightless eyes staring back. He reached down and gently closed them. There would have to be a burial and he would have the bleak task of telling the man's family and friends what had happened. Getting hold of a coffin to bury him in would be a challenge in itself. So many had died that coffins were in scarce supply and there was often now a long wait. He had even heard rumours that in Skibbereen they had started to use a coffin with a hinged bottom. There was a lever on the side which could be pushed; the bottom would fall away, and the corpse would drop down into the grave. The coffin itself could then be re-used. Michael shuddered and peered again at the body. The man's face seemed somehow familiar. Then he realised – it was the man in his kitchen earlier that day, the one who had spoken with relish at giving Clifton a dig in the ribs with his hurling stick. He had obviously decided to kill himself, to deliberately walk into the sea and let it take him. Poor fool.

Spent, Michael threw himself down on the wet sand and lay for a while staring up at the sky. It was a clear, cloudless night, the sky studded with stars. How often as a child had he lay on the ground staring up in exactly this way, filled with hope and wonder, his whole life ahead of him? Now all he felt was despair. He could feel himself tilting and falling into a deep depression. He had felt this before and knew that once in its grip, it might be weeks before he surfaced again. Each time it was as though he had been pitched into a hole, its sides too smooth to climb and far above, a single distant shaft of light from the entrance. Why did he think pitching a rock through Clifton's window would stop anything? He couldn't change what was happening. It might give Clifton pause for thought for a while but once his greed resurfaced, he would push on as before. Michael couldn't save Mullangar. He couldn't save this poor soul, the wretch who lay stretched out beside him. How could he have thought he could save a village? No, he was a fool. Sorcha was right; he had put them all in jeopardy and they would pay a heavy price.

*

It was almost dawn when Michael returned to the cottage. His clothes were still wet, and he shrugged them off onto the floor, his skin still damp as he slid back beneath the sheets. Sorcha seemed to be asleep, but he guessed she must be feigning. His entrance had been too noisy for her not to wake. He turned in towards her warmth and tucked an arm around her waist.

"I'm sorry. I know I'm a fool sometimes, but I love you."

Sorcha felt her eyes moisten.

"And I love you, Michael, always have done, always will – however much of an eejit you are."

She pulled his arm tighter around her.

"There was a man in the sea – he drowned. I tried to save him but couldn't get to him quickly enough. I brought him ashore, but he was already dead. It was one of the fellas from last night. I don't know if you noticed him. God forgive me but he was an ugly fella – had a face like a blind cobbler's thumb."

"No, I don't remember him. There was one of them who seemed awful noisy – had a lot to say for himself. Was that him?"

"Yes, that probably was him. Well, he's a lot quieter now."

"God have mercy on his soul. It's an awful way to go but then there's worse again."

"Yes, there is – far worse. I'll have to talk to his people this morning…let them know."

Michael…it's a risk having them here, but you can't turn them out on the road."

"No…even less so now. But we can't feed them either. We can offer shelter but for food they'll have to fend for themselves. Are you sure about this, Sorcha? If Clifton finds out, then we'll all be on the road."

"Yes, I'm sure. They're the same as us…I would hope someone would look out for us in the same way if it came to it."

"The truth is they probably wouldn't…folk are too scared and who can blame them?"

"I know…God is good. It'll work out somehow."

Michael didn't answer. The suffering he had seen had destroyed his belief in God; for him it was just another fairy story, as real as all the other ghosts and fairy nonsense people believed in. There was no God. They were alone in the world and there was no-one watching out for them. He envied Sorcha her faith and had never shared how he now felt but he could sense its bitter truth deep inside him, souring his thoughts and clouding his mind with a terrible darkness. He hated Father

McNamara; everything he told his congregation was lies. *Care not for this world*, he said. *Put your faith in God and think only of the next.* Well, there was no next; this was all there was and if there was a Hell then they were already in it and the priest was right there with them.

"I had watched the progress of the famine policy of the Government, and could see nothing in it but a machinery, deliberately devised, and skilfully worked, for the entire subjugation of the island—the slaughter of a portion of the people, and the pauperization of the rest."

Leader Writer for The Nation, 1847

"I thought it not right or good to restrain off the soldiers from their right of pillage, or from doing execution on the enemy."

Oliver Cromwell commenting on his soldiers' massacre of the local population in Wexford in 1649

CHAPTER SIXTEEN

Mary gazed around her. There were so many people in the room that Michael had asked Liam to help him move a heavy chest against a wall and Michael now stood on it so everyone could see him better. Liam had joked that the room was so crowded the only way his dog had managed to squeeze in was by leaving his fleas at the door.

Michael held a copy of *The Nation* folded in front of him. Two days had passed since the incident with Clifton, and all of those present in the room were aware that he had delivered the message. A number of the villagers had elected to stand, but some simply sat on the cold stone floor, too fatigued for the effort of standing and content to listen rather than having to peer over the shoulders of their neighbours so they could see Michael. Candles had been placed both on the kitchen table and in crude metal holders set into the walls.

Mary loved poetry and she had asked Michael if she could read a poem which had been published in the newspaper. He had readily agreed. She spoke hesitantly at first, unsure as to how the poem would be received, but seeing the appreciative nods from several people in the audience, she grew in confidence.

"He found them there, the young, the old,

The maiden and the wife;

Their guardian brave in death were cold,

Who dared for *them* the strife.

They prayed for mercy, God on high!

Before *thy* cross they prayed,

And ruthless Cromwell bade them die

To glut the Saxon blade!"

It was quiet for a moment when she had finished. A very tall man standing close to Michael coughed to clear this throat and then spoke.

"Cromwell was a bastard alright!"

Maggie Doyle who stood close to the front of the crowd, looked encouragingly at him. Eamonn Fitzgerald was known as the historian in the village; he was in his eighties with heavily pouched and rheumy eyes and a long, gaunt face. Everyone loved him not only because he was a source of endless tales about the past, but because he also had a keen and mischievous sense of humour. Sometimes, listening to him, it was hard to distinguish truth from fiction; Eamonn had never let the truth get in the way of a good story. Sensing he now had the full attention of his audience, he spoke again.

"His troops – the New Model Army – massacred a church full of women and priests in Wexford. Then there was the Siege of Drogheda – the commander there was beaten to death with his own wooden leg once the walls had been breached. It was rumoured there was gold in the leg as well, which made it extra heavy –"

Laughter rippled around the room.

"Did they find the gold?" asked Liam.

"They did, of course – sure didn't they beat it out of him? Well, out of his leg anyway."

They all laughed. Eamonn was on good form tonight.

"Now, is this a true story or another one of your yarns?" asked Liam.

Eamonn looked reproachfully at him.

"A true story, of course – have you ever known me to lie to you?"

"I have, of course."

"But on important matters, Liam? Have you ever known me to lie on important matters?"

"Especially then."

Eamonn grinned. "Well, sometimes the truth is not as interesting – I prefer to tell things as they should be, rather than what they are. It's more entertaining – do you follow?"

"You're a rogue, Eamonn," said Michael, "– and you'll come to a sorry end."

"Arra, I think I passed the sorry end some time ago. Anyhow, Drogheda was no laughing matter. Cromwell and his men massacred most of the town's inhabitants – except for the Protestants, of course; they murdered innocent women and children – they were either shot or put to the sword. That's why there's a street there called Scarlett Lane, so much blood ran down it. The English were so pleased with his handiwork, they instituted a Thanksgiving Day. And when he was finished with Drogheda, he fell on poor Wexford. They burned the Friary there and the priests inside it. A priest dead or captured was worth twenty pounds – just imagine it, twenty pounds."

The crowd had fallen silent, fascinated by Eamonn's speech. Sean Gallagher, a man in his early thirties, broke the silence.

"Michael – tell us more about Young Ireland; what are they after – is it just repeal?"

"They want repeal of the Act of Union right enough, but they want more than that – they also want land reform. They want a man to own his land rather than rent it from a landlord who spends most of his time in England. They want Ireland to rule itself, to have its own Parliament in Dublin, rather than be beholden to the English one in Westminster. They also want to bring Protestants and Catholics together rather than being at each other's throats. It's England, which is the enemy, not ourselves."

"The English will have us all in the grave if these evictions carry on!" said Sean, fiercely.

"Yes," said Michael evenly, "but some of these landlords are Irishman as well – don't forget that."

"Well, Clifton's no Irishman and he's the one about to put me and my family out!"

"Clifton's a bastard," said Michael, "and there'll always be bastards, repeal or no repeal. Anyhow, I have a feeling he won't be doing anything in Tyrone…"

Maggie spoke. "I'm tired of politics – it's making my ears ache. Would you not give us a song, Michael?"

Michael looked at her with amusement. Maggie was a young woman with unkempt black hair and mischievous blue eyes. He smiled and in a light tenor voice, started to sing.

"'Tis the last rose of summer,
Left blooming alone;
All her lovely companions
Are faded and gone;
No flower of her kindred,
No rosebud is nigh,
To reflect back her blushes,
Or give sigh for sigh."

It was a slow, haunting air and as Michael sang, Jim Murphy reached down to where he had left his fiddle leaning against the wall and started to accompany him. Michael nodded in appreciation and as his voice found a firmer foothold on the melody Jim was now playing, it became stronger and filled the room.

Sorcha and Mary had been stood together near the front and as Michael started the second verse, Mary joined in. Perhaps because they were siblings, the harmony of their two voices together was bewitching, and everyone in the room was enthralled. It was a song their mother had often sung and it had a particular poignancy for both of them because of this.

"I'll not leave thee, thou lone one!
To pine on the stem;
Since the lovely are sleeping,
Go, sleep thou with them.
Thus kindly I scatter,
Thy leaves o'er the bed,
Where thy mates of the garden
Lie scentless and dead.
So soon may I follow,
When friendships decay,
And from Love's shining circle
The gems drop away.
When true hearts lie withered,
And fond ones are flown,
Oh! who would inhabit
This bleak world alone?"

Tears filled Mary's eyes as they sang the last lines of the song. Michael was looking directly at her and knew she was thinking about Owen and he couldn't stop his own eyes from also welling up. To cover his embarrassment, he put his head down for a moment and turned to the side, wiping his eyes quickly with one hand. Sorcha saw and her own eyes were pricked with tears as well. Outside, snow was still falling and lay in thick drifts around the walls of the cottages. Most of the other cottages were in darkness, but there was a soft glow of candlelight from the windows in Michael's house which gave it an almost magical, evanescent quality, a bubble of light in a dark and brooding landscape. In the distance, there was a low drumming noise, which faded and then grew stronger.

CHAPTER SEVENTEEN

T he hammering was so violent, the door shook against its hinges. Immediately, a hush fell over the room, those nearest the door moving instinctively away. Mary rushed to take the copy of *The Nation* which Michael had been holding and passed it to Liam. It was then hurriedly spirited away from hand to hand down the room. It was finally passed to Kathy O'Herne, an elderly widow standing close to the back of the room, who, unwrapping her shawl, shoved it down the front of her heavy woollen dress, arranging it so it rested against her breasts and above a thick rope belt which cinched in her dress at the waist.

Once this had been done, Michael nodded to Jim Murphy who, putting down his fiddle against the wall, lifted the heavy wooden bar placed across the door and pulled it open. In the doorway stood the sheriff, Flynn, and behind him, having just dismounted, several policemen with their distinctive stovepipe hats. Behind them again and barely visible against the dark bog, there were a small group of soldiers still on horseback.

Murphy could just make out the glint of their bayonets. Flynn shoved roughly past him followed by the policemen. The room was already crowded, and their passage forced people back against the walls. Sorcha was alarmed to see that her two sons had opened the door to their bedroom and were looking on in terror. With effort, she pushed through her neighbours and ushered them back into their room.

"Back into your room, boys, and I'll come and see you again in a moment."

"Mammy – there's soldiers," Rian cried, his voice high and frightened.

"Well, what of it? Sure, they'll be gone again in a minute. I want youse both to stay very quiet. Can you do that for me? It's a game, right? See who can be the quietest for me and I'll give you both treats in the morning. Declan, look after your brother, will ye? I won't be long, I promise."

She returned to the main living room, closing the door to the bedroom behind her.

Flynn was screaming at Michael.

"Michael McGuiness! You're under arrest for plotting sedition and rebellion."

"You're having me on – when did getting together for a few laughs and a sing song become sedition?"

Flynn glanced briefly back at his men. This was his stage, not Michael's and he wasn't about to be made a fool of. He was a scrunched-up figure of a man, with lined, coarse features, his back bent as though he had just been unfolded from a suitcase.

"Take him and search everyone in this room!"

Two of the policemen moved forward and grabbed Michael roughly by his arms, pushing him back towards the door.

Sorcha let out a cry of disbelief.

"No – you can't…this is wrong! Stop…you can't!"

Flynn wheeled towards her.

"Shut up or we'll arrest you too!"

"Do it then, you coward…do it! What use am I without Michael anyway?"

Michael had not yet been forced through the door and was pushing back hard against his captors. On hearing his wife's voice, he craned his neck round anxiously to try and find her in the crowd.

"Leave her alone!" he cried. "You have no right!"

"If you arrest her then you can take me as well," said Mary pushing in front of her sister-in-law.

Eamonn Fitzgerald also moved forward.

"Aye – take all of us if you've a mind too. Michael has done nothing and nor has anyone else in this room."

"Don't tempt me – I could well have you all arrested. Get McGuinness out of here and take him into custody. The rest of you get this room and everybody in it searched – you can start with that trunk."

Michael was steered through the door and his arms were forced back so he could be shackled. The shackles were painful and bit deep into his wrists, but he had little time to dwell on this as he was shoved up into a cart. A policeman climbed up bedside him and the cart sprang forward. With the sudden momentum, Michael found himself tipped onto his side and had to struggle to right himself, so he was at least in a sitting position. As he forced himself up, he could already see his village disappearing in the distance. The soldiers accompanied the cart, their horses trotting alongside and behind, the deep rumble of the cart partially masked by the jingling of harness and spurs.

Back at the house, a policeman lifted the lid of the heavy oak trunk and began emptying its contents on the floor. First came some frayed grey blankets and then some pale blue china plates which were carelessly dropped so they smashed on the stone floor, pieces spinning away against people's feet. Whilst he was engaged in this, three others struggled to pull people out of the crowd to try and search them. Such was the crush of people in the room, they found they had to manhandle them outside the house and then conduct the search there. They ran their hands roughly over people's clothes, hoping to find at least something that might incriminate them – a knife or, better still, a gun.

Flynn had told them before the raid that they needed to find copies of *The Nation* or any other seditious material but if not this, at least something that might be used to bolster the charges made. They enjoyed unashamedly groping some of the younger and more attractive women but when they came to the ancient and stooped figure of Kathy O'Herne, they were much less enthusiastic. She fixed them with a level stare as if daring them to molest her. One of the bolder policemen moved towards her anyway but he contented himself with the most cursory of searches and his hands skittered over her breasts with all the nervousness of a virgin on his wedding night. Kathy stared fiercely at him as he searched her, but her heart thumped so madly in her chest she thought she might pass out with fear. The policeman stepped away and turned to his next victim and she dared to breathe again. The sheriff had been watching her closely. He strode across and, seizing the top of her dress, pulled it savagely down. The newspaper flopped to the floor. Kathy's hands flew up to hide her now exposed breasts. There was a gasp from the crowd.

He glared at the policeman who had failed to search her properly.

"I want this done right! It's not for me to do your work for you."

One of the other policemen then spoke.

"Do you want her arrested as well?"

"No – she's more trouble than she's worth. Just finish what you're doing."

In the trunk, they also found some notebooks, and these were brought across to Flynn to examine. He glanced briefly at them, noting they seemed to be household accounts. There were details of grain bought and sold, the prices of seed potatoes, rental amounts due on his tenancy – what was important was that they provided enough samples of Michael's handwriting. Finding a copy of *The Nation* was good, he thought, but getting a conviction that might hang the man now depended on whether they could successfully match Michael's handwriting with that on the note to Clifton. Still, the law was a pliable thing, he had found, and you could go a long way with very little, particularly where sedition was involved.

CHAPTER EIGHTEEN

Trevelyan swept imperiously through the lobby of the Salt Hill Hotel just outside Dublin. Two ancient colonels already enjoying their first whisky of the day peered with interest at him. He had arranged to meet with Twisleton, the Chief Poor Law Commissioner, in a lounge area towards the rear, where he had been told they wouldn't be disturbed.

"So, why no plan then? You were expressly charged with producing one and yet it seems that task must now fall to me."

Twisleton looked incredulously at Trevelyan. "Sir, you have spent but two days in Ireland. I have spent the last year here and witnessed at first hand the terrible effects of the famine and the appalling conditions in the workhouses. Now, I see you have closed the soup kitchens and want to stop the provision of relief outside the workhouses. This is complete madness and yet you want me to produce a plan to implement it! I don't have a plan, and nor do I intend to provide one."

Trevelyan looked coolly back at him. He had not met

Twisleton before, although they had corresponded by post, and he had conjured up a mental image of what sort of man he might be; the reality was worse than he had imagined. Twisleton had fine, dark hair which was badly receding. He had compensated for this by cultivating longer sideburns, but the overall effect was unimpressive. His features were soft, and betrayed weakness, in Trevelyan's opinion. He knew Twisleton had a classics degree and he seemed too much the academic, a man unused to the rigours of the real world.

"These are not my policies," said Trevelyan. "They are the policies of the Government and legislation has been enacted by Parliament to ensure their implementation. We are both paid servants of that Government and we therefore have a duty to carry out those policies. You may think they're harsh, but the reality is we cannot afford to go on paying for relief in Ireland. As you must be well aware, the financial crash has crippled our own economy and Ireland must stand on its own two feet."

Twisleton shifted in anger. "But landlords cannot collect the rates you need to pay for poor relief because their tenants not only have no money but are so reduced in circumstances as to be close to starvation and death. Wood may insist on the collection of rates by horse, foot, and dragoons – as he so nicely put it a letter to Clarendon – but you're fishing in an empty pond."

Trevelyan gave a thin smile. "Irish property must pay for Irish poverty."

"I'm familiar with your views – I read your article in *The Times*. You've upset quite a few people, writing as you did."

"By quite a few, I take it you mean Clarendon and Sir John?"

"Amongst others…"

"The only views that matter are those of myself, the Chancellor, Sir Charles Wood, and, of course, the Prime Minister, Lord Russell, and you'll hardly be surprised to learn that we are all – all – in complete agreement as to the way forward."

Trevelyan leaned back in his chair. He was beginning to enjoy Twisleton's obvious discomfort. He could see the man was angry, but he knew that Twisleton would be compelled to do his bidding whatever his personal feelings on the matter and this amused him. Twisleton was like a small animal caught in a trap, frantically racing around, looking for a possible escape route but ultimately doomed.

"And what might that be?" asked Twisleton.

"Very simple, actually…the workhouses were set up to ensure their inhabitants carried out some form of useful labour in return for shelter and food. The children were to be educated and so on –"

"That might well be, but the reality is very different –"

Trevelyan cut him off. "If the reality is different, it's because of the incompetence of the Union officials responsible for them. The point is this – what I want you to do is ensure the workhouses only house the able-bodied, those capable of work. Those who cannot work because of infirmity or age must be expelled. We will then allow for a modicum of relief for such people, but solely in the form of cooked food. Entrance to the workhouses must be made as difficult as possible – we only want those capable of work."

"This is madness! The Irish only enter the workhouse as a last resort – many of them already prefer to die in a ditch than enter such places. They think of them as prisons and they're right to do so – if they try and escape and are caught, then they're charged with stealing. A number of the workhouses are rife with disease and fever – to enter those is a death sentence. It's only the sick and infirm who are desperate enough to want entrance – the able-bodied are the very people least likely to want to end up there."

Twisleton was glaring at Trevelyan and his agitation was such that he was clearly having trouble staying seated. His face was flushed, and Trevelyan could also see that his hands were trembling a little. Twisleton noticed Trevelyan's glance and quickly lowered his hands below the edge of the desk.

Trevelyan was always both astonished and irritated by the inability of others to control their emotions. He prided himself on only very rarely giving way to anger and he knew that once this happened in others, they had already lost, their emotions sweeping away any remaining capacity for rational argument. He also suddenly felt exhausted; he had had a long and difficult journey. There had been a particularly rough sea and he was not a good sailor at the best of times. Initially, he had tried to rest in his cabin, but he had still been nauseous, vomiting several times into a steel bucket, which he had been careful to place beside his cot before retiring. The rank smell of this and the violent movement of the ship had eventually forced him up onto the deck where he had hung limply over the rail, only feet above the huge waves which besieged the ship on all sides. Oddly, here he felt a little better and he had stayed on deck for several hours, oblivious both to the cold and the wind-whipped spray stinging his face.

He had not yet eaten since disembarking and he was beginning to feel lightheaded. His previous good humour had now entirely vanished, and resting a hand on his brow, he closed his eyes. When he spoke again, it was as though he were addressing not only Twisleton, but all of his critics.

"There is a much bigger picture, Twisleton – much bigger – of which you are entirely ignorant. I also have neither the energy nor the time to give you a basic primer on the economics of the situation. Yes, I'm aware there will be some short-term suffering – some discomfort, if you will – but, ultimately, Ireland will emerge the stronger and better for it and, as a result, better able to care for all of its people without the need to fall back on us for help. So…I've told you what needs to happen, and I've also prepared a written briefing with clear directions on this. You and Sir John just need to ensure it's enacted…"

Trevelyan opened his eyes and moved his hand from his brow so he could look directly at Twisleton, who held his gaze briefly before quickly looking away. Twisleton seemed broken, physically reduced in size.

"I've registered my protest…and I know Sir John will also… but, as you wish."

"Thank you – and now, if you don't mind, I've had rather a long journey and I need to get some rest."

"No, of course…I perfectly understand…it's not an easy journey."

"Well life isn't easy is it? But then, it's not supposed to be either."

Twisleton had already half risen from his chair with the expectation that not only would he escort Trevelyan out, but they would both at least observe the tradition of shaking hands. In this, he was to be frustrated because by the time he had completed the process of standing up, his nemesis had already gone, disappearing quickly through the ornate panelled door at the far end of the room. Twisleton continued to stare at the door but it was with unseeing eyes. He had thought Trevelyan was someone who could be reasoned with, but he now realised this was not the case. Instead, he had been plunged into a world which followed the logic of the madhouse; up was down and down was up. Where it would end, he shuddered to think.

CHAPTER NINETEEN

G erard felt numb with the cold. His clothes were soaked through and he could barely feel his fingers gripping the barrel of his gun. He had chosen a snow-filled hollow close to the lake on Clifton's estate. He knew the grounds well from his poaching exploits with his father. He also knew that Clifton often walked the circumference of the lake with his dog, a grey wolfhound standing three feet tall at the shoulder. Gerard had borrowed his father's gun, a flintlock musket of dubious vintage. It was an awkward gun to fire. Gunpowder from a cartridge had to be tamped down in the barrel with a ramrod, the musket ball sitting on top of this. More powder had to be poured into the pan which sat below a steel piece of metal called the plate; when fired, the flint would strike the plate, igniting the powder in the pan and barrel, which in turn propelled the lead ball. It took time to reload and fire again so Gerard knew he would only get the one chance. Now, it appeared the wretched dog had scented his presence; it had come to a stop less than ten yards away and was emitting a low growl. Clifton also stopped. He seemed to stare directly at Gerard.

"What is it Zeus?"

Zeus's growling grew louder. Gerard knew he had little choice but to try and get his shot off now. Adrenaline surging through him, his arm shook as he lifted the gun and sighted down the barrel. It was a poor shot, hitting Clifton in the shoulder. The landowner spun to his left and fell to the ground. Enveloped in the acrid smelling smoke of the blast, Gerard struggled for a second to see what effect his shot had had. The smoke cleared, and he could see Clifton had fallen, his dog barking in excitement by his side. For a moment, Gerard was ecstatic but that quickly turned to dismay when he saw Clifton slowly raise himself up on one elbow and peer across at him.

"I know who you are, you bastard!" he screamed. "I'll see you hang for this!"

Gerard got to his feet and abandoning his gun, fled. The dog immediately ran after him and using its head almost like a battering ram, knocked him to the ground. Gerard lay face down. The dog sunk its teeth into the side of his neck. He howled in pain, twisting round and trying to shove his splayed fingers into the dog's eyes. The dog bit deeper, severing his carotid artery. Blood spouted into the dog's mouth, almost choking it, and it leapt back in surprise. Gerard's head fell back. He felt both the odd warmth of his own blood and the icy cold of the snow at the same time. There was a smell of piss laced with an odd coppery tang of blood. He realised to his shame that he had wet himself. His eyes closed. Michael was right, he thought – Clifton was much bigger than a rabbit and I still couldn't do the job. He pictured Clifton for a moment as a rabbit; he did have a rabbity face he thought. Nonsense words filled his head: *rabbity rabbity, rab, rab, rab.* It was funny how if you repeated a word often enough, the stranger it sounded. *Rabbity rabbity rabbit, rab, rab.* Slowly, he rolled to one side. The snow around him was splashed with his blood and he thought it oddly beautiful. It seemed to him that his soul was leaking back into the earth, becoming one with the landscape around him. The priest would like that, he thought; could make a sermon out if it. He smiled and closed his eyes.

CHAPTER TWENTY

"So, the handwriting doesn't match up with the note?" said Clifton.

"No, it doesn't, which is not good."

Clifton turned to Johnson. His shoulder ached and was heavily bandaged. He had only suffered a flesh wound from the bullet fired by Gerard but it was still a constant reminder of how close he had come to being killed.

"Johnson, you've been very quiet through all this – what do you think?"

Johnson leaned forward a little in his chair.

"I think the handwriting could be made to match the note."

"How's that?" said the sheriff, sharply.

Johnson paused for effect and fixed both with a level, confident gaze.

"You have the handwriting samples from his house – all we have to do is produce a new note. We three are the only ones who have seen it after all, and we all have an interest in making sure the man behind the attempt to murder you now hangs. Is this not the case?"

Flynn stared at Johnson and slowly stood up. He walked to the window and stood with his back to the other two men, gazing out over Clifton's estate. Still turned away, he spoke.

"It might work but is it enough to hang the man? We still have no direct link to the murder attempt."

"Well, at the very least it shows a conspiracy," said Johnson. "But in any case, I have more – there was a man present at the meeting that produced the note who will not only swear he saw McGuinness write it, but that it was McGuinness who encouraged this man, Gerard, to try and kill you."

Clifton was astonished.

"Is this true? Where did you find this man – this informer? And who the hell is he?"

Johnson smiled.

"Liam Foley. I got Moran to make some enquiries – find out what anyone knew about the note. That brought him to Foley – a man afraid of his own shadow. It wasn't difficult to get him to blab – in return for a bit of cash, of course. We've leaned on him a little harder and now he's prepared to swear it was McGuinness who put Gerard up to murdering you as well. To be frank, the man would give up his own mother for the price of a loaf of bread."

Clifton looked triumphant.

"We have him – we have the bastard."

Flynn was still turned away, staring out of the window.

"It certainly looks that way. However, it's all very well this man Foley saying this stuff now. Would he still be prepared to say it in public – in a courtroom in front of his neighbours and friends? You said he was afraid of his own shadow – well, it won't be shadows he'll be facing in court."

"I've thought of that," said Johnson. "He'll have no choice – either he gives up McGuinness or we tell him we'll drag him into all this and make sure he hangs himself."

"So, when can I see him? I'll need to interrogate him to make sure he'll hold to his story. A man so afraid might jump five different ways in a morning, depending on who's in front of him. I want to make sure he'll be a credible witness."

"I'll get Moran to bring him in tomorrow for you. We'll fetch him around dawn when the rest of the village is still asleep, and we can get him out without anyone seeing."

"Makes sense – a man half-awake is also easier to talk to, if you get my meaning."

"So, we have a plan, gentlemen," said Clifton. "And a hanging to look forward to. Johnson, will you take care of the note?"

Johnson looked at Flynn.

"If you can come and see me this afternoon, I'll give you the samples I took," said Flynn.

"Good man. Then I'll have a new note ready by tomorrow."

"Will you have a glass of port, gentlemen?" said Clifton, rising to his feet.

"I won't," said Johnson, "it's a little early in the day for me."

Flynn looked greedily at Clifton.

"That would be very pleasant."

"There's also one more item of business I'd like to discuss with you both. I want McGuiness's house levelled to the ground, every stone taken down and his family tipped out onto the road." Clifton turned to Johnson. "When can you arrange it?"

"We can have that done by the end of the week"

"The sooner, the better – I'll make that family rue the day they decided to take me on. Another glass perhaps?"

"Yes, that would be grand – thanks," said Flynn.

"One more thing – Moran tells me a number of the villagers from Mullangar have crept back into the village and put up scalpeens against the ruins of their cottages. I want them cleared out and if they find a ditch to hide in afterwards and try to turn that into a shelter, I want that cleared as well – I want them all off my land. Tell Moran to take five of his men there today and tell them to bring clubs too, if necessary. Once the McGuinness family has been dealt with as well, then we'll look at evicting the other tenants at Tyrone."

"I'll go and arrange that now," said Johnson. He left the room, glancing briefly back at Clifton and Flynn as he closed the door. They were leaning together; Clifton having put a hand on Flynn's shoulder as though to pull him closer. He had softened his voice so it seemed little louder than a whisper, seemingly anxious that Johnson shouldn't overhear him. What fresh devilry are you plotting now? he wondered.

The housekeeper showed Johnson to the front door. She was a plump, simple soul and Johnson thought that if she had any more chins, she'd be wearing them around her waist. He knew that Clifton's wife had hired her; she made sure none of the hires were comely enough to tempt her rogue of a husband. The woman seemed anxious, he thought, almost afraid. He wondered why this was. Still, not my problem. I've got more important things to worry about.

CHAPTER TWENTY-ONE

"God, my back hurts…God forgive us, that's bad."

Father McNamara glanced at his housekeeper. He was sat at his desk trying to write the sermon for the next morning's mass. Eileen Dolan stood holding her back with one hand, and a dusting cloth in the other. She had been his housekeeper for more than a decade but was now in her seventies, a stout, good hearted woman with grey straggly hair and the strong hint of a moustache on her upper lip. He was mildly offended by her blasphemy, but if he called out everyone in his flock who took the Lord's name in vain, then he would have no time to talk to them about anything else.

"Well it might be bad, but our Lord suffered far worse," he said evenly.

"Yeah, but then he was a lot younger than me, he could put up with the suffering."

Despite himself, McNamara laughed.

"Eileen, you're a caution…I'm sure when you die, God is going to struggle to know what to do with you."

"Well, the first thing he can do is sort out my back. He did a great deal of turning water into wine, but I don't remember him doing an awful lot with backs. Whatever you do, don't get old, Father. I do tell the children that, but I might as well talk to the wind for all the listening they do."

"Maybe that's because they have no choice in the matter… they're all going to get old, whatever you say."

"You're right, of course, Father, but then you're always right. Only the Pope is more fallible."

McNamara laughed again.

"Infallible, Eileen, the Pope is infallible."

Eileen looked confused.

"Well, whether he's in it or out of it, he speaks for God. Anyway, I have some news for you."

"And what news is that?"

Eileen paused for a moment for dramatic effect. She instinctively lowered her voice to a stage whisper, as though she might be overheard.

"Mary Hogan has taken up with a Protestant. The whole village knows. They're walking round together as brazen as you like, holding hands and pawing each other and God knows what else in private. It's a terrible thing to see, Father. I would rather be blind than have to see it."

"Mary, speak up woman…you know I'm deaf now and I only heard half of what you said. What about Mary Hogan? What Protestant?"

Exasperated, Eileen was now virtually shouting.

162

"She's seeing a Protestant, Father. And brazen with it...she doesn't care who sees them."

McNamara immediately felt depressed. Following the excommunication, he had felt a terrible guilt. That poor woman, he had thought. What have I done? I even cursed the poor woman's unborn child, the same woman I had held in my arms and baptised when she was a baby herself, a little scrap of a thing who stayed silent throughout, looking up at me with those wonderful green eyes of hers. And then she loses her own baby. I can blame the bishop; he urged me to do this, but I could have said no, told him I wouldn't do it. But I was too proud and arrogant, wanting to please him and show my flock what a great man I was, how much power I wielded over them. It's my fault...all my fault. God forgive me.

Eileen seemed oblivious of McNamara's sudden descent into gloom and prattled on, excited by her own sudden passion.

"You have to say something tomorrow...you need to condemn her, Father, from the pulpit, in your sermon."

The priest felt a sudden flash of anger.

"Condemn what? What would you have me condemn...I've already cast the poor woman out of the Church. What more can I do which is worse than that?"

Eileen was startled by the sudden outburst and instinctively backed away.

"But other people, Father...you have to say something... otherwise they'll all be at it. It's wrong...it needs to be stopped."

"No, Eileen...nothing needs to be said and nothing needs

stopping. Now leave me – I need to finish this thing and your…"

He didn't finish. He wanted to say "nonsense," but he was afraid of upsetting her.

"Of course, Father…I'll be back this evening, prepare you some food. I think there's some pork left in the larder we could try…"

"Thank you, Eileen…you're a good woman and you'll…"

"Get my reward in Heaven…yes, I know, Father. Well, I'm certainly not getting it on earth that's for sure."

"None of us are, Eileen," said the priest sadly, "None of us are. Sometimes I think it's Purgatory we're in, but no-one's bothered to tell us."

Eileen hesitated.

"Sometimes I think God has forsaken us altogether."

"Perhaps he has…but if we're being punished, it's for a reason, Eileen. God's ways are mysterious and it's not for us to question him."

"No, you're right of course." Still, she thought, I might be tempted to give him a piece of my mind when I do see him. He's a man after all and its always men that create the mess in the first place, leaving the poor womenfolk to clear up afterwards.

"Do you want a bite to eat, Father? Pardon me for saying this but you're looking awful thin – you are looking after yourself, aren't ye?"

"Sure, how can I walk round looking like the best-fed man in my parish when everyone else is on the edge of starvation? That wouldn't be right, would it?"

"Well, you'll be no use to them if you drop dead yourself through want, will ye? And then who will there be to do the Mass and offer communion?"

"There are no wafers left for me to use anyway and I don't think I'll be getting fresh supplies anytime soon. I was thinking of giving everyone a piece of brown bread instead – what do you think?"

"What do I think? What do I think? Well, you're the priest. If you don't know then there's no use asking the likes of me, is there?"

McNamara laughed.

"You have the right of it, of course. I should be asking the bishop, but I've an awful feeling he would say no. He's a terrible prig of a man, God forgive me."

"Well, I'll say one thing – there's more goodness in brown bread than one of them thin wafers – they do stick to the roof of your mouth something awful. You tell us we're not supposed to touch them with our teeth, so I spend the rest of the mass trying to prise them off with my tongue. Of course, there's several people in the church have no teeth anyway, so it's no difference to them – they have to suck on everything as it is. That's why their mouths are so pinched."

"I thought it was smoking a pipe did that."

"It's both; the pipe and the wafers."

"Thinking about it now, I don't think I've got any sherry left either."

"Well, you could always try giving them potcheen – I'm sure

they'd all be crowding into the church to get some of that."

"You're an awful woman – when you see Saint Peter, I think you might need me beside ye to get you in."

"Just say a prayer for me at Mass, Father – that will be powerful enough to get me in, I'm sure, and if it's not, I'll take my chances with the devil. If your prayer's that weak, you'll probably be seeing him yourself."

"Whatever the case, I don't think he'd last very long with you," said the priest. "You'd see him off before he'd managed to take off his coat."

"So, you'll have some food so?"

"I don't think you'll give me any peace until I do – well alright, bring me a cup of buttermilk. We'll save the bread for communion so. We'll have to do with water for the sherry."

"He's turned water to wine before so perhaps he can pull the same trick."

McNamara sighed. "I'm thinking it might be best if you saw me for confession first before the Mass tomorrow."

"Well, as long as you don't pretend not to know me when I'm in the cubicle – I know fine you know it's me and you give me a double penance because of it."

"Let me have a loaf of the bread," said McNamara. "I'll walk it down to the Kiely's house. They have sore need of it because they've got the largest family in the village, nine children last time I counted and there's probably another one on the way now."

CHAPTER TWENTY-TWO

"What do you want from me?"

"Very simple, Michael – I want a confession. I want you to tell me it was you put young Gerard up to trying to kill Clifton. And it was you behind this note."

He held out a crumpled piece of paper in front of Michael.

Michael peered at it with his one good eye. The butt of a rifle to his forehead the previous night had left a deep cut in his brow and a black eye which was now sealed shut by the swelling. Although his vision was poor, it was sufficient to see that this wasn't the note he had delivered to Clifton curtesy of a rock. Someone had replaced it and changed the handwriting.

"What are you talking about? Why are you showing me this and what's this about Clifton and Gerard? The only thing I'm certain of is that I shouldn't be here – you've arrested an innocent man."

Flynn smiled. "I don't think so, McGuinness. I think we have it just right – this is your handwriting. I matched it myself to the notebooks I took from your house. And we have a witness to you both writing the note and conspiring with Gerard Lynch to murder poor Clifton."

Michael felt a chill run through him. If they really had a witness, he was done for; they would need very little to make a case against him and a witness prepared to lie in court would see him hanged.

"You're bluffing – you have no witness and no evidence."

"You're a fool, Michael, full of piss and wind like all of your kind. You think you're a revolutionary, a man of the people, an Irish Robespierre. You're nothing of the kind – you're a poor deluded peasant with barely enough wit to get up in the morning. Your kind disgust me; you're all just vermin, filthy rats, and I mean to get rid of every last one of you."

He nodded to the gaoler who had stood silent during the interrogation at the rear of the dimly lit cell. The gaoler grunted and, lifting the heavy set of keys hanging from his waist, turned and opened the cell door. Flynn left first followed by the gaoler.

Michael had been sitting up but now he fell back, leaning against the damp cell wall. His only bedding was a mound of wet straw which, ironically, was also alive with the rustle of rats. There was a small window high on the opposite wall covered by a rusted iron grid. It was too high for Michael to see out of, but he could at least glimpse the leaden sky through it. I'm a dead man, he thought. They've forged a new note and they've managed to trump up a witness prepared to lie. Who the hell could it be? He sighed – the truth was it could be anybody;

desperate people do desperate things. It could also be a woman, doesn't necessarily have to be a man. And Gerard? Where was he in all this? If he had been caught, then, surely, they would have brought him here? But there had been no mention by Flynn or his gaolers of him being taken in and wouldn't they have wanted to taunt him with that? Unless, of course, Gerard had been killed himself in the attack; poor Gerard if that was the case and what about his father? This would finish him off as well – Gerard was the only thing he lived for. And what will Sorcha and the boys have to live for if I'm hanged? What will become of them? What have I done? I've ruined us all with my stupidity. God help me, God help us all.

CHAPTER TWENTY-THREE

"I'm really worried about him."

"I know you are – and the business with Gerard won't help either."

"Poor Gerard. No – I'm sure they'll try and pin what happened on Michael. He could hang, Simon. They've hung men for a lot less."

Mary turned to Simon, her eyes wet with tears. They had taken to walking alongside the river; for some of its length the footpath was shaded by trees and they found it both peaceful and, perhaps more importantly, rarely used by other walkers. It was a spate river with both the bogs and mountains draining into it. The melt water from the recent snows also meant that it was running fast and full, its waters spilling out into adjoining fields.

Simon hugged her to him. She was small and frail in his arms and it felt as though if he hugged her too tightly, he might crush her. She buried her face in his shoulder and now her tears came more freely; her body shook, and she sobbed, cried for Michael, for her lost child and for herself.

"Let it out, Mary, let it out…it's alright…it's alright."

"I have to save him…I couldn't save Owen or my baby, but I have to save Michael – I can't let him die. I can't…if he dies, then I'll die as well. I can't live without him. I just can't. He's everything to me."

"I know that, Mary, but what can we do? How can we help him? They won't even let you see him in prison."

"I don't know but I'll find a way – I have to, I have to find a way of saving him."

"Alright, let's think about this – what evidence do they have about him? There's reading *The Nation* to people, but I can't see that's a hanging offence – otherwise half the county would be in prison. Then there's the note delivered to Clifton and the attempt on his life, but they have no evidence for either of these – it was Gerard who shot Clifton and it could have been Gerard who delivered the note. So, what do they have really – nothing. They have nothing."

"They must think they have something, otherwise why is he still in prison and why is everybody talking about hanging? There has to be something."

"Well, we could make a start by trying to find out. I could talk to people…see what I can find out. I could speak to Jeremy – he's well connected, will surely know something."

"Can you? I'll see what I can find out as well – if I can find anyone in the village willing to talk to me. Half of them shun me now because of the anathema and then me picking up with you as well."

"I'm sorry, Mary – I know how hard it's been for you. I could wish I hadn't been born a Protestant. In any case, I'm not even sure what I believe anymore."

Mary hesitated. "Well, despite everything, I still believe in God."

"You're a better person than I'll ever be."

"Perhaps I'm just a lot more foolish…still, I have to believe. If I didn't, I think I would go mad."

"But the anathema –"

"I don't believe God will turn me away when I arrive at the gates. Priests can curse you but they're human after all – it's God who'll make the final judgement."

It suddenly started to rain. Mary glanced up. The sky immediately above was still blue, although it was framed by darker clouds.

"Great – now we'll get soaked. I hope this isn't one of his judgements…"

"It's just a shower, Mary – it'll pass soon enough."

Even as he said this, the rain became more intense. Within seconds they were both wet through, their clothes clinging to them.

Despite herself, Mary laughed. She swept her wet mane of hair back off her face.

"Just a shower is it? I'd hate to be with you when it really rained."

Now Simon was laughing. He leaned towards her and kissed her, pulling her towards him and wrapping his arms around her. He could smell the damp wool of her dress mingled with the earthy smell of the bracken crushed beneath their feet.

"Trust you to get romantic when I'm like a drowned rat!"

"A very beautiful drowned rat."

"Do you think we might find some shelter? God knows I don't think I could get any wetter but even so –"

"There's an overhanging ledge of rock over there," he said. "I think it might be dry underneath – we could try it anyway."

The ground beneath the rock was dry and covered in rough grass and heather before this petered out to a mottled red sandstone deeper within the recess. The ledge above them was too low to allow them even to crouch and so they lay down. In front of them hung a curtain of rain.

"I think we might be stuck here for a while," said Mary.

"Indeed, we will – we'll just have to find some way to amuse ourselves."

He kissed her again.

"I love you, Mary."

"And I love you Simon, so I guess we're sorted so. How lucky are we? Except, of course, you're a Protestant and we can never marry."

"In my church –"

"No – I could only marry in a Catholic church and that would never be allowed, even if I were allowed back into the Faith."

"Is that possible? Could they let you back in – cancel the anathema?"

"It's possible, but I doubt it will happen – getting together with you doesn't exactly help either. Let's not talk about it – live for today."

She pulled him closer. "Make love to me."

Simon looked at her. Despite being in his mid-twenties, he was still a virgin and had not gone further with Mary than a few chaste kisses.

"Are you sure?"

"Yes – I'm sure, I'm sure. Anyway," she laughed, "I need to get these wet clothes off me."

Simon was so tentative that in the end Mary had to guide him inside her. He came immediately and hurriedly pulled out.

"Sorry – not very good at this. I've never –"

Mary smiled up at him.

"Never what? Sorry, I'm teasing you – I'd guessed already. Don't worry so – you'll get better."

"When?"

"Two or three years perhaps? No, seriously – let's give it half an hour, maybe less…"

"The rain's stopped."

Mary laughed and pulled him closer.

"No – I think you'll find it's starting up again."

*

Simon had felt invisible almost from birth. He was the youngest of three boys and felt eclipsed by his older siblings. He had no doubt that his parents loved him but it also seemed to him that although they hid it, they were also disappointed in him. His oldest brother had gone on to become a doctor, the other a sea captain. Both were loud and boisterous and embraced life to the full. Both were also now married with a clutch of children who delighted their grandparents. Simon had become a schoolmaster and showed a diffidence with women which meant he was mercilessly teased by both his own family members and his peers.

Mary was his first serious relationship and it felt as if her love had brought him into existence, had made him visible to both himself and others. He could scarcely believe his good fortune and was terrified of losing her; what was worse, he sensed that Mary's love was that of an affectionate sister; she was with him because of a sense of obligation. He had saved her life, had been sent to her as an emissary by God, and it was her fate to therefore be with him. He figured that what she felt was an intense gratitude which had softened into fondness but it was not real love and never would be. It was the secret sorrow at the heart of their relationship, a canker he feared would eventually poison it.

CHAPTER TWENTY-FOUR

Mary stared at Sorcha. She was shocked by how gaunt and crushed she looked. Sorcha ushered the two boys to play outside whilst they talked, and Mary waited until they had gone before speaking.

"How are they holding up?"

"Not great – I've told them Michael's had to go travelling, to see some cousins in Ballina, but they're not daft – they know there's something wrong and they keep asking after him, wanting to know when he'll be back, why is he so long? It breaks my heart to lie to them, but I can't tell them the truth either."

Mary reached over and held Sorcha's hand. They were seated around the kitchen table which had been painted white. It was pushed against the wall and the adults sat awkwardly around it, Sorcha and Mary on the only two chairs in the house, and Simon on a log which was raised off the floor on rough wooden pegs. He spoke again.

"Where's he being held?"

"Cranmore in Sligo."

"Have you been allowed to see him?" asked Mary.

"No – I've tried, but they're not allowing any visitors."

Mary gave an anguished look at Simon.

"Do you know when the trial is?" she asked.

"No – I've heard nothing. I don't even know what's he accused of –"

"I've spoken to Jeremy," said Simon. "You know – the minister at the church I do voluntary work for. He made some enquiries for me – he knows the sheriff, Flynn."

"That gobshite – he's got a face on him that would drive rats from a barn," said Mary, in disgust.

"He may be a gobshite but he's the one with all the power and he's also in Clifton's pocket. Flynn told Jeremy that Michael stands accused of sedition and a conspiracy to murder Clifton."

"They can't think Michael's mixed up with Gerard shooting Clifton. Michael was in prison, for God's sake, when it happened" said Sorcha.

"Doesn't matter – they're arguing Michael put poor Gerard up to it. Gerard hadn't got the wits he was born with, so it's not a difficult argument either. Then there's the message delivered to Clifton – Flynn says the handwriting on the note has been matched to Michael's."

Sorcha felt her stomach fall away. She felt faint. She had known in her bones this would happen but the realisation that it had actually come to pass was almost too much to bear. Mary reached across and hugged her. Sorcha immediately burst into tears. Her whole body shook as grief overwhelmed her.

Mary was in shock herself, struggling to control her own feelings and a rising sense of panic. She forced herself to calm down and pleaded with Sorcha, even while tears ran down her own cheeks.

"It will be alright – they haven't got him yet – there has to be a trial. Please, Sorcha – you have to have hope –"

"There is no hope! They'll hang him and then what will become of us? He's the only man I ever loved, the only man who would look at me with when I was younger, who could see past my crippled leg. What will happen to us Mary? How will we survive?"

"We'll get through this – we will. We have to – we can't let them win. Simon, we must be able to do something –"

"There's a defence lawyer in Sligo we might use, Daniel Smethwick. He has a very good reputation – I could try and speak to him."

Mary turned to face him.

"Could you? When could you travel? Can I come with you?"

"I could go tomorrow. And yes, of course, come with me. Two voices are better than one and you might be better able to persuade him than I can."

"Sorcha," said Mary, "Did you want to come?"

"I can't – I need to look after the boys. You can borrow my horse though."

"You're sure you don't need her?" said Mary.

"No – not for a few days anyway. Take her – you won't get a better horse this side of the mountains."

"Thanks – I will. Simon, what time could we leave tomorrow?"

"First light would be best because it's a long ride."

"First light it is then."

CHAPTER TWENTY-FIVE

Moran was none too pleased to be dragged out of bed by the sheriff at such an ungodly hour. It was still dark outside, with sunrise not expected for another couple of hours at least. The air was damp and although the snow had stopped, enough had fallen again overnight to make picking their way across ground on their horses a slow and tedious process. Flynn had brought two constables with him and Moran had mustered another three of his own men; not enough if they encountered any real resistance but since it was a mopping-up operation with villagers who had already spent a week outside in harsh conditions, he doubted there would be any fight left in them. Flynn had also told him that in a few days they were to take down McGuinness's house. He was looking forward to that; he was also hoping Michael's sister would try to intervene which might present him with an opportunity to become a little more intimately acquainted with her. He had long been an admirer of Mary and had been more than a little put out when she took up with and then married

Owen. Still, Owen was in his grave, wasn't he, and the way was now clear for himself. He had little hope she would ever want to have anything to do with the likes of him, but there were other ways to get a woman to do your bidding.

When Moran had opened his door that morning, Flynn had greeted him with a broad smile. In his hand he waved a bottle of brandy.

"Something to warm us up before we get started."

"Good man," said Moran. "Come in – the wife's still asleep so keep your voice down. If we wake her up, I'll be sleeping in the barn when we get back."

Once Moran had found some glasses, Flynn poured out a generous measure for them both which they then greedily drank.

"This is a gift from Clifton," said Flynn. "He said to make sure all the men had a good drink of it before we reach the village."

"Well, I think we're both entitled to a second sup given we have to lead them into battle," said Moran.

"True enough – it's fierce cold out there and brandy's the best for warming you up. I've left the men at the bottom of the lane; we'll give them the brandy before we set out."

"The more drunk they are, the better they'll do their duty anyway," said Moran.

"Well, with that in mind I have a second bottle in my saddle bag."

Moran laughed and slapped him across the back.

"You're the man, Flynn. With a bit of drink inside him, a fella would follow you to Hell itself."

＊

The dogs in the ruined village were the first to sense the approach of Moran's men. Their barking was soon followed by the clatter of horse hooves. The villagers, still groggy with sleep, staggered to their feet. Even as they rose, the branches they had used to build their inadequate shelters were clubbed to the ground, showering them in sticks and dirt. A pig ran squealing in terror.

"Kill that bloody pig," shouted Moran.

One of his men stood in front of the pig, arms spread wide to try and slow it down. A second raced across and clubbed it savagely across the head. It sank screaming to the ground and was quickly dispatched by a second blow.

"Well, at least we'll have some pork and bacon tonight," laughed Moran. He looked round and saw a cart close to one of the now ruined shelters.

"Dump it on the cart and we'll take it back with us. You can hitch one of the horses to it."

"Have pity on us will ye," cried an old woman, her back bent double with age so she had to peer up at Moran.

"Too late for that – you can all clear the fuck out of it."

Children stood crying, bewildered, some clinging to their parents, others prostrate on the ground, their eyes shut tight against the horrors around them.

The villagers had gathered together in a group. None of them had a weapon; they were too broken for that. Flynn now addressed them.

"Collect your children and leave now. If any are left behind, we'll clear them out ourselves."

Parents rushed forward to coax their children to come with them. The menfolk picked the children up where they lay and, murmuring softly to them to try and calm them, carried them over to the group. Then, as one, all of the villagers turned to leave. Many of the villagers were barefoot. One or two winced at the pain of stumbling through the snow; others seemed indifferent, their heads down, their meagre belongings slung in canvas sacks over their shoulders or carried in front of them in wicker baskets.

"Set fire to the branches," said Moran. I don't want them sneaking back. Tomorrow, we'll do another search of the land to clear out any of them who try to build new scalpeens in ditches or woodland. The entire estate has to be cleared."

He shivered against the bitterly cold wind. I need to get home in front of a warm fire, he thought, or it will be me perishing out here, never mind them.

CHAPTER TWENTY-SIX

Four days after clearing Mullangar again, Moran and three of his men rode out to Tyrone. This time they had waited until mid-day; it was just the one house and they didn't need the element of surprise. Moran was indifferent as to whether anyone else knew of their plans. He was so confident, he had told the sheriff that he wouldn't need his help; he would manage it with his own men.

The four men dismounted close to the edge of the village, tied up their horses to a nearby tree overlooking a brook, and strode nonchalantly through the muddy lanes towards Michael's cottage. Taking down a stone building would not be easy, so they had brought sledgehammers and thick rope. Two children looked fearfully at them from a doorway, a boy and girl dressed in patched rags and perhaps no more than ten or twelve years old, although they looked much older. Their mother came out and, seeing the men, hurriedly ushered them in and shut the door. Otherwise, the streets were completely empty.

Moran reached Michael's house and banged fiercely on the

door. Immediately, it was flung open and there to his shock stood the village priest, McNamara. Sorcha stood looking over his shoulder behind him. Behind them again stood her two children, their arms wrapped tightly around their mother, their faces buried in her dress.

"So, what brings you here, Andrew, on a cold wintry morning such as this?"

"I could ask the same of you, Father – why are you here?"

I'm here to say Mass and offer succour to poor Sorcha and her children; her husband has been arrested, as you know."

"Have you anyone else with you?" Moran said, trying to peer past the priest into the dark interior of the house.

"No – but some of the neighbours are at your back."

Moran heard a shuffling behind him – he turned and saw a ragged band of people stood shivering behind him, most of them hugging themselves in a vain attempt to stay warm. One or two looked more defiant, carrying cudgels mirroring those carried both by himself and his own men. He felt nervous but reflected that none of them would be much of a match for his men, despite their numbers. He gave them a contemptuous look and turned back to the priest.

"We have a warrant from the Court to seize this property and destroy it. The family cannot stay and will have to leave the village."

"Is that so?" said the priest coolly. Show me the warrant."

Moran dug into his pocket and pulled out a thin sheet of paper which had been folded in half. He carefully unwrapped it and, stepping nearer to the priest, raised it up to his face so he could see what was written there.

"Satisfied?" he asked with a sneer.

"This shows arrears of £5 covering 12 month's rent. Is this right Sorcha?"

"No, that's impossible – Michael always paid his rent straightaway. He owes nothing, I'm sure of it."

"Well," said the priest, "Sorcha is a good God-fearing woman. If she says there are no arrears, then I'm afraid your warrant is wrong, and you have no business here."

"Damn you, McNamara. This has been issued by the Courts – we have legitimate business here – stand aside."

Moran had been holding a thick wooden cudgel and he now raised this, waving it rudely in the priest's face.

There was a murmuring in the crowd and suddenly Moran was struck fiercely in the back; he gasped and fell to his knees. Next moment, there was a second blow, this time to the side of his head. Roaring with pain, he collapsed on the ground.

His own men looked anxiously at each other. There were around thirty of the villagers gathered around them and they looked angry enough to tear them all apart. They were weak and hollowed out by hunger, but a fierce anger had given them renewed strength and purpose. They all knew what had happened at Mullangar and they had heard as well of the way in which Moran and his men had chased the poor villagers off Clifton's land.

"Ronan – stop! You'll kill him!" screamed McNamara.

Ronan gazed unseeing at the priest. In his hand he held the loy he used for digging potatoes and ploughing up his land. He had hit Moran with the heel of the spade but now he stood with his arms raised above him, as though he were about to plunge the narrow steel blade of the loy into his prone body.

"Ronan!" he screamed again.

It was too late. Ronan brought down the blade of the spade with a guttural cry, plunging it deep into Moran's neck. Thick arterial blood shot into the air, spraying both Ronan and the body with a shower of dark crimson.

"Ronan, what have you done?" cried the priest. "May God have mercy on you, you've killed him. You've murdered him."

"They murdered my son! Murdered my poor son – what is there left for me? What?"

A man stepped from the crowd and very gently took the spade from Ronan's hands. Ronan didn't resist. Sorcha had been standing behind the priest but now moved forward. She clasped Ronan by the shoulders and with tears in her eyes, pulled him towards her, holding him in a firm embrace.

"Quiet now. Quiet – say no more. Say no more – come inside."

Slowly, she led him back into her house, the priest moving aside to let her in.

Moran's men stood like statues, glancing uneasily at each other. One held a cudgel but the other two had pulled out long-bladed knives which they brandished in front of them. As the priest looked at them, a line from Shakespeare's *Othello* suddenly came to him: "Keep up your bright swords for the dew will rust them." He had never really understood the words before, but their meaning now had a startling clarity.

"Go home," he said. "Go home – we'll take care of the body. You're not wanted here."

For a moment, they looked uncertain, still dazed by the horror of the death. Then they turned and, without a word, walked away.

Foley now stepped forward from the crowd. He glanced with horror at the body and then looked at the priest. He looked scared, his body trembling.

"The body, Father – what do we do with it? What will happen when Clifton –"

The priest cut him off.

"We'll leave that in God's hands." He turned away from Foley and stared at the crowd. "I want men to lift this body and get it into a cart. Then we'll take it to the sheriff and explain what happened. After that – well, we'll have to see."

As Sorcha led Ronan inside, her two sons shyly crept forward from the back room. Declan was ten years old, Rian had just turned six. Both looked frightened, their eyes wide in their head. They had heard the noises outside, but their mother had made them stay in the back room with the door shut and with strict instructions only to come out if she called their name.

"What's happening, Mam?" said Declan. "Why is Ronan here?"

"He's hurt, darling, so we're looking after him for a little bit."

Sorcha carefully guided Ronan to a bowl of water set out on a dresser, stripped off his shirt which she let fall to the floor, and with a cloth she had salvaged from one of Michael's older shirts, started to clean the blood off him. The bowl became dark red very quickly and she carried it carefully outside and emptied it onto the ground. She lifted the lid on a barrel of water which stood close to the door, rinsed the bowl, and then refilled it. As she rinsed, she watched the residue of blood in the bowl turn the water a pink milky colour and sighed, knowing the barrel would itself need to be emptied and refilled from the stream once she had finished. Then she turned to go back into the house. Satisfied finally that she had got off all of the blood, she fetched another bowl of clean water, pushed Ronan's face down into it, and with soap, started on his hair which was matted thick with Moran's blood. Through all this, he said nothing and appeared to be in a state of shock.

Although Rian was six, he occasionally still sucked his thumb. His parents had decided this was a comfort thing and made no attempt to dissuade him. No doubt he would grow out of it in time. He had become increasingly anxious with Michael's disappearance. Sorcha had told them he was visiting a cousin in Sligo but neither child believed her; Michael had never been absent from the house for such a long period before.

Now Rian looked nervously at his Mother.

"Where's Da?" he asked. "When is he coming back?"

"Soon, darling – very soon."

"When is soon?"

Sorcha hesitated.

"A week or two, perhaps – maybe a little longer."

He stared up at her.

"I don't believe you – you're lying. They say he's been arrested for trying to murder someone; they say they'll hang him."

Sorcha got up from the table where she had been looking after Ronan and hugged Rian to her waist. He was now noisily sobbing, trying to get words out but his voice kept catching.

"Hush, child – Dad will be alright. Don't you go worrying about it and don't pay any heed to what people are saying either. They don't know anything and should keep their mouths shut."

"I've heard the same things, Ma," said Declan. "Everyone is talking about it. Sean Murphy's Dad works at the prison – he says Dad is there because of Gerard trying to kill Clifton."

Sorcha took a deep breath to try and compose herself before she next spoke.

'Look, don't go believing what other people are telling you. It's true Dad is in prison, but he never tried to murder anyone. Gerard did try and kill Clifton, but that's got nothing to do with your Dad. There'll have to be a trial and that will prove Dad is innocent – you have to cling to that, boys. I said he would be home soon and he will.'

"I miss him," said Rian, tears welling up.

"We all do, darling, we all do. Now take yourselves out and play – you've been cooped up in here all morning and you're under my feet, so ye are. Go on – go on out and play, play snowballs or something."

Declan took Rian's hand. Rian had wedged his other hand back into his mouth again, sucking hard on his thumb.

"If you keep your thumb in your mouth like that," said Declan, "I'll be getting off twice as many snowballs as you, if you even manage one."

As they moved towards the door Sorcha suddenly realised the snow outside would be stained with Moran's blood. She looked at the priest who had been standing quietly just inside the door. He knew immediately why she was alarmed and moved to block the door.

"Hold on, boys – I think you need your coats before you go out. It's fierce cold out there."

Sorcha rushed to fetch their coats and made a great show of putting them on, taking her time to do up the buttons on Rian's coat.

McNamara stepped briskly outside, closed the door, and hastened over to the area which was still stained with blood. He kicked more snow over it until all traces of the blood had been erased and then went back into the house. He nodded briefly to Sorcha to let her know it was now safe for the boys to go outside.

"Right, boys, off you go and be careful you don't get frostbite. Declan, look after your brother, now, won't you?" she said.

When they had gone, the priest looked at Ronan who was sat in front of the fireplace trying to warm himself. Despite the heat, he was shaking uncontrollably. He had wrapped his arms around himself and was staring sightless into the fire.

"Ronan, they'll be coming for you soon. You shouldn't be here – it will alarm the boys and may get Sorcha into trouble as well. And God knows she has enough of that as it is."

Ronan said nothing and continued to stare into the fire. The priest realised he hadn't heard a word he had said. He touched him gently on the arm.

"Come on now – we need to get you home."

Ronan turned to look at him and then slowly stood up and allowed himself to be led out of the house.

"Once he's settled, I'll be back, Sorcha."

Sorcha hesitated.

"Father – Michael's sister, Mary."

The priest stared at her.

"I understand, but I can't revoke it – the bishop, you see –"

"Can't or won't?"

"I'm sorry, I just can't. The British are determined to see Catholicism crushed in this country. Look at Maeve Kelly – she's sending her two daughters to Protestant schools. She's attending their church services and has been fed their poison; she's foresworn the Virgin Mary. If we don't send a message, where will it end?"

"You baptised Mary– she was in church every Sunday. If she took the soup, it was only to feed her unborn child. Do you not see that? And now she's lost the baby – she's in Hell and only you can save her."

"I can't, I can't do it. I'm sorry – if I could I would."

Sorcha turned angrily away.

"Go then – get away from here because we have no need of you."

She was close to collapse but hid it from him. She needed to stay strong. When he had gone, she couldn't stop the tears falling. She went into the bedroom and fell, sobbing, onto the bed.

CHAPTER TWENTY-SEVEN

The Reverend Lloyd was starting to think they had overstayed their welcome with the Fitzpatricks. It had started to snow again, and it was uncomfortably cold. Although it was only four in the afternoon, it was already dark. He glanced back through the glass window of the carriage at his son Percy. He had taken care to lay a blanket over him before they left, and he was already asleep. At that moment, two men appeared from the field to his left, one of them grabbing the bridle of one of the horses to bring it to a halt whilst the other stood pointing a pistol straight at him. Both their faces were concealed by scarves so only their eyes were visible.

Lloyd felt his heart pounding in his chest, almost as though it were trying to physically break through his skin. Despite the cold, he was also sweating, perspiration streaming down his back. He tried to speak but nothing came out; he felt as though he were choking. The man with the pistol fired. His aim was wild, but the bullet struck Lloyd in his shoulder. He clutched at it, but the gunman was already firing again and this time he struck him in the belly. Lloyd fell backwards and toppled from the carriage into the road. The gunman coolly dispatched him with another shot to his head. He flung open the carriage door and stared in at the terrified boy.

"Out!" he shouted. "Get out of there!"

He levelled his pistol at the boy to show he meant business. Trembling, the boy stepped down from the carriage. He was too frightened to speak. The man gestured with the pistol to the driver's seat. Percy scrambled up and the other man, who was still holding the bridle, caught hold of the reins and passed them up to the boy.

"Drive," he said.

"What?" said Percy nervously.

"I said drive – go on, get out of here."

Gripping the reins, Percy motioned the horse to move. At fourteen, his father had let him take the reins on a number of occasions so, despite his shaking hands, he was confident enough to put the horse into a smooth trot. Not once had he glanced down at his father's body and nor did he look back now. In minutes, he was out of sight of the gunmen and had been swallowed up by the darkness.

CHAPTER TWENTY-EIGHT

"Tyrone's a sorry business."

Twisleton turned to stare at Trevelyan. He had been studying a report on the collection of the poor rates, something he was now responsible for overseeing. The news wasn't good; uncollected poor rates now stood close to a million pounds, a staggering figure. Many landowners had simply stopped paying and in some districts, rate collectors were actually being attacked. A rate collector in Galway had been besieged by a large crowd, many of them armed with sticks cut from the hedgerows and whatever stones they could find on the road. Children had scurried back and forth looking for the largest stones they could find to arm their parents. An 1843 law had made Irish landlords financially liable for every tenant who had land valued at £4 or less. Irish property must pay for Irish poverty had been the mantra, but it seemed Irish landlords did not share this sentiment.

"Is it? Why?" Twisleton asked.

"You must have heard, surely? The murder of the bailiff in Tyrone? The attempted murder of his landlord?"

"No, I haven't, I'm afraid. I've been distracted with other matters." Twistleton waved a hand over the thick pile of papers littering his desk.

"Ah, yes of course – I forgot to congratulate you the other day on your promotion– you must be very pleased."

"It was unsought, I assure you," said Twisleton wearily.

"Still – Chief Poor Law Commissioner, quite the step up."

"So, what about Tyrone?" said Twisleton impatiently. He wished Trevelyan would leave him in peace; he had yet to have a conversation with him that hadn't left him feeling agitated and annoyed. On a number of occasions, he had wanted to punch his smug face. He would probably have been instantly dismissed but, sometimes, he thought it would still have been worth it. He hated his job and fools like Trevelyan certainly didn't make it any easier.

"We're going to have to do something about it," Trevelyan said. "The rule of law is the only thing that keeps civilisation from collapse. Without it, there would be anarchy. These people must be taught a lesson."

"And how do you propose to do that? Isn't this already being managed by local police and officials?"

"It's not enough to punish the villains who carried out these vile acts; their families and friends must also suffer. People have to be taught that if they break the law, then it's not just themselves that will suffer – only that way will we bring this anarchy under control. I've spoken to the Home Secretary and it's been agreed that a platoon of the 8th Hussars will assist the local police in clearing the houses in Tyrone. It's also been arranged for them to stay on for the hangings to ensure there is no more dissent."

"Colonel Jones has knowledge of this, does he?"

"Jones takes his orders from London. The troops leave tomorrow."

Twisleton sighed. "I see – well thank you for sharing but I really must return to my labours."

Once Trevelyan had gone, Twisleton rose from his desk and stared out into the street. The sky was a leaden grey. It seems low enough to smother us all, he thought, a fat pillow on the face of Dublin. He had never known a land where it rained so much. And when it wasn't raining, it was snowing. Even now, there was a tiresome drizzle; not bad enough to warrant an umbrella but you still ended up soaked if you stayed out in it long enough. Everything seemed infected by damp or mildew – the floorboards beneath his feet, even the clothes in his wardrobe. In the distance, he could just make out the central spire of St Patrick's cathedral. He had been told it was a magnificent structure. I really must try and visit it one day, he thought, if only I can get away from these wretched mounds of paper. He sighed again and turned back to his desk.

CHAPTER TWENTY-NINE

The day after Moran's murder, and in the dead of night, Tyrone's villagers were woken up by a piercing, screeching sound. Peter Furey stirred and opened his eyes. He shivered. It was the souls of the dead, he thought, come back to warn them. Something horrible was about to happen, he was sure of it. Sorcha too heard it; it was so loud; it was as though the sound was coming from somewhere inside the house. She heard a scuffling sound and then the quick patter of bare feet on the stone floor. Declan and Rian stood at the foot of the bed.

"Mammy, we're scared – can we come in with you?" asked Declan.

Without a word, Sorcha threw back the covers. The children slipped in beside her and she hugged them tightly.

"There's nothing to be frightened of – it's nothing, I'm sure. Some crows getting excited is all."

"It's the banshees, Mammy" said Declan. "Christy saw one the other night, hiding behind a tree. She had a long grey cloak and red hair. Someone's going to die – I know it."

"Hush your nonsense – that's a fairy tale and Christy should know better. He's a stook and a muppet. His own Da has disowned him, so ashamed of him he is."

"It's not just Christy, Mam. Old Ma Kelly has seen them too."

"Ma Kelly has more rubbish in her head than flies on shite. Don't be listening to her either or people will start looking at you sideways as well."

Rian giggled.

"You swore, Mammy".

"I fecking didn't."

"Isn't fecking a swear word?" asked Declan.

"Fecking isn't swearing at all – it's a way of not swearing and the priests are perfectly happy with it. They use it themselves, of course, although not during Mass."

"What's sideways, Mammy?" said Rian.

Sorcha sighed.

"It's upside down is what it is. Now go to sleep the pair of you. I'm worn out and ye must be too."

Sorcha woke at dawn. The terrible noise had stopped. It was quiet – too quiet really. She slipped out of bed, put on a shift and coat, pulled on her shoes, and went outside. What she saw filled her with horror. The fields were littered with the bodies of crows; the lane outside was thick with them and she could scarcely walk a yard without standing on them. She peered at the ones closest to her. Normally, crows were fat-bodied creatures, but she could see these were starved, mere skeletons. She shuddered. Perhaps Declan was right after all and there were bigger creatures than crows who would soon be dead.

CHAPTER THIRTY

Smethwick, the defence lawyer, was in his early thirties with a mane of sandy hair swept backwards from his forehead. He spoke with an easy confidence and very quickly won Simon and Mary over. Simon could see how a jury might warm to a man like this.

His desk was piled with papers and buff folders and the oak bookcase behind him was lined with leather-bound law books, some new, some where the leather had split and faded. Smethwick himself didn't stay seated for long but stalked around the room, becoming more and more animated as Simon and Mary explained what had happened.

"And you say no-one's been allowed to see him?"

"No," said Mary. "It's only through a minister – a friend of Simon's – that we even know what charges are being brought against him."

"I'll try and arrange and see him tomorrow. I'll also ask that you be allowed to see him – they shouldn't be denying you access."

"That would be wonderful, if you could," said Mary. "We've all been so worried about him."

"Do you think they can make these charges stick?" said Simon.

Smethwick hesitated.

"The fact they have a witness isn't good. The handwriting match doesn't help either but that can be argued; it depends how close a match. But the witness is bad news – do you have any idea who it might be?"

"None at all," said Mary. "Nor can I think of anyone who would want to harm Michael in this way."

"These are desperate times. Only two days ago, a vicar was murdered in Roscommon. He was a landowner as well as a reverend and, as you know, landlords are none too popular at the moment. He was murdered in front of his son. And then, of course, there's the bailiff's murder, Moran. I understand you know the man who killed him, Mary."

"Yes, I do – Ronan Lynch. He's a good man but I think his son's death has driven him out of his wits. He was so gentle – I can't believe what he did."

"We're all capable of it if provoked enough. And in most murders, you don't need to look any further than the immediate family."

"Oh God, how did it come to this?" said Mary.

Simon put a comforting hand on her shoulder. Tears ran down her face and she hastily wiped them away with her fingers.

"I'm sorry, I didn't mean to upset you," said Smethwick.

"Don't worry, I'll do everything I can to try and free your brother. We'll start with getting you access. We must also try and find out who this witness is – people in your village must have their suspicions. Do you or Simon really have no idea?"

"No – no, I don't. I've tried speaking to people, but no-one seems to know anything."

"Someone must know something – I'll try and make my own enquiries, see what I can find out. I also need to get a look at this so-called note and compare it myself with samples of your brother's handwriting. I know they took samples away when they raided his house but let me see anything else you have – it could be very important."

"I'm sure I can give you what you need – I'll look when we get back. How do we get them to you though? Should we ride out again?"

"No – don't worry. Tomorrow I'll try and see your brother but the following day, I'll come to your village. I want to talk to as many of the villagers as I can – see what we can find out."

"I'll get Michael's wife, Sorcha, to introduce you to some of them – I don't think they'll open up to a stranger otherwise. I have to warn you though – because of what happened to Moran, many of them are now terrified, too frightened to speak to anyone. I can't speak to them myself either – since I took up with Simon…he's a Protestant, you see."

"I understand. I'll need to speak to Sorcha as well anyway."

Mary hesitated, as though weighing something in her mind. "With Moran's death, I think they'll clear the village – make an example of us. It'll happen soon I'm sure – I think it might be better if you travel tomorrow and see Michael the day after."

"You're right – we'll leave first thing tomorrow. You'll both need accommodation for tonight, I imagine."

"Don't worry," said Mary. "I'm sure we'll find somewhere."

"You can stay with me – I have a large enough house and there's plenty of room."

"Are you sure, sir?" said Mary. "We don't want to be a bother to you and you've already done more than we could have hoped for."

"It will be my pleasure. My wife is always complaining we don't entertain enough. We have two dogs, I'm afraid, and there's my son but if you think you can put up with them – the dogs, I mean, although my son can be a handful as well…"

Mary smiled.

"We both love dogs – and children as well."

"That's settled then."

*

Mary lay in bed, listening to the gentle sound of Simon's snoring. He was lying on his back; she remembered Owen had also invariably snored if he did the same and she would often nudge him, hoping he would wake up and turn on his side. She thought about nudging Simon but decided against it. He was clearly very tired and needed his sleep. She had never before slept in such a comfortable bed with a thick mattress, cotton sheets, and woollen blankets. A fire burned in the grate, its soft glow casting flickering shadows against the ceiling.

She felt safe but she couldn't sleep. Her mind kept returning to her miscarriage, the horror of it. She hated her own body; she felt it had betrayed her. She had wanted this baby so badly, had imagined it growing up, its first steps tottering around the kitchen, its first smile, its first words. Owen had died but part of his soul would have lived in this baby; it would have had his eyes, the way he sighed when he was dissatisfied with something, his kindness.

She felt so wretched and alone; how was it possible to feel like this and yet still be surrounded by people? It was as though you were trapped in a dark cave. Beyond the shadows you could dimly perceive people laughing and dancing; you could hear the sound of a fiddle, someone else singing. But you couldn't join them; your feet were paralysed and if you called out, no-one would hear you. There were only one or two people she felt really close to, where it was possible to let them know how you felt with a single exchanged look, no words spoken, just that mute understanding between you. Michael was one of those people and Owen had been too. She would be thinking of something and start to speak about it and before the words had even left her lips, Owen would start to talk about the same thing, as though they had but one shared mind, a river, sometimes diverging into smaller brooks or tributaries but always destined to come together again, the river now stronger and more powerful, its course more certain, sweeping down towards the sea. And what was a child but that same river? The mingling of their souls, the outpouring of their love.

She cried, the tears running silently down her cheeks. She had lost Owen and she had lost her child; she couldn't afford to now lose Michael. If she did, then she herself was lost. Simon was a good man and she had started to feel she could love him, but he was not Owen and nor was he Michael. Michael was the north star of her soul and she would follow him wherever he led, even if that meant death and an unmarked grave.

CHAPTER THIRTY-ONE

A rmed with a switch he had cut from a bush, Declan thrashed at a clump of nettles. Once he thought he had enough, he carefully put the mashed leaves into a wicker basket, cradling them in an old linen cloth to avoid being stung. In the past, his mother would have given it body by adding potatoes; now it would be made up as a thin green gruel.

Suddenly, he heard a clattering of horses in the lane below the high bank on which he stood. He lay down on his stomach to make sure he wasn't seen and peered down. What he could see looked like soldiers with white gloves and gold brocade adorning their jackets. He could also see the swords hanging from a scabbard at their waists. He felt a tingle of both excitement and fear. Behind them and also on horseback, sat what he was sure were Clifton's men and several policemen, drably dressed, in comparison with the splendour of the soldiers, in silver-buttoned black tunics and peaked caps. Wriggling backwards on his stomach, he stood up and ran. The soldiers and police would need to follow the lane's path around the base of the hill, and he knew he would be able to get back before they reached the village.

"Soldiers!" he cried.

A small group of men who had been idly chatting turned to stare at him. For a moment they looked bewildered. Then, realising the peril they were in, they ran to their cottages. Hearing his cry, Sorcha was already at her door, Rian peering anxiously out around her.

"Soldiers, Mam – just up the lane." Declan pointed back the way he had come.

"Get inside – quick," said Sorcha.

Although frightened, she stepped out into the lane, closing the door behind her. Many of the other villagers joined her and she noticed Ronan was among them. He should be hiding she thought, or better still, trying to escape into the hills.

They heard the low rumble of the troops and horses before they saw them. Sorcha gasped at the number of troops and men before them. Mounted at the front were Flynn and Clifton's land agent, Johnson. Flynn spoke first.

"Mr Lynch – we have a warrant for your arrest."

Ronan stepped forward from the crowd. He was holding a long pike, the blade glinting in the light. Flynn noticed there were others in the crowd armed with pikes and the sharp-bladed sleans used for cutting turf. Others held scythes or heavy sticks; still others were carrying rocks and stones.

He shifted uneasily in his saddle.

"We don't want any trouble now – give yourself up, Ronan, and we'll then leave these good people in peace. You can start by throwing down your weapon and that goes for all of you. My men are armed and the troops here will cut youse all to ribbons before the breath is out of your mouths. There's been enough violence – let's not make it worse. Many of you have families, young bairns – do you want to make orphans of them?"

The crowd stirred and looked at each other.

Ronan stepped forward.

"What do you know about family?" he said contemptuously. "Look around you – how few children there are. It's not because they're hiding – no it's because most of them are dead, dead with the hunger and disease. What do we care for your guns and your swords? We can choose to die today or tomorrow but die we all shall anyway – what is left for us? Do you think we fear death? No, it's life we're afraid of – a life you and your kind have turned into Hell itself."

With those words, Ronan rushed forward and before the sheriff and the others could react, he swept Flynn to the ground with his pike. There was a gasp from the crowd and, for a moment, everyone stared. The pike's blade was embedded in his throat, Flynn clutching at the wound around it and trying frantically to stem the blood which spewed out of him, blackening the ground. He tried to sit up, making a strange gurgling sound, then fell back. The noise stopped.

As one, the troops surged forward on their horses, sweeping their swords from their scabbards, knocking men and women to the ground and savagely laying about them. Ronan was one of the first to be killed, a soldier dismounting and plunging his sword into his stomach almost up to the hilt. The crowd had fallen back before the onslaught but then rallied. Men ducked beneath the blades and used their sleans, scythes, and pikes to swipe at the horses' legs, crippling them and bringing them to the ground. Some of the soldiers lay trapped beneath their mounts and the enraged villagers fell upon them, stabbing and cutting, careless of the wounds they inflicted, intent only on killing the invaders. One soldier was caught in the face by a rock brought down on the back of his head by one of the women and fell to the ground, killed instantly by the blow. The villagers, although driven by desperation, were still no match for the troops. Shots rang out as the soldiers fired their weapons at point blank range. The air was filled with the acrid smell of gunpowder and smoke from the guns swirled up into the air.

In a matter of minutes, it was all over. Dying men screamed and moaned. Around them lay those who were already dead, their bodies contorted, their eyes lifeless. Some of the villagers fled, racing as quickly as they could up into the hills surrounding them. The slower among these, either limping badly from leg wounds or handicapped by other injuries, were quickly cut down by a ragged volley of shots from the troops.

Sorcha and a number of the other women had fallen back as soon as the fighting had started, looking on in horror at the carnage in front of them. Now they pressed forward again. One of the women rushed to attend to her husband's wounds, oblivious to the soldiers who still wheeled about her, their horses' hooves dangerously close as she bent to look at her husband. A soldier swung his sword, slashing into her face and neck and she fell, lifeless, to the ground, lying stretched over her husband's body. He screamed and tried to rise but the same soldier rode his horse deliberately over him, not even glancing back as he then steered his horse towards the women clustered at the edge of the slaughter.

"Run!" screamed Sorcha. Around her the women stared with disbelief and then darted away, racing to their cottages and flinging themselves inside. Sorcha was limping and knew she was too far from her own cottage to chance it. She hoped to God her own two boys had managed to get back there. Stumbling, she made her way into the long grass edging the village and tumbled down into a ditch. A shallow stream ran through it and she lay there, hardly daring to breathe, the cold water numbing her limbs.

She started to get up but stopped. She knew if she exposed herself, she would be cut down as surely as that poor woman who had rushed to tend to her husband. She could still hear the muffled screams of the dying and the noise of battle. Pray God the boys did get away and are safe, she thought. Either way, I have to live if I'm to help them – I can't do that if I'm dead.

Johnson gazed around him. He had dismounted from his horse and was armed with a single pistol.

"Captain Ellis," he shouted, "we need to clear these cottages."

Ellis had only recently been given his commission. To

Johnson he looked like a mere boy and yet he was in charge of a platoon of thirty men. Ellis was still on horseback but was pale and sweating and his nervousness had infected his horse, which wheeled and pawed the air with its front legs. Struggling with the reins, Ellis fought to stay in his saddle. He realised events had spun out of his control and screamed above the slaughter.

"Stop – I command you to stop – stop, for God's sake! I'll have your hides for this."

No-one heard and his shouts were drowned out by the noise of battle around him. Johnson had heard though. He had clear instructions from Clifton and this fool wasn't going to stop him.

"Clear these cottages," he shouted. "Get the villagers out and set light to the roofs."

Wooden torches tipped with pitch were hurriedly passed out amongst his men. One of them pushed his way into the nearest cottage and lit his own torch from the hearth fire. Returning, he used this to light two of the other torches and these in turn were used to light the rest. The torches were flung up on to the roofs of the cottages which were poorly thatched with straw. In seconds, the whole village was ablaze. Both the soldiers and the bailiff's men were careless as to whether anyone was still in the cottages. Villagers who had tried to take refuge emerged stumbling and choking, their eyes blinded by smoke. Small children ran screaming into the street. The men emerging were struck down by gunfire or the slash of a sword. One of the soldiers slashed at a woman's belly with his sword; she fell with a moan to the ground. Now there was a kind of frenzy;

other women were struck and some of the older children also fell, struck with swords or the stout blackthorn sticks wielded by the bailiff's men. The smaller children tried to run, darting around their assailants, desperately trying to keep away from the horses whose legs mashed the air, hooves thumping against the earth. The air filled with the sound of screams and the roar of the fire. Freighted with ash and sparks, smoke billowed upwards, hiding the sun.

Ellis dismounted and ran, grabbing the arm of a soldier who had lifted his sword above his head, about to strike a young boy who had fallen to the ground. He looked back at him, but his eyes were crazed, unseeing. He tried to wrest his arm free from Ellis's grip. Ellis struck him hard across the back of his head with the butt of his sword. The soldier staggered.

"You bloody fool – I'll have you court-martialled!" Ellis screamed.

This seemed to bring the soldier to his senses. He lowered his own sword and stood staring at Ellis. He could see the calculation in his eyes. Suddenly, the soldier lunged forward. Ellis had been anticipating this and sidestepped, plunging his sword deep into the man's belly. He fell, moaning, to the ground. Ellis wrenched the sword free and stabbed again, this time into the man's chest. The ground was quickly soaked with blood and the soldier clutched at his stomach, desperately trying to keep his entrails from spilling out through his tunic. The life went out of his eyes and he lay dead at Ellis's feet.

*

Lying face down, Sorcha craned her head upwards to try and understand what was happening. She could see and smell the smoke.

There was a sudden rustling sound. Someone grabbed the collar of her shift and dragged her to her feet. She screamed and tried to claw at her assailant's face by reaching backwards but he easily dodged her flailing arms.

"You're a feisty one, aren't you? I like my women to have a bit of spirit."

He pushed her to the ground beside the brook and settled himself on top of her. She could feel the cold steel of what must be a knife pressed against the side of her throat.

"Now we can do this the easy way or the hard – I don't mind which, but if it is the hard then you'll suffer the more. Do you understand me?" he hissed into her ear. "Are you going to be quiet or what?"

Sorcha went still. Her heart was leaping fit to burst out of her chest and her blood roared in her ears.

"I'll be quiet," she said. "Please don't hurt me."

Her attacker laughed.

"Well, that's more sensible – now we can enjoy ourselves."

He sat up, straddling her haunches. She could feel his erection pushing against her. He pulled up her dress and loosened his trousers, grunting with the effort of undoing his belt whilst he leant with his full weight on top of her. She screamed.

"Noisy little bitch, aren't you? Shut the fuck up or by God I'll make you shut up."

The soldier closed his hands around her throat and squeezed.

CHAPTER THIRTY-TWO

"I imagine you're aware of the riot in Tyrone."

Twisleton glanced up from his desk. Trevelyan looked anxious; he also looked as though he had slept badly, dark shadows beneath his eyes. Trevelyan appeared not to have shaven either, which for a man so punctilious about his appearance was remarkable in itself.

"I am yes," said Twisleton. "It was murder, plain and simple –"

"You misunderstand – it was not murder. Those troops had no choice but to put down that uprising, their own lives were at risk. Some of them died. The government will need to act –"

"Act? To do what exactly? How would you expect a people to behave faced with losing their homes and being driven out onto the roads like that? Many of them were already suffering from starvation and fever; how many of them would survive in the open with no shelter at all?"

"It's not happened elsewhere –"

"And why is that? Because the population is so worn down

with disease and hunger, they can barely stand, never mind try and resist the police and a troop of soldiers. And there have been problems elsewhere – only last month there were riots in Kerry; shops were ransacked, officials assaulted –"

"Which is precisely why we cannot allow this to pass – troops are being sent to hunt down those who escaped and bring them to justice. We'll have to hang a few as a warning to others. The rest will be transported."

Twisleton sighed.

"Will you now? You're a hard man, Trevelyan. Have you no pity?"

"Of course I do – I have as much sorrow for what has happened as the next man. Unless punishment is meted out though, unless a warning is sent that this sort of thing won't be tolerated, the violence we're seeing elsewhere will only get worse. Kerry was not an isolated incident. Barges were blocked by rioters in Dungarvan to try and stop a shipment of grain. Buildings were set on fire, merchants beaten –"

"And what then happened?" said Twisleton angrily. "Troops opened fire – people were killed and for what reason? They're starving but we're still shipping food – food they desperately need – to England. What do you expect?"

"What I expect…what I expect is for you to show me a little more courtesy and to curb your temper, Mr Twisleton."

"Oh, to hell with it – what's the point in arguing with a man like you. If you don't like what I'm saying, speak to your friends in the Treasury and have me cashiered – frankly, I no longer care."

Twisleton stood up, flung the file he had been working on to the ground and left, banging the heavy door behind him. There was a room at the end of the passageway which he knew would be empty, the occupant having travelled to Galway to inspect the relief works there. He stood in there for a while, breathing heavily. He buried his face in his hands; he could feel them trembling.

I must calm down, he thought. Trevelyan was now responsible for relief operations in both Ireland and Scotland. He was a powerful man and incurring his wrath could only end badly. I must apologise, he thought – I have a wife and family to care for; I can't wreck my own career because of pride. Slowly, he began to recover his composure. He opened the door and stared up the corridor. The door to his own office was still closed, which meant Trevelyan must still be there. He walked carefully towards it and opened the door. Trevelyan was stood at a window staring out at the rain, which was hammering at the glass in a fierce downpour. He could see that already the streets were flooded, pedestrians ankle deep in water.

"So, you're back – have you calmed down a little?"

"Yes – I have. I owe you an apology…"

"No – no need for that. We live in difficult times – it's bound to get to all of us occasionally. I'm not inhuman, Twisleton, whatever you may think of me. It's just that I have a job to do; it may look callous but that's not my intention. It might surprise you to know but my ancestors were from Cornwall, so I have Celtic blood in me. I'm not insensible to the suffering the Irish people are facing, but I have to take the long view. The famine – terrible as it is – will allow the economic reform of this country and, in time, everyone will prosper as a result, not just the landowners but everyone. If I have an issue, it's not with the Irish people as such but with Irish landowners. Take Skibbereen for example – I've just read a Board of Works report on the situation there and it's the most awful thing I've ever read. A local Catholic priest has predicted that a third of its population will be in their graves by April. And why is this? Is it the government's fault? No, the reason the situation is so grim is that there is no local relief committee. Without this, there's no mechanism to distribute provisions – those are the guidelines laid down by the Treasury. And why is there no relief committee? None exists because the local landowners are unwilling to put their hands in their pockets to set one up. Wrixon-Beecher in Skibbereen has an annual rental income of £10,000. You could buy up a good part of London with that. These people aren't really Irish; they were settled in Ireland two centuries ago as a deliberate policy to establish English rule and English culture. I'm more Irish than they are. Half of them don't even set foot in this country; they're in London or the shires drinking themselves to death on port and gorging themselves on the very produce produced by this country. I know well that people are starving whilst vast quantities of grain and pork and beef are shipped out of the country to end up on their tables. However, that's the economic reality and we have to deal with it."

"Well, if the problem is so severe in Skibbereen, why not ask the local depot to simply open their doors and give the corn away? Why are we letting these people starve?"

Trevelyan looked sadly at him.

"If we were to do that, then other towns would demand the same – there would be a run on our supplies which would then be quickly exhausted. We can't afford to make exceptions like this, even though the consequences are so dreadful."

Twisleton could feel himself becoming angry again. I have to stop this, he thought, I need to calm down.

Trevelyan glanced across. Although Twisleton was trying to hide it, he could see the anger bubbling up inside him again. He affected not to notice.

"I retrieved your file – I've put it back on your desk. You might need to spend some time putting your papers back in order though. He smiled briefly. "I do understand your anger. There are times I become angry myself. I would dearly love to pick Wrixon-Beecher up by the heels and shake him until every last penny had been wrung from his pockets. It is these people who stand by, pretending to care that are the problem, not us. Look, I don't want to continue this now. Let's leave it – it's late and we both need our sleep – well, at least, I do anyway. We can talk again in the morning. I hope you sleep well because I almost certainly will not."

Once Trevelyan had left, Twisleton opened his desk drawer and pulled out a small flask of brandy. Usually, he would content himself with a couple of sips. This time though, he took a long slow drink. He felt the fire hit his throat and sighed. Trevelyan was a mystery. He had thought him completely without humanity, a soulless automaton, like one of those mechanical puppets the French were so fond of. A friend had told him of a flute-playing automaton in Italy and had shown him a sketch which had been published in *The Times*. It looked both sinister and hideous at the same time. And now, impossible as it seemed, there did seem to be a glimpse of humanity in the man. He seemed genuinely concerned about the plight of Ireland's population. The pity of it was that he was so straitjacketed by dogma, so convinced that he was right, that he was unable to break through this. If Twisleton were to open up Trevelyan's chest, he wouldn't have been at all surprised to see not a warm beating heart, but a mere assemblage of wires and levers, a clever facsimile of a human being. Trevelyan seemed to have empathy but was pursuing policies which were destroying the lives of thousands of people. Now it seemed the Scots were also to be the subject of his tender ministrations. Well, God help them, he thought – at this rate there won't be a single Celt left alive in the whole of the British Isles – except perhaps for Trevelyan himself, he thought bitterly. Yes, except for him.

CHAPTER THIRTY-THREE

"What have you done? You bloody fool – first Moran and now Flynn; two men murdered because of your stupidity. And worse, you're also responsible for the deaths of all of those poor women and children in Tyrone. How can you live with yourself? You disgust me – I can't stand to look at you."

It was nearly noon, but Clifton had only just dragged himself out of his bed, having elected, as was so often the case now, to sleep in a bedroom as far away from his wife as he could manage without actually having to leave the house. Even then, he had briefly contemplated sleeping in the barn; at least there he might have been safe from her continuous rants. The woman was hysterical, he thought, quite mad.

The mad woman now stood in front of him in the kitchen whilst he sat cowed in a chair, his hand to his brow, unwilling or unable to look at her. He had gone to bed drunk and he was still drunk now, having availed himself of a half bottle of whisky as soon as he surfaced from sleep. He remembered placing the bottle on his bedside table when he had gone to bed but when he woke, he couldn't find it. It had taken a long period of anxious searching before he finally located it trapped underneath the sheets at the foot of the bed. His wife also spent more and more of her time drunk, imbibing copious amounts of the sweet sherry they called Madeira. When they were both inebriated, it was not a recipe for harmony at the best of times and this was far from the best of times.

"Leave me alone, woman – I have a fierce headache and you're not making it any better."

"Poor you – well, try taking your head out of a bottle – that should go some way towards mending you."

"You vicious bitch – I should have left you years ago. And I still might, yes, I might still do exactly that."

"And who the Hell would have you if you did leave me? You're not a man; you're a cringing coward who gets others to do his dirty work. Don't threaten me – if anyone leaves this marriage it will be me, not you, you spineless eejit."

Clifton stood up – he still felt very unsteady and had to lean heavily against the wall to stop himself falling. Desperation spurred him on though and he began to push roughly past his wife.

"I don't have to listen to this – get out of my way."

"And where do you think you're going? You daren't display your face in public and you can't even walk your own estate without someone trying to kill you. Worse, I can't go out in public either because I'm your wife and they would as soon murder me as well."

She manoeuvred to block his exit.

"I'll only say this once more," Clifton growled. "Get out of my way."

"Or what – is the little manikin going to hurt me?"

Enraged, Clifton stepped towards her and punched her just above her brow with a closed fist. She reeled back with shock and pain. He moved towards her to strike again. Emma stumbled backwards against a low oak table. She almost fell but managed to right herself. There were two drawers in the table's side and, turning quickly, she opened one and grabbed a long carving knife. Clifton grabbed her hair while she still had her back to him, forcing her head back.

Fear drove her on and, ignoring the pain, she wrenched herself free, so she was now facing him. She plunged the knife into his chest. She was amazed at how easily the knife slid in. Now it was Clifton's turn to look shocked, his eyes bulging in his head. Blood bloomed across his white shirt. He grabbed the knife with both hands as though to try and pull it out, then fell heavily forward, dropping to the stone floor and driving the knife even deeper into his chest. He gave a loud groan; his body shook and then he was still. Emma gazed down in horror. Blood was spreading in a wide pool around his body. She hastily stepped back as it pushed towards her feet. What have I done? she thought. I've murdered him.

She heard hurried footsteps in the corridor and Sarah, the housekeeper, flung open the door. Sarah screamed, a long piercing sound which never seemed to end. Emma stared at her. She wanted to scream herself but was struggling to breathe as panic and fear overwhelmed her, forcing her to lose consciousness. Emma struck her head hard against the stone floor and was still.

When she woke, Sarah was kneeling beside her, oblivious to the blood now soaking her clothes. She gently raised Emma's head and brought a glass of water to her lips. Emma drank too quickly, choking and coughing water back up across her neck and face.

"Try and drink more slowly, Ma'am."

Emma nodded and raised herself a little more so she could drink without choking. As she lifted herself, she caught sight of Clifton's body lying beside her. Horror filled her.

"He attacked me…the knife…I didn't mean to…oh, Sarah, what am I to do? I've killed him…I've killed him."

Emma was crying now, hot tears running down her cheeks. Sarah could see she was starting to become hysterical.

"Shush, shush," she murmured. "It will be alright. Shush now, calm yourself."

"How can it be alright? I've murdered him, I've murdered my husband. They'll hang me, they'll hang me for this, Sarah." Fear consumed her and she started to shake.

"No, no-one's going to do anything, Ma'am. We'll fix this, I promise. We can fix this."

"How can we fix this? How can anyone fix this – he's dead, he's dead."

"Trust me – we can fix this."

*

Sarah hurried from the kitchen and returned with an ornate Persian rug she had taken from Clifton's study.

"Help me roll him into this."

Emma dragged herself to her feet. They spread the rug on the floor. Kneeling beside him and straining with the effort, they eased him over and onto the rug. Clifton had been an enormously obese man and by the time they had managed to roll him up into the rug, they were both breathing heavily. Sweat trickled freely down both of their backs. Clifton's blood, sticky and warm, coated their clothes, hands and arms. Sarah pushed her hair back from her face and behind her ears, blood smearing her face and hair.

"I'll fetch the carriage and horses," Sarah said. "We won't be able to lift him into the carriage, but we can use it to drag him to the lake using a rope tied to the rear axle."

"I could get Johnson to help," said Emma.

Sarah shook her head quickly. "No, no – we can do this ourselves and Johnson can't be trusted to see this in the right way. No, it must be just you and me, Ma'am. We need to fasten rope around both ends of this rug. There's some in the stable we can use, and we can use it as well to drag him behind the carriage."

By the time they had finished, the sky was already darkening outside. Sarah was pleased; it would mean they should be able to arrange everything without being seen. Johnson's cottage was on the far side of the lake and was hidden from view by a small copse of trees. He would therefore be unable to see any activity taking place at the front of the house. There would be a risk if he decided to walk his two dogs around the estate, something he often did, particularly at first light and then again in the evenings.

Sarah brought the carriage and two horses round. They wrapped a rope around the rug's circumference and then tied another rope lengthways, arranging it carefully around each loop of the first rope so it couldn't slip. They tied the body by a third length of rope to the carriage's axle. Both women climbed up into the carriage and Sarah flicked the reins, encouraging the horses to set off in a slow trot. She glanced around anxiously to make sure the ropes tethering the body hadn't worked themselves loose. There was one awkward moment when the body snagged against a fallen branch and she had to jump down to free it, but it wasn't long before they arrived at the lower end of the lake. She stopped and looked across at Emma who had elected to join her at the front rather than sit in the enclosed carriage.

"We'll leave it here," said Sarah. "It's beside a footpath and it won't be long before one of the groundsman or Johnson himself finds it. We need to untie these ropes though and find somewhere to bury them; we can't risk someone finding them."

"I can't do it," said Emma. "I can't bear to look at him – you'll have to do it."

"Yes, Ma'am. You stay here."

It took Sarah a while to free the body from the ropes; it had already started to stiffen with the onset of rigor mortis. Dead bodies are strange, she thought. How quickly life vanishes, as though a candle had been blown out. She stopped and stared at the body for a moment. His face looked hollowed out, as though whatever inhabited him, his spirit or soul, had somehow fled. A light fills a room, she thought, and in an instant, it's gone, snuffed out by the wind, leaving just darkness and shadows. God, he's heavy. What a fat bastard he was. Grunting with the effort, she finally managed to untie the last rope. She looked back across the field from where they had come; it was fine when they were on the estate road, no marks were left, but the field was a different story. The grass had been heavily flattened where they had ridden through, a trail of breadcrumbs leading directly to the body. There was also a strange smell of shit; she put her fingers to her nose but quickly pulled them away in disgust. How? She thought, and then glancing down, noticed the brown marks seeping through the seat of his trousers. She stood up quickly and walked back to the carriage. She knew Emma could smell it because her employer gave a tiny grimace and looked away.

Without speaking, they turned the carriage back towards the house. Emma couldn't shake from her mind her last image of her husband. God help us, she thought – what have I done? How has it come to this?

*

At first, Murphy couldn't be sure what he was seeing. He could see one of the bailiff's men lying across a man or a woman and he appeared to have his hands gripped around their throat. As he moved closer, he realised with a start that it was Sorcha; she was wearing a coarse linen shift which had been pushed up around her waist but in her hair was the distinctive red ribbon she often affected to give some colour against the drab grey of the dress.

He knelt down and scrabbled around him in the long grass, searching for a rock or large stone. He was barely ten feet from the couple so he reached as softly and blindly as he could whilst keeping his eyes on them in case the man heard him. His hand fastened around a rock. He felt around its circumference and then gently tried to prise it up from the earth. He managed to lift one edge. Risking a look down, he saw that the rock could be gripped easily in one hand. It didn't have any sharp edges which might have made it a more effective weapon, but it would do. He rose carefully to his feet and then rushed forward.

The man heard the sharp rustle of the grass behind and twisted his head round to see what had disturbed it. It was too late; Murphy smashed the stone against his skull, just above his ear. He screamed with pain, but the blow had not been enough to kill him. He lurched to his feet and with a fierce cry, launched himself against his assailant. Sorcha lifted herself on to her elbows so she could watch. She was too exhausted anyway to try to stand and flee but she was also anxious to see what happened.

The man had toppled Murphy to the ground and, pinning his body to the ground, he started pummelling his face with his fists. Murphy reached up and, clawing at his face, managed to push a finger hard into one of the man's eyes. He easily knocked Murphy's hand away and went back to the business of bludgeoning Murphy's face.

In the periphery of her vision, Sorcha could see her attacker's knife lying on the ground beside him. She grabbed it and, lifting herself painfully from the ground, limped forward. The man hadn't noticed her; he was too busy trying to finish his grim task of smashing Murphy's face to a pulp. She had no time to pick a spot or to think about where best to try and stab him. On pure instinct, she stabbed downwards as hard as she could into his neck. He howled with pain. Blood spurted out around his wound, quickly covering his back and face. He fell to the ground, moaning. For a moment, he lay on the ground staring at the sky. It was the last thing he would see.

Grabbing the rock Murphy had been using, Sorcha knelt beside him and smashed it as hard as she could into his face. He screamed again. Savagely, she reached across and, using all her strength, yanked the knife from his neck. She plunged it into his chest; his body arched upwards in pain and terror and he gasped. It still took him a while to die and Sorcha took a grim satisfaction in watching. Finally, he was still, and his agonised breathing stopped.

She stood up. Murphy had managed to lift himself to his feet and move forward to where she still knelt. She stood up and hugged him hard. His face was a bloody mess and it would take some time for his wounds to heal but for the moment they were alive. They looked at each other. One of Murphy's eyes was too swollen for him to see anything out of, so he squinted at her with his remaining good eye.

"Are you alright?" he asked.

"Yes – are you? Your poor face."

She lifted a hand to gently caress the side of it.

"Yes, although it will be a while before I play the fiddle again."

He lifted his right hand to show her; two of the fingers were badly swollen, with one bent awkwardly to the side. It looked broken and it was quite likely that the other swollen finger was broken as well.

Despite the grimness of their situation, she laughed.

"Well there's always the tin whistle."

"Assuming I get can my fingers around the holes."

"Well, perhaps the bodhran then."

"You saved my life."

"You saved mine."

"I've never seen a woman with your courage."

"Wisht, Jim. I just lost my rag, is all."

"Well, I hope you never lose it with me!"

Sorcha started to laugh but it died on her lips as quickly as it had started. She realised her whole body was trembling.

"He would have raped me, Jim."

"Yes, I know. Still," he said grimly. "He'll never bother anyone again."

Sorcha looked down at the body. She turned to Murphy, a

sudden look of panic in her eyes.

"The boys! Have you seen them?"

"No, no, I haven't. I hope to God they managed to get away."

There was a catch in his throat as he spoke and he started to cry, the tears falling silently down his cheeks, quickly stained with the blood from his wounds.

"Jim – what's happened?"

"The soldiers have gone but the village is destroyed; there's not a house left standing."

"My God, oh my God."

He hesitated. "And there's worse – a lot of people have died, Sorcha."

He stared at her and she felt a chill pass through her. She turned away and started to run as fast as her limp would allow back towards the village.

"I have to find them."

"Sorcha, wait – I need to come with you."

She stopped and looked at him. "Well, come on then."

She had started to run again but Murphy hurried after her and caught her by the arm.

"Wait. Wait, please for the love of God."

She turned towards him.

"Wait – wait for what?"

"There are some terrible things – I don't want you to see them. No-one should see such things."

"What are you talking about Jim – what things?"

"Some people were trapped in their houses by the bailiff's

men when they set light to them –"

She stared at him as the meaning of this sank in.

"I still have to go – I have to find them. It's up to you if you come with me."

"No, we'll go together – please don't run; my old limbs can't keep up with you. Take my arm and we can hold each other up."

There was an acrid smell of smoke as they neared the village. Dogs raced wildly up and down, barking furiously. As they neared, Sorcha and Murphy noticed another smell. Sorcha sensed it was familiar but, at first, she couldn't place it. She realised to her horror what it was; it was the smell of cooked meat. Even as the realisation dawned, they saw the charred remains of their first corpses. Buried by ash and scorched timbers, the bodies were unmistakably human, their limbs splayed at grotesque angles. Sorcha forced herself to look more closely at one of them. The flesh had been stripped from the face revealing the skull underneath; the teeth were still intact, but the mouth was open and gaping, a rictus of agony. She felt her stomach heave and bending over, unable to stop herself, she vomited. Murphy held her gently by the shoulders.

"It's alright Sorcha, it's alright – let it out."

"Those poor people. Monsters, they were monsters to do this. How could they Jim? How could they?"

Murphy hugged her.

"I have no words, Sorcha. I –"

He sobbed, unable to finish the sentence. Sorcha was also in tears and for a long while, they simply held each other.

"Jim, take me to my home – I need to see it."

He nodded and they made their way up the lane, taking care now to look only at the ground in front of them, not daring to glance around, letting their peripheral vision help them to orientate themselves, to work out how close they were to her cottage. Finally, they reached it and Sorcha lifted her eyes to gaze upon the ruins. She anxiously scanned the interior, now open to the sky, a mess of tumbled and blackened stones and charred wooden beams. Her heart lifted a little; as terrible as the scene was, there were no corpses here.

"Jim –"

"I know – they must have escaped, maybe got out before the soldiers reached your place. God willing, they'll be alright, up in the hills somewhere with the others."

"We have to find them. I have to know they're safe."

"We could start by travelling up the footpath at the back of your house – that would be the obvious way to go."

"Right, let's go then. It will be dark soon and then it will be impossible to find them. We need to start now."

CHAPTER THIRTY-FOUR

It was the following morning when Johnson found him. The dogs, both lurchers, had raced ahead out of sight. He was used to this because they were keen hunting dogs and often went in search of rabbits or foxes. Sometimes they were so caught up in the excitement of the chase that it was difficult to call them back. He understood their temperament and didn't chastise them when they sometimes responded to his call a lot more slowly than he ideally would have liked. They barked excitedly and he hurried to see what they had found.

The dogs were excited by some object lying upon the ground, dancing around it, closing to sniff and then darting away before coming back again to repeat the cycle. The sun was just breaking over the horizon and its glare made it difficult for him to see properly, even when he attempted to shield his eyes. As he neared, he realised why they were so excited. The object was a body. He moved closer.

"Marley, stop your nonsense now – sit."

He grabbed Ludo by the collar.

"The same goes for you – sit. Sit – that's better. Good boy."

Johnson hastily drew two small pieces of bone from his pocket, shards of meat still clinging to them and used these to lure the dogs away from the body. He fed them the bones and then walked back.

The body was on its back, its face badly swollen. The crows had already made short work of the eyes and dried crusts of dark blood smeared both its face and limbs. He knew immediately who it was. How had this happened? he wondered.

He gazed off to his left. The grass around the lake was only cut once in the autumn to provide feed for the sheep and cattle. Since it was still early in the year, it was nearly a foot high, but he could see it had been flattened by something, a path cut through it. He stared at the ground beside the corpse. Here, near the lake, it was muddy and wet. There were deep weals in the mud. He knelt and looked more closely. They were the tracks of either a cart or a carriage. He stood and looked off again at the path which had been cut through the grass. He followed it up for a hundred yards to where it seemed to disappear. Horse shit lay on the ground and he gently prodded it with a stick. The outer layer was skinned but he could see the interior was much softer; he knew this meant that horses had come through here not that long ago, certainly during the night anyway.

Closer to the house, the grass had been cut much shorter and it was more difficult to discern the route the cart or carriage had taken. He knelt again and looked carefully at the ground. There had been a hard frost that morning and the ground was frozen;

even so, he could still make out the shallow indentations which could only have been made by wheels. A gravel path led up to the house and there were a number of shallow depressions in this, but these might have been made last night, this morning, or just as easily some weeks ago. Still, he thought, this doesn't look right; there's something very wrong here. It looks as though someone wanted to make it look like Clifton had been murdered down by the lake, but who would that be and what were their motives? More importantly, why did the tracks of the cart or carriage which had dumped him by the lake seem to lead back to the house?

He decided to walk around the side of the house to the stables. Clifton kept five horses there and two carriages, one of which was much grander than the other and was kept as Sunday best for visiting other landowners. His instinct told him that if a carriage had been used to move the body, it was likely to be the smaller one. He threw back the two stable doors to allow as much daylight as possible into the otherwise dark interior. He could hear the horses shuffling nervously in their stalls. A pungent smell of horseshit mingled with the sweeter smell of hay. He stepped closer to the carriage and examined the floor where the coachman would normally sit. There were dark stains in the wood which seemed recent; he licked his fingers and rubbed them into the stains. Then he walked back towards the entrance where the light was better. His fingers had a dark reddish stain. This looks like blood, he thought. So, if this was the carriage which was used, then someone within the house must have been involved in moving the body. It was possible that someone had broken into the stables, stolen the carriage, and then moved the body, but it looked as though Clifton had been murdered either inside or very close to the house. And if no-one connected to the house was involved, why had they gone to the trouble of not only moving the body down to the lake but also taking the carriage back to the stables? Wouldn't they have abandoned the carriage by the lake as well? Or, more to the point, why didn't they just leave the body where it was, outside the house?

No, the more he thought about it, the likelier explanation was that someone inside the house had killed Clifton and then moved the body down to the lake to make it look as though he had been murdered by members of the Molly Maguires or some of his evicted tenants. So, who did that leave as a possible culprit? One of the servants perhaps or…? Mrs Clifton, he thought; if Clifton had been murdered in the house, it was impossible that she wouldn't have been aware of it, heard his cries at least, or heard someone trying to move the body from the house. The only possible conclusion was that she had been involved; she had killed him herself or she had been involved in arranging his death. Either way, what should he now do with that knowledge? Should he call the police and have her arrested or was there another way he might turn this to his advantage? He thought for a moment, and then turned back towards his cottage.

CHAPTER THIRTY-FIVE

Sorcha and Murphy found a number of the villagers huddled together in a shallow valley in the hills immediately overlooking the village, a little distance from one of the footpaths. The villagers were hidden from view from anyone below, either still in the village itself or moving upwards towards them along its flanks.

Eamonn O'Neill rose to meet them. He was a tall man, still in his thirties with an untidy crop of blond hair, his face smeared with ash and dirt.

"Sorcha – you're alive! We've been so worried."

"The boys – where are they? Are they here?"

Rian had been staring disconsolately at the ground, aimlessly scratching at the dirt with a stick. On hearing his mother's voice though, he ran across and hurled himself against her, sobbing noisily.

"I thought…I thought you were dead. I couldn't find you – we were so scared –"

Sorcha knelt down and looked at him, carefully wiping

the tears from his face.

"It's alright, Rian, you're safe now – no-one can hurt you. Where's your brother?"

"He went…he went to find you."

"Went? Went where? Where did he go Rian?"

"To…to the village."

He pointed.

"Down there."

"Merciful Heavens, oh my God. I have to go – Eamonn, look after Rian for me." She turned again to her son. "How long? How long ago was it?"

"I don't know…a while…when we got here."

"That would be half an hour or more," said Eamonn.

"I have to go –"

"Your leg – let me go with you," said Eamonn.

"No, I'll be fine. I'll be fine, honestly."

She turned and started to run. Her limp slowed her down, but she compensated by trying to keep all her weight on her good leg. She slipped on the steeply banked hillside a couple of times, landing heavily, but she immediately rose up again and, ignoring the pain, pushed herself forward.

When she came to the first ruined houses in the village, her pace slowed. She was terrified of what she might find. Running down the hillside, her only thought had been to get to the bottom, to reach the village as quickly as possible. Now she was here, she realised how frightened she was of the possibility of coming upon his body, of finding him dead. Her heart was beating furiously, and she was finding it hard to breathe. She struggled on.

From the corner of her eye, she saw a flash of blue. She turned. Declan's body lay in the lane to one side of her. He was wearing the blue linen shirt she had dressed him in that morning but now it was stained with blood. She knew immediately he was dead. Sobbing, she knelt down and lifted him to her chest, hugging him tight. She let him gently down to the earth again and lay across his breast. Smoke continued to swirl around them, and ash began to settle, coating them in a thin grey film. Sorcha had stopped crying; exhausted, she had fallen asleep across his body. Now there was neither movement nor sound. The ash continued to settle. Darkness fell.

CHAPTER THIRTY-SIX

"**M**r Johnson, Ma'am"

Sarah ushered Johnson into the room, stood behind him for a moment and, unseen by Johnson, gave Emma a meaningful look. She curtsied and left.

Johnson coolly appraised Emma. She had asked Sarah to walk over to Johnson's cottage that morning and ask him to come and see her as a matter of urgency. She had given strict instructions to Sarah to say nothing of her husband's murder; if he pressed her as to why he was being asked up to the house, and by Emma, rather than Clifton himself, Sarah was to tell him she simply wasn't privy to that information.

"Mr Johnson, thank you for coming so promptly. I'm afraid I have had some terrible news – my poor husband has been murdered."

Johnson pretended to feign surprise and shock.

"But this is terrible – when did this happen?"

"I'm not sure – it looks as though it might have happened last night – the stable boy found the body down by the lake early this morning; as you know, he comes up first thing to feed and tend to the horses. I was up early myself and discovered my poor husband wasn't in the house. When Hedges arrived, I asked him to search the grounds for me – my husband has trouble sleeping and often is out early with the dogs. Initially though, I thought he might be down in the stables – that's the first place Hedges looked. I then asked him to look round the grounds and that's when he found him – murdered down by the lake –"

Her voice broke and, covering her face with her hands, she started a noisy sobbing.

Johnson looked at her with mild disgust. Not bad, he thought – you should really have considered a career on the stage; you would have probably been second rate at best but I'm sure some people might have appreciated your modest talents. You might make a passable Lady Macbeth, for example.

"This is terrible news. Poor Clifton. Is there anything I can do? Have you notified the police – we need a doctor as well so he can certify the death."

"No, not yet…that's why I asked Sarah to bring you here – I need you to do this. I can't…I just can't…"

"I understand. I'll make the necessary arrangements."

He looked at her. Should I go and comfort her, he wondered? Take her in my arms to console her? No, he decided. It would be too difficult to do it without revealing his true feelings.

"I'm so sorry this has happened. I'll go and find Sarah and ask her to sit with you; I don't think you should be left alone."

*

It took several hours for the doctor to arrive. At last, his carriage pulled up on the gravelled path beside the lake. The driver leapt down to open the door and the doctor carefully stepped down. Johnson heaved a sigh of relief. There were two doctors in the district, one a complete fool who must have been in his eighties at least and who was so stooped his patients often felt that perhaps it would be better if they treated him rather than the other way around. O'Connor, on the other hand, was still in his early thirties and well-practiced in his trade, despite the fact that he looked a little strange. His appearance was at odds with the keen intelligence shown in his eyes. Johnson often thought O'Connor looked as though he had been assembled from God's rubbish tip; the stuff left over once everyone else had been assembled. O'Connor had a parrot's nose and a wide, sensuous mouth, which might have sat better on a woman. He also had large jug ears and once you had noticed them, it was impossible not to become fixated on them, your fascination such that you didn't hear a word the fellow said.

O'Connor slowly knelt and put his hand lightly on Clifton's forehead. It was cool to the touch. He lifted an arm and then gently dropped it down again. It was stiff but didn't hold its position, slowly settling down on to Clifton's chest. It had been a cold night and O'Connor knew that often delayed the onset of rigor mortis. He sighed; this wouldn't therefore be of much use to him in determining the time of death.

"Mr Johnson – I need your help on this. We need to roll the body over."

It took considerable effort to do this. Once turned, the doctor then eased Clifton's blood-stained shirt up from his britches, exposing his buttocks and flanks.

"Look there. See how the blood has settled down around his back, those dark purple patches. That's what happens after death – the heart can no longer pump blood around the body, so it sinks down. The pooling didn't shift either when we turned him over."

He gently pressed his thumb into the flesh of Clifton's lower back. There was no blanching – the skin stayed a stubborn and vivid purple. The doctor grunted and rose to his feet.

"The fact that the skin didn't pale when I pushed into it means the pooling is fixed. This means Clifton must have died between eight to twelve hours ago."

O'Connor pulled a brass pocket watch from his waistcoat and lifted the lid. Johnson admired it and thought he must try and acquire one himself.

"It's still early, around ten. So, this means the time of death would have been either just before midnight or shortly thereafter. As to the cause –"

They both stared at the body. The whole of its front was a sticky mess of blood. O'Connor opened the leather black bag he had brought with him; using long-nosed scissors, he carefully cut through Clifton's shirt, exposing his torso. There was a large ugly gash just below his rib cage.

"This is a knife wound," O'Connor said. "It also looks as though it must have been thrust upwards towards the heart. If the heart was pierced, he would have died very quickly. I can't be definite about this – I'll have to carry out a post-mortem to determine the exact cause of death – but that's what it looks like anyway. Have the police been informed?"

"Yes, they should be here shortly."

"Good. Well, look, I think I'm finished here. Once I've done the post-mortem, I'll produce a report for the police. They'll let you know what I found."

"Thank you, doctor – I realise this must be a very unpleasant business for you."

"Believe me, I've seen far worse."

"Well, still – I'm very grateful."

Johnson gazed up towards the house. For a moment he thought he saw a figure standing in one of the upstairs windows observing them. Then it was gone.

CHAPTER THIRTY-SEVEN

It had already grown dark when the relief committee convened at Reith's house. Their carriages stood idle in the gravelled grounds immediately in front of the house, the horses having been taken to the stables to be watered and fed. Reith's house was even more imposing than Clifton's, the huge pillars of stone at its entrance gleaming faintly in the moonlight. The house overlooked a vast swathe of closely mowed lawn sweeping down to a river. Johnson stood for a moment, admiring the view; the beginnings of a hard frost were evident and the lawn shimmered with a white glaze. He walked over and tentatively pressed down on the coral spiked grass with his foot. It gave a satisfying crunch. In the distance, he could just about discern the noise of the river as it rushed over a weir. He smoked the last of his cigar and tossed the butt onto the ground.

A servant, who had been discreetly standing in the shadows, ushered him through into a hallway and from there into a large room. Paintings of Reith's ancestors hung on the walls. High above Johnson's head loomed an oak timbered ceiling. He could see the other guests already seated at a table and walked across to join them. At the table's head sat Simmons, the Justice of the Peace for the district. His thinning grey hair was swept backwards, and his face appeared to have collapsed downwards into his chest, rolls of fat where his neck should have been, deep grooves carved into his jowls and either side of his nose.

"Right, before we begin, most of you already know each other but that's not the case for everyone here, so I'm going to go around the table and ask each of you to introduce themselves. I'll start – my name is Brian Simmons and I'm the Justice of the Peace. So, on my left we have?"

"Father McNamara – sorry, Patrick McNamara. I'm the Catholic priest for this diocese."

"Derek Johnson – land agent for the late Mr Clifton."

"You're very welcome, Mr Johnson," said Simmons. "Mr Clifton was a very able member of this committee and will be sorely missed. Have the police yet managed to identify who might have killed him?"

Everyone turned expectantly in Johnson's direction.

"No – their enquiries are still continuing –"

He was interrupted by Reith, who had yet to introduce himself.

"Something must be done to stop this – none of us are safe until these murderers are caught. Clifton was attacked before – now they've managed to kill him. Where will it end?"

"Mr Reith, calm yourself – I'm sure the police will catch these people. It may take longer than you would like but I'm certain they won't be at liberty for long. If I may, can we continue with the meeting. Now I've told everyone who you are, perhaps you could explain your role on this committee?"

"I apologise – it's just…my name is Frederick Reith – I own the estate neighbouring Clifton's."

"Hence your concern, no doubt," said Simmons. He nodded to the man sitting next to Reith.

"Kevin Saunders – I'm a local merchant."

"You're very welcome as well, Mr Saunders," said Simmons. "And last, but certainly not least, we have?" He inclined his head towards a man sat at the far end of the table.

A small squat man with hooded eyes nodded and then spoke. "Father Spence – Jeremy Spence – I'm the parish priest for St Michael's."

"Right then, perhaps we can turn to the main business this evening. As you know, there has been a clear directive from the government – from Mr Trevelyan – that corn from the depot cannot be sold below market prices. He also gave a second directive – some months ago – that corn should only be purchased in the United Kingdom. This was to ensure traders did not find themselves competing against the government in overseas markets. Now, all of this was quite rightly to protect the mercantile trade in this country; unfortunately, though, this has also had unforeseen consequences."

"It has indeed had unfortunate consequences," said McNamara. "People are starving – so many have died there are no coffins to bury them; they're being buried wrapped in rags or even newspaper. And then, what do the landlords do to alleviate their misery – why, evict them of course, turn them out on the roads, and, worse still, stoop to murder."

He turned to glare at Johnson who studiously ignored him, staring straight ahead.

"People were murdered in Tyrone by government troops," McNamara continued, "not just the menfolk but women and children. I repeat – women and children. How have we descended to such savagery?"

"He's right," said Spence. "I don't know whether it's incompetence or malign intent but whichever way you look at it, people are dying, and government policy seems designed only to make matters worse. We try and help, providing soup for the worst affected, but much, much more is needed than what we can do."

"We know all about your soup –," said McNamara contemptuously. "Handing out the soup with one hand and tracts vilifying Our Lady with the other."

"Gentlemen – squabbling amongst ourselves like this is scarcely helping, is it?" said Simmons. Although it was a large room, the table they sat at was relatively small and he realised that this had forced everyone to sit uncomfortably close to one another. It didn't help either that two of the people in the room – Reith and Saunders – were grossly overweight. Both men were sweating profusely and every time one of them shifted in their chairs, there was an ominous creaking. He was beginning to bitterly regret ever agreeing to be a member of the committee, let alone having to chair it.

"The point is this," Simmons continued. "Government policy on the prohibition of buying meal from foreign suppliers has been lifted and I am hopeful our requests for further supplies to be sent as a matter of urgency will now be met –"

McNamara snorted.

"And what use is it even if new supplies do arrive? People can't afford what you've got at the moment – none of them have money to pay for the meal. Only a fraction are employed in the public works schemes and even these don't earn enough to buy corn for their families. The corn should be given away – no-one should pay a penny for it."

"If I may speak?" said Saunders nervously.

"Mr Saunders – yes please do. What's your opinion on the matter?"

"If the corn is given away, then that will ruin us. That will put an end to all supplies of corn other than those provided by the government through the depots; that hardly seems a desirable outcome to me."

"All you care about is making a profit – you don't even see the people dying of starvation around you – all you see are the figures in your ledgers," said McNamara.

"Have a care, sir – all you hand out to your congregation are prayers for a better life after this one. People can't live on prayer alone but that's all you give them. At least I put food in their bellies."

"But that's precisely what you don't do – you spirit away grain and pork in front of their noses, in carts guarded by soldiers, to feed bellies in England and abroad, but not one ear of corn is left for the people who grew it."

"Gentlemen," interjected Simmons, "this is scarcely solving our problems. If you want to have a row, then you both can continue outside. However, if either of you is genuinely concerned with finding a solution to our woes, then you'll allow others to speak."

"I apologise – I do want a solution, that's why I'm here," said McNamara.

"I also apologise – although I was severely provoked," said Saunders, glancing with disdain at McNamara.

Johnson intervened.

"My understanding is that even though this prohibition has been lifted, it's very unlikely that new supplies of meal will arrive that quickly. Indeed, it could be months – the French and the Belgians have been buying up all the corn to alleviate their own food shortages. The Government is struggling to purchase Indian corn from either the United States or the Ukraine. Don't forget the potato crop has failed in Belgium as well. Both Holland and France have also suffered."

"So, what are we to do?" asked Hughes. "The situation is already desperate – people are dying in their thousands. Corpses litter the roads, whole families are found dead in their cottages. We can't just stand by –"

"There is something we can do," said Johnson.

They all looked expectantly at him.

"Look – the situation is this. Tenants don't have the rent to pay their landlords and yet the landlords themselves still have to find the poor rates. No wonder half the landlords in this country are already bankrupt. It is true the Government has given loans to landowners to finance public works schemes to improve their own estates but, at some point, it will want those loans repaid or, perhaps worse, it will look at imposing still greater taxes on landowners to reduce the financial burden on her Majesty's government. But there may be a way out – landlords could pay their tenants to emigrate –"

Reith looked at him keenly. He knew such a scheme would cost money but with fewer tenants, his rates bill would reduce significantly.

Johnson caught his look and knew immediately what he was thinking.

"Look," Johnson went on, "landowners want to make their estates more productive by introducing modern agricultural methods. The potato crop has already failed two years running and there have been catastrophic failures too in the past – take 1821, for example. Many people died then as well from starvation. Landlords will benefit hugely from introducing a more commercial approach to agriculture but to do this, they first have to clear their lands. Moreover, they're already paying more in rates than they would by paying for their tenants to emigrate. With emigration, the tenants and their families get the opportunity to start new lives elsewhere and the landlords can modernise their estates. If landlords are unwilling to bear the cost of shipping their tenants to Canada or the States, then they can pay for them to travel to Britain, pay their packet fare to Liverpool. If they really want to cut their costs, they can put them on the cattle boats to Liverpool; there are also lumber ships going out to Quebec – much cheaper than the passenger ships. The merchants pay to fetch lumber in and refit them to take a human cargo back."

"Why should people have to leave the land of their birth?" said McNamara. "For what – to take their chances on the high seas in coffin ships – because that's what those lumber ships are? I've heard tales of the suffering and disease on those boats. Very few survive the journey. Why should people have to risk their very lives? Leave their families behind, brother separated from brother, grandparents from their children and grandchildren, perhaps never to see them again? Did you know that when someone goes abroad, they hold a wake for them, the same as a funeral, because to their families and friends they might as well be dead? What sort of a solution is that? Why can't we just lower the prices of the corn we have left in the depot until new supplies arrive? That's what's happening elsewhere. I've even heard of some depots simply giving away the meal. Why can't we do the same?"

"Because it's against government policy and if we fall into disfavour in this way, then they may cut off future supplies altogether," said Simmons. "I'm afraid it's really quite naïve of you even to suggest this."

"Even if we did reduce the price, not only would you be undercutting local merchants, but the little supplies we do have would be quickly exhausted and what then?" asked Saunders, addressing his remarks to Simmons, and avoiding McNamara's eye.

"I'm sorry," said McNamara, "I can't stomach any more of this nonsense. You'll have to continue without me – I can't be party to this…this…evil." He stood up, reached round for his chair, and slammed it into the table. "Good day to you all and may the Lord have mercy on your souls."

The room was silent for a moment. Reith gave a sigh of relief and turned to Simmons.

"Well, I, for one, am pleased he's gone," said Reith. "Perhaps now we can have a civilised debate on this issue. Mr Johnson, I think there may be some merit in your suggestion, and I'd like to explore this further with you."

"By all means," said Johnson smoothly.

CHAPTER THIRTY-EIGHT

It took a while for Smethwick's eyes to become accustomed to the gloom. The stench as the lawyer entered the cell was like a physical assault; stale sweat, damp, and the overpowering smell of shit. McGuinness had been lying motionless in a corner but rose unsteadily to his feet when the lawyer entered the cell. Smethwick could hear what he took to be rats skittering away to the far reaches of the cell. McGuinness had a deep gash above his eye and bruising to his face, which was a livid purple and yellow. It appeared to Smethwick that the wound, although clearly not recent, was not healing either and was probably infected.

"Who are you?" asked Michael, his voice hoarse and barely above a whisper.

"My name's Smethwick – I'm a lawyer. Your sister, Mary, has asked me to act in your defence."

"Mary – how is she? Is she well? Can I see her?"

"I've spoken to the new sheriff and they're not allowing you to see anyone – they don't have a choice with me of course."

"The new sheriff? What happened to –"

"Flynn? I found out today he's dead, murdered when troops were trying to remove the tenants at Tyrone."

"Murdered? By who? My home is in Tyrone – my wife and two sons. What in the devil has happened to them? Are they safe?"

"I'm sorry but I don't know. I only know what I've been told this morning by the new sheriff. I can try and find out –"

"Please, you must find out – I need to know they're safe. I need to know."

"Mr McGuiness, I know this is a shock for you, but you must calm yourself – we don't know what's happened. Pray God they're safe. I'll find out as a matter of urgency and come back and see you."

Michael could feel his heart pounding in his chest, and he was struggling to breathe. He fell back against the wall. Tears sprang from his eyes.

"Please, you must find out…I cannot endure –"

Smethwick grabbed him by the shoulders and looked deep into his eyes.

"I promise you I'll do everything I can. As soon as I leave, I'll ask Mary to ride back to your village to find out what's happened and where your family are."

"Thank you…I…"

"I know. I understand. You must have hope – you must cling to that."

Michael took a deep breath and felt a little calmer.

"If anything's happened to…I swear I'll slaughter –"

Smethwick interrupted him.

"That's for the future and, God willing, they're alright. It's in God's hands now. Mary will find out. If she rides out this afternoon, she should be back before it's dark tomorrow. I'll arrange to see you again as soon as I have news." He hesitated. "So, can we talk about your defence?"

"What is there to say?" Michael's tone was bitter. "They've made up their minds to hang me and there's nothing more to be said."

"There's a great deal to be said. Mary tells me you've been accused of delivering a threatening note to Clifton and conspiracy to murder him. And there I have some more news for you. Clifton has been murdered. They found his body on his estate down by the lake – apparently he was beaten to death."

"Clifton? Beaten to death? But by who? Or have they added that to the list of charges against me? They already have me down for his attempted murder. It's marvellous what a man can achieve locked up in a cell. I'm thinking tomorrow I might murder every landlord in the country – why not? Why wouldn't I do it given the magical powers I appear to have?"

He laughed but only briefly because he was immediately convulsed by a coughing fit. He recovered and spat a ball of green phlegm onto the floor.

Smethwick looked away to cover his disgust. "No-one knows, but the suspicion is that it must be one of his former tenants or perhaps the Molly Maguires themselves making good on their threats."

Michael laughed again. "Well, if it is the Molly Maguires, let's hope they catch them soon and let me off the hook. Anyway, I'm not going to pretend I'm not glad he's dead or Flynn, for that matter. They were both nasty pieces of work and were always going to come to a bad end sooner or later."

"Quite. Shall we go over the evidence they have against you. Obviously, there's the note –"

"Look, I delivered that note, let's not pretend otherwise, but I was also careful to disguise my handwriting – I wrote it with my left hand, do you see? But they've forged another note which does match my handwriting – they must have produced it from the handwriting samples Flynn took from my home. Then there's this witness – they say they have someone who will swear that I conspired with poor Gerard to murder Clifton."

"I know about the witness – do you have any idea who it might be?"

"No, no I don't. God knows who it is."

"Well, that's where I'll start; I'm going to do my best to find this so-called witness and see what they have to say for themselves. As to the note, I'm less confident – they may have forged it but how do we prove that?"

"We can't," said Michael despairingly. "We can't. Oh God, I'm so tired – I just want this to be over. I no longer care what happens to me. As long as Sorcha and the boys are alright then that's enough for me – I'd give my life if it meant they could live. You must find out how they are"

Smethwick put a hand on his shoulder. "I'll find out, hopefully by tomorrow night – I'll then see you first thing the following day. Have courage Michael – you will get through this."

Michael turned away and buried his face in his hands. "Easy for you to say – leave me, I want to be left alone."

"Alright, I'll go. I hope to see you again the day after tomorrow. Take care, Michael – there are a lot of people who love you and want you freed. Hang on to that."

Smethwick turned to the cell door; it was oak with a small iron grid through which the occupants of the cell might be viewed. He hammered on it to get the jailer's attention. Almost immediately, the jailer appeared and peered through the grid. Smethwick wondered if he been outside, listening in to their conversation. There was a rattling of keys and the door swung slowly open.

CHAPTER THIRTY-NINE

As they neared the village, Mary slowed her horse to a slow trot. It had been a hard ride from Sligo, and they had galloped for long stretches to reach Tyrone as quickly as possible. The horses were panting and lathered in sweat but that wasn't the reason she was now going more slowly. Even from a distance, they could see black smoke drifting into the air, and she became afraid. She was terrified what she might see as they entered the village, whether Sorcha and the boys were there or had run into the fields and hills around them. What she feared most was that they were dead.

They land sloped upwards just before the village itself and as they came to the crest of the hill, they stopped and stared down. They both gasped in shock. It was a scene of utter desolation. Not a house had been left standing; all they could see were blackened ruins. But there was still worse; bodies lay fallen all over the village. Nothing moved and there was an eerie silence which unnerved them both. Mary suddenly realised why it was so quiet; there were no birds. She could not hear them and, looking up, she couldn't see them either; the skies were completely empty. It was as though the birds themselves had realised the depth of the evil here and fled. Nor were there dogs; they too seemed to have vanished.

She shook the reins and her horse picked its way slowly down the hill towards the village, carefully stepping around and over the many rocks which lay in their path. Simon followed on his own horse; as they got closer, he eased his horse in front of her as though to shield her from at least some of the horror which lay before them. Despite her fear, Mary anxiously scanned the faces of the dead which lay around them. Where they lay face down or had their faces turned away from her, she looked at their clothes and whether they were a man or a woman. Some were children. She could feel tears streaming down her face and as she looked at Simon, she realised he too was crying. They reached the end of the village; there had been no sign of Sorcha or her children. They peered up into the hills around them. Was it possible they had escaped the slaughter? Had at least some of the villagers managed to make their way into these hills without being followed?

Without a word exchanged, Mary nudged her horse with her knees and it moved forward, Simon following. As it became steeper, they realised they would be safer going on foot, so they dismounted, tied the horses' reins to blackthorn bushes bordering the path, and slowly picked their way forward. It was hard going and the path was so steep in places that they had to claw their way up using both their hands and feet. Finally, they crested a summit and looked down.

It was already dark, clouds scudding across the face of the sickle moon like shadows fleeing the scene. A lake shimmered beneath them. Camped beside the lake were an array of rough shelters, some overlaid with branches and turf, with walls of torn sheets and blankets, still others open to the skies. A large fire formed a centrepiece around which a number of the villagers huddled for warmth. They could hear the sound of a fiddle which someone must have salvaged as they hurriedly made their escape. Someone else had a tin whistle as accompaniment. Above it rose a beautiful but mournful lament. Mary and Simon hurried down and the figures seen as mere shadows from the crest of the hill became their friends and neighbours who gasped in surprise and rose to greet them. The music came to a sudden halt.

Murphy, who had stayed resting on the ground, slowly got to his feet. Mary stared at him and immediately knew something terrible had happened. He started towards her, hugged her and began sobbing.

"He's dead…he's dead – I'm so sorry."

Mary looked at him in alarm. "Who's dead? Who's dead – tell me, tell me, Jim."

"Declan – poor Declan. The soldiers –"

Mary stared at him, unable to take it in, her heart pounding in her chest, her legs trembling so violently she could scarcely stand.

"But is Declan alright, Jim? Tell me he's safe?"

"He's dead, Mary – dead. He's not alright, he's not alright. I'm so sorry. I'm sorry. I'm sorry –"

"Sorcha? Where's Sorcha? Is Rian alright? Where are they? I must go to her. Tell me where they are?"

"Mary – she's not the same. Not the same – her mind has gone."

Mary stared in horror.

"Take me to her."

Murphy led her across to the far side of the camp. There was a rough shelter roofed with some timbers the other villagers had carried up from their ruined village. Hay and bracken had been thrown on the ground to make a bed.

Mary crouched to enter. It was dark inside, but she could see a figure stretched out on the makeshift bed; it didn't stir.

Simon had followed Mary and Murphy as they made their way but hadn't spoken. There would be time later to console her, but he knew that now she was too immersed in her grief to even notice his presence. Both he and Murphy waited outside the shelter.

Mary knelt and rubbed the shoulder of the prone figure. It made no movement, didn't glance up to see who crouched beside her.

"Sorcha, Sorcha – my poor love. Oh, Sorcha – how in merciful God can this happen?"

Sorcha was silent and unmoving. Her eyes were closed. Mary knew Sorcha was awake but still she didn't stir. Mary continued to gently rub her shoulder. She wanted to lie on the ground beside Sorcha and clutch her to her chest, but she also knew it would be unwanted. There was something terribly wrong.

"Sorcha – I'm going to leave now but I'll come back, I will come back."

There was a break in Mary's voice and tears fell silently down her cheeks. She wiped them away with her hand and then slowly backed out of the shelter. Murphy motioned her to move away so they couldn't be heard.

"She hasn't spoken since it happened, not a word has passed her lips. Nor has she eaten. She looks at you but doesn't see you, there's nothing there, Mary, nothing there –"

Now he was crying. He hugged her again, speaking in sobs, his head resting on her shoulder.

"She didn't come back, you see. She went down to the village in search of Declan but didn't come back. Me and Liam went down to find her. She was lying across his body – it was awful, awful. May I never see such a sight again. I've lived a long time, Mary, and I've seen some terrible things but nothing like this, nothing like this. I wish God had struck me blind rather than this. It would have been better for me. We got her back to the camp. Some of the other men brought Declan's body up – we buried him in a field over there, no priest to say a prayer for his soul."

"Rian? Where's Rian?"

"Maggie Doyle has got him – she's looking after him. I can take you to him if you like?"

"Poor child – yes, let me see him."

Simon had been standing beside them and now spoke.

"Do you want me to come with you?"

"No, stay with Jim. It's better if I see him on my own."

*

Maggie's shelter was worse than the one thrown together for Sorcha. Branches and bracken had simply been laid over a small hollow. Bracken had also been laid upon the ground inside the shelter. Rian lay under a blanket towards the rear. For the first time, Mary noticed how cold it was.

Before entering, she glanced up; heavy dark clouds had drifted across, blocking the sun. The air felt damp; it was about to rain, and it looked as though it would be a heavy downpour. How were they all to cope out in the open like this?

Maggie stood up as Mary stooped to enter. The ditch was too shallow to allow either woman to fully stand and, after briefly hugging, they both knelt on the ground. Rian sat up. He threw off the blanket and standing, hugged Mary, the top of his head resting against her belly. She pulled him closer and then knelt to look at him.

"How are you, darling?"

Tears ran down his dirt stained cheeks.

"Where's my Mam? Have you seen her?"

Mary glanced up at Maggie, who hesitated and then briefly nodded her assent.

"Yes, I've seen her. She's resting, Rian, she's very tired and needs her sleep."

"I want to see her."

"I know, darling – Maggie will take you to her, she just needs her rest, is all."

"Have you seen Declan?"

Maggie shot her a warning glance and Mary understood in an instant that Rian didn't know his brother was dead.

"No, no I haven't but I'm sure –"

Maggie quickly interrupted.

"He's with your Ma – we've already spoken about this Rian. He's fine but like your Ma, he's still very tired."

"But I'm not tired – why are they tired?"

"That's because you've got too much energy," said Maggie. "Sure, no-one can keep up with you."

Rian looked up at her. Mary could see that he didn't believe her, he somehow knew something was very wrong. Children saw more than they let on; they were eternally vigilant, always on the alert for anything that might threaten or disturb the fragile props of their lives. Rain suddenly fell in a steady roar which made further conversation impossible. The two women grimaced. Already heavy drops were falling on them, the roof of their frail shelter quickly breached by the rain's heavy onslaught. They needed better protection but there was none. They huddled together, their heads bowed, Rian between them to give him at least some shelter. Their clothes were quickly soaked, water dripping from their hair, puddles forming beneath them. There was nowhere to go, nowhere to hide, so they simply waited. This would pass, thought Mary, but unlike the rain, their grief would always be with them, the ghost of her unborn child now joined with that of Declan, ghosts who would haunt their thoughts until they themselves were dead, linking hands, at peace at last.

CHAPTER FORTY

"What did the police say?"

Emma Clifton had moved away from him, gazing unseeing through one of the drawing room's sash windows which stretched from floor to ceiling, affording magnificent views of the mansion's grounds. She had spoken with an affected casualness, as though she had little real interest in what he might have to say. Her heart, however, was beating furiously and a sheen of sweat coated her hands and trickled slowly down her back.

Johnson studied her closely; he was a keen observer of people, of the subtlest shifts in their features which might betray their true feelings.

"They were non-committal. I said I thought he must have been murdered by someone local, perhaps poachers on your lands or tenants your husband had evicted from their homes."

She relaxed a little and turned to face him, her confidence now returning.

"You were there, weren't you?"

"Sorry, Madam, I don't understand –"

"At Tyrone – where my husband's men – including you – murdered those poor villagers."

"It was the soldiers who killed those people – I, we, had nothing to do with it. We tried to stop them but –"

"I don't believe you," she sharply interrupted. "You led the slaughter, you wanted those people dead, God have mercy on their souls."

Johnson struggled to control his anger.

"I'm not going to dignify what you said with a response. However, I do have something to say to you – your husband wasn't murdered by poachers or villagers. No, he was murdered by someone within this household."

Emma felt a chill run down her spine. She was filled with a mixture of anger and fear, but it was anger that won out.

"How dare you – get out, get out of my house. Leave now or I'll ask the servants to throw you out."

"Not so fast, my lady. I said little to the police but there is a great deal I could – and still may – say to them."

Emma was becoming more and more alarmed. The wretched man looked entirely at ease and was looking at her with frank contempt.

"What do you mean? What might you say to them? You have no evidence –"

"Ah, but I do – I have more than enough evidence to see you hanged and, perhaps, your housekeeper as well."

"What do you know? There is nothing to know – my

husband was murdered by intruders – that's it. What else is there to say? Now please leave."

"I'm afraid not – I think we need to reach an understanding first. Do you have any port? From memory, I think your husband kept some in that cabinet there."

He gestured towards a dark walnut cabinet near one the windows.

"How dare you presume – I told you to leave. Get out! Get out!"

Furious, she stepped towards him.

Johnson smiled. "I think you'll find I'm a little more difficult to dispose of than your husband." He turned his back to her, moved towards one of the armchairs surrounding a low table and sat down. "Might I suggest you join me? There are some things we need to discuss."

Emma hesitated but she also suddenly felt her confidence drain from her.

Johnson saw this and smiled. "Perhaps you could fetch the decanter of port and two glasses."

She turned away and walked across to the cabinet. Her hands trembled as she folded back the doors. She couldn't see it at first and wondered if perhaps her husband and his cronies had consumed it all. She pushed aside some bottles of whisky and gin and found the decanter at the back of the cabinet. Taking two heavy crystal glasses which sat on top of the cabinet, she walked slowly back to where Johnson was sitting. Sitting carefully opposite him, she placed the decanter and glasses on the table. Johnson reached across, removed the stopper from the decanter, and poured both of them a drink. He pushed one of the now full glasses towards her and lifted his own glass to his lips.

"Look, I know you murdered him, and you must also have had help moving the body. If the police were to interview your housekeeper how long would it be I wonder before she cracked and gave you up? Anyway, all of this is beside the point. I have no interest in handing you over to the tender mercies of the police."

He paused for a moment to let this sink in.

Hardly daring to breathe, Emma spoke. "What do you want?"

"Ah, indeed, what do I want? Well, what I want is very simple – I want us to get married. You're obviously a very dangerous woman so I can't pretend you wouldn't need watching. Tell me – how did you kill him?"

Anger again got the better of fear. She rose to her feet and glared down at him.

"How dare you. Why would I marry a filthy commoner like you? I told you I had nothing to do with his death – one of his tenants must have killed him. God knows they had reason enough."

Johnson sighed and sat back.

"You really are being very tedious. Look, I found blood on one the carriages in the stables. I also found the tracks of a carriage down by the lake. Let's not waste our time pretending;

272

five minutes with your housekeeper would confirm it all anyway. I'm afraid she doesn't have your acting skills. As to me being a filthy commoner, well that's rich coming from you. I've heard you were a whore in London who Clifton took a shine to – after all, no-one else would want a man that ugly, unless of course he had money and whores love money."

He could see the wheels turning as she thought everything through. Slowly, she sat down again. Her eyes glinted. "You said I was a dangerous woman – I didn't kill him but you're right about that, at least. You would be a very foolhardy man to marry me; everyone has to sleep at night."

To her amazement, he burst out laughing. "Well done – you're even more formidable than I first thought. Who knows what we might do together? Look – you don't have to say anything now. Think on what I've said. You know where I am. Don't take too long though. I have a powerful itch to tell the truth; just how I was brought up, I'm afraid."

He laughed again. He liked this woman. She was attractive and she had spirit. A little plump perhaps, but he liked his women to have some meat on them. He was becoming aroused and it was uncomfortable enough that he had to shift position in his chair. She had noticed; there was that same glint in her eyes, and she smiled. A dangerous woman indeed, he thought, but that was what really excited him, that and the power he now held over her. He rose to his feet.

"Your husband was a poor fish. I think I might be a better catch for you."

CHAPTER FORTY-ONE

Smethwick was startled by Mary's appearance. Her face was drawn and grey and the life had gone out of her eyes. She seemed to have visibly aged. Simon stood anxiously at her side. He quickly related what had happened, the eviction of the villagers, some of them murdered, poor Declan's death and Sorcha's grief. He said he had given shelter to Mary, Sorcha, and her son Rian in his own house. He had also taken in another woman Maggie, to whom Rian had seemed very attached and who had looked after him at their camp. Mary said nothing; she stared listlessly around the room. Smethwick was both shocked and worried.

"The trial is next week," he said. "On the Thursday. How can I tell Michael what has happened? He will abandon all hope, do nothing to save himself."

At the mention of Michael's name, Mary looked at Smethwick. For the first time since they had arrived, she spoke, although it seemed to require a huge effort, as though she had to drag the words out of her own body.

"You can't tell him; it will drive him insane. We must hide it from him. If he wins at trial, then we can tell him. If not…"

She couldn't finish and stared again at the floor.

"I understand," said Smethwick gently.

"We're both very worried about Sorcha," said Simon. "She's said nothing since Declan's…passing. She doesn't eat. She sleeps most of the time. Maggie looks after Rian. If it wasn't for her –"

Mary had been sitting with her head bowed but now she looked up. "She has me now Simon. I won't let any harm come to her, not while there's breath in my body."

Simon touched her arm. "Yes, she has you and no-one could have a better friend."

There was silence for a moment which was broken by Smethwick. "Look – it's now Friday. I think you both must stay here until after the trial. I've been speaking to the sheriff; he'll allow you to see your brother on Monday. I'll come with you. Simon, I'm afraid you can't come; I struggled to persuade him to allow a visit from his sister."

"What about Sorcha and Rian? Mary asked. "I can't leave them."

Simon spoke again. "Maggie will look after them – Sorcha is dead to the world; she won't even notice you've gone, and Rian adores Maggie. They'll be fine, Mary – your place is here now. The ride back will be long and hard. You're exhausted; you need to rest up a while, get back your strength."

Smethwick nodded approvingly. "Simon is right – it's your

brother now you need to focus on. I have a trial to prepare for and I may need your help."

"Yes – whatever you think is best," said Mary.

She fell silent again.

"Look, I'll ask the housekeeper to prepare a meal for you both," Smethwick said. "Then you should both rest – you'll need all your strength now over the next few days. You both need to be well."

Simon looked at the lawyer. "You don't have to do this – I can find rooms."

"No, I insist – you must stay here. There's very little accommodation now anyway because of the…"

He left the sentence unfinished, glancing sharply at Mary.

"Rest," he said. "You both need rest. That and food. Wait here – I'll have the beds made up and speak to the housekeeper about arranging a meal."

They were shown to the same bedroom as their last visit. The white china bowl still sat on the oak dresser filled with dried lavender scenting the room. The room was wallpapered with an elaborate Chinese motif, all swirling blues and pinks, pagodas and acers, small arched wooden bridges above trickling brooks. Sorcha looked out from one of the sash windows which backed onto the garden. It was growing dark but there was still enough light to see the neatly trimmed box hedges bordering the lawn, the stone fountain with its gentle cascade of water dominating the middle of the garden, and towards the rear, a vegetable plot, tall canes leaning against each other for support. All of this was a world away from the lives of her family and friends. Two days ago, she had slept on damp bracken and hay. Tonight, she would sleep in clean linen and a soft bed. She pulled across the heavy brocade curtains and climbed into bed beside Simon. He nestled against her and, resting his hand on her shoulder, bent to kiss it.

"No," she whispered.

He sighed and turned away.

CHAPTER FORTY-TWO

"Where did you find it?"

"In a chest of drawers in one of the front bedrooms – it was tucked underneath some shirts."

There was the obvious question as to why Sarah might have been looking through Clifton's things, but Emma decided to let that go for the moment. In her hand she held the note which had allegedly been left by the Molly Maguires.

"I don't understand," Emma said. "I thought this had been handed over to the sheriff?"

Sarah hesitated. She had thought long and hard about giving her mistress the note, especially in the light of her now closer relationship with that devil Johnson, but this was too important to ignore, especially with the McGuinness trial starting in a few days' time. She had found the note some weeks ago and had been too frightened to do anything then but now Emma and she were bound to each other and she saw herself almost as an equal.

"Neither do I. I was hoping you might be able to explain it."

Emma stared again at the note. How could it still be here? she thought. Then a realisation dawned. This was a different note – the handwriting was unlike that of the original note her husband had finally showed her. There, the handwriting had been that of someone who had clearly been well educated; it was neatly done with confident flourishes on a number of the letters. On this new note, the handwriting was an almost illegible scrawl, with the final sentence in block capitals to drive home the threat – "And now we'll destroy you." She felt instinctively that this had been the original note. But if that was the case, where did the second note come from?

She looked blankly at Sarah.

"There must have been two notes," Emma said. "But why? I still don't understand – unless…"

"Unless what?"

"Unless, the second note is a forgery."

Sarah suddenly realised what had happened. "It is a forgery! It was done to frame poor McGuinness – someone wrote it afterwards and…your husband must have known."

"My God – I thought he was evil but to stoop to this –"

"We have to tell the authorities. This could stop McGuinness being hanged."

"Wait – let me think a moment. What you say makes sense but what if the sheriff was in on it? What if my husband and Moran concocted this between themselves?"

"There's a lawyer – Smethwick's his name. He's been

appointed to defend McGuinness – perhaps we should give it to him."

"Yes, yes, that would be better. I must speak to Derek and see what he thinks."

*

Emma didn't find an opportunity to speak to Johnson until that evening. Johnson had moved into the house. He had also moved into her bed, where he was not entirely unwelcome. He proved to be a more enthusiastic and better lover than Clifton had ever been and took as much pleasure in her enjoyment as his own. He had done things with her no other man had done, had gone down on her and taken her into his mouth for minutes at a time. He had lain her on her front and run his tongue along her spine and then followed the same track up her skin with his breath, blowing gently until she gave an involuntary cry of pleasure.

Now though, he looked grey with exhaustion.

"You look terrible – are you alright? What have you been doing?"

"Seeing the new sheriff – I needed to discuss the McGuiness trial with him. Pour me some whiskey and then perhaps you can tell me about your day. It's bound to have been better than mine. It was a long ride as well with a heavy rain at the end which made the lanes almost impassable – the horse didn't seem to mind but I was not only soaked from above, I was also soaked from below, coated with mud from the bloody great puddles it splashed through."

Emma hadn't noticed before but as she now looked him up and down, she could see how mud-smeared his clothes were. She didn't want him taking his ease in the library in that state – he might ruin one of the sofas she had been at such pains to choose when her husband had first bought the place.

"I'll run you a bath and bring the whiskey up to you – you'll need to get out of those wet clothes."

"You're an angel – fetch me the Bushmills; I prefer that to the Scotch."

"I'll bring it up in a second – I might have a glass of Madeira with you."

*

It wasn't until the following day that she managed to find an opportunity to discuss the note with him.

"Sarah came across something interesting yesterday."

He was only half listening. She could see he was deep in his newspaper and she had long ago realised how effectively men could screen out half of what a woman said; with Clifton she had found she had to repeat something two or three times before she could be sure he had really taken it in. He would often do something which indicated that he couldn't have heard a word she'd said.

"She found a note – one which was almost identical to the one thrown through my bedroom window."

Now she had his attention. He glanced up sharply.

"What note? What are you talking about?"

"The note from the Molly Maguires – if indeed it was them."

"Sorry, I'm not following you – of course it was them, led on by McGuinness."

"Yes, I know," she said impatiently, "but there seem to be two notes."

She thrust the note across the table to him. He picked it up and stared at it. He appeared shocked. However, she also noticed something else, a glimmer of calculation in his eyes.

"But how? Where did this come from?"

"Sarah found it in one of the front bedrooms, in a chest of drawers, hidden under clothes."

She quickly explained what she thought it meant, why she and Sarah had agreed it should now be given to the lawyer defending McGuinness. At the end, he agreed with her and said he would take the note to him himself, thought it safer to do that rather than show it to the new sheriff.

After breakfast, he wandered into the library and carefully closed the door. He lit a cigar and then walked over to the turf fire burning in the large stone fireplace. It had been made up earlier by Sarah and was now burning brightly, the smoke curling upwards into the chimney.

He took the note from his pocket and threw it into the fire.

CHAPTER FORTY-THREE

Mary held her brother in her arms for a long time. He felt so frail, she felt if she hugged him any tighter, he would collapse inwards like the dry husk from a grain of wheat. They were both crying, and she was struggling to speak, the words choked and stillborn in her throat. Smethwick stood at her back and he too had tears in his eyes. Finally, she pulled away from him.

"How have you been?' she asked.

"Fine so – I'm fine, Mary; all the better for seeing you."

"Have they been feeding you?"

He grimaced. "I wouldn't say the food was great, but I've eaten worse."

She knew he was lying but said nothing.

"So – what news do you have?" he asked.

Smethwick now spoke. "Nothing, I'm afraid, nothing has changed. I know both Mary and Simon have tried to find out who the so-called informer is but without success."

"Well, I didn't expect you would find out – no doubt the first time I clap eyes on the lying gobshite will be in court."

He turned to Mary and looked anxiously at her.

"How are Sorcha and the boys?"

She looked away as she spoke; she didn't dare look him in the eyes because her expression would immediately betray her. "She's fine, you know – worried about you, of course. She's had to lie to the boys, say you're away visiting your cousin in Sligo, but I think they know anyway – the other children…" She trailed off staring at the ground.

"Do they indeed? My life means nothing to me but they're my heart's blood, the only thing stopping me from –"

Tears sprang from Mary's eyes again. This was agony – she wanted to flee, be alone with her sorrow. She couldn't bear to see him in pain like this and have to lie to him. He hadn't needed to finish his sentence; she knew full well what he meant.

"You must have hope, Michael," said Smethwick. "We'll find a way through this somehow."

"And how would that be? Fine words won't save me, will they? And that's all you have for me; bloody words – words, words, fucking words."

He thumped the cell wall with a fist. Pain shot through his arm and as he drew it back, he could see he was bleeding.

"Your hand Michael – your hand!" screamed Mary.

He held it with his other hand and brought it to his lips, sucking it to relieve the pain. The anger had gone out of him as quickly as it had arrived.

"I'm sorry – I know you're trying your best. It's just –"

"It's alright, Michael – I understand. There's still two days before the trial. We won't give up; while there's breath in my body I'll fight for you."

Michael looked up. "You're a good man, I know you'll do what you can. Will you come again before –"

"I'll be here every day."

"And you, Mary? Will they let you…?"

Mary glanced at Smethwick. "If they let me, I'll be here."

"I'm sure they will," said Smethwick. "They can hardly deny you – you're his sister."

Even as he spoke, he knew they wouldn't let her see him. He would have to bribe the gaoler; it could be done, he was sure; the gaoler looked a greedy fat bastard and Smethwick had met his type before.

"We have to go now," Smethwick said. "We'll be back in the morning."

Mary hugged her brother again. "I love you, I love you, even though you're an eejit."

He gave a brief snort of laughter. "That I am, Mary, that I am – only an eejit would get himself into this sort of trouble."

Mary whispered to him. "Tomorrow then, we'll see you tomorrow."

CHAPTER FORTY-FOUR

Johnson arrived back long after midnight. Emma had stayed up waiting for him, but she had finally given up and retired to bed. She lay awake for a while, thoughts churning in her head, alert to even the whisper of a sound that suggested he might be back. But she heard nothing and fell asleep. Johnson had decided to sleep in one of the guest bedrooms to avoid disturbing her.

Emma woke early; she had not fully closed the curtains and a shaft of light shone against the wall just above her bed. It shimmered and she gazed at it, entranced; motes of dust floated within the beam of light, dancing into the light and then out again. She suddenly realised that he wasn't in the bed with her; the blankets on his side lay flat and undisturbed. She got up and, wrapping a silk dressing gown around her, walked out of the room.

It was a large house with six bedrooms. Sarah occupied one of these, the furthest away from her own bedroom. Emma knew she would have been up at dawn, making up the fires in the kitchen, library and drawing room and then preparing breakfast. Each morning she baked fresh soda bread and plucked eggs from the hen's nests in the coop at the end of the small walled kitchen garden. Emma quickly searched the remaining rooms, opening the doors and then gently closing them again. She found Johnson in one of the south-facing bedrooms and she noticed with distaste that it was the one favoured by her husband when he wanted to get away from her. He was lying on his side and appeared to be asleep. As she came closer, he turned towards her and his eyes opened.

"Did you sleep well?" she asked.

"I did, thanks – I came in here because I didn't want to disturb you – I was back very late, I'm afraid."

"And how did it go? Did you see his lawyer?"

"Yes, I saw him. I was impressed actually – he struck me as a very shrewd and capable individual. I doubt McGuiness could have found better."

"What did he say?"

"He was very pleased – thought it might make all the difference. There's still the matter of the witness against him of course but this undermines his testimony."

Emma felt a surge of relief. McGuinness, she knew, was a good man and a good tenant – he had never fallen behind on his rent, was always polite and respectful to her on the few occasions their paths had crossed.

"Will they need me to appear at his trial do you think?"

"No, no – I don't think that will be necessary. It's a long

journey in any case – should they need you, I'm sure his lawyer will be in touch. Come to bed – I've missed you."

She smiled and stood to throw off her dressing gown. She paused momentarily to let his gaze linger on her body, enjoying his frank admiration, and then slid between the sheets.

His lovemaking was rougher than usual; he dispensed with foreplay and thrust himself into her almost as though he was angry with her. It was uncomfortable and it hurt. As he laboured, bringing himself to a hasty climax, he bit hard into her shoulder. She screamed with pain. He apologised and lay on his back for a moment gazing unseeing at the ceiling. Then he got up, dressed quickly and left. Other than his apology – which itself felt perfunctory – he had said virtually nothing.

Emma got up and went to the full-length mirror to examine the bite on her shoulder. She saw with shock that it was bleeding. She held a tissue to it and retired back to bed, lying on her back so as not to stain the sheets. Her mind whirled; he had never behaved like that before, she thought. It was not just that he seemed to want to punish her, but it was almost like an exercise in power, as though he wanted to show her that it was he who held the whip hand, that if he wanted he could destroy her as easily as swatting a fly. Well, she was a lot tougher than he thought so if he wanted to play that game, then he might get his own nasty surprise.

*

Part of that surprise came later that morning. Emma wasn't sure where Johnson had disappeared to when he had left the bedroom but since he didn't reappear, she assumed he must have again retired to one of the other guest bedrooms. She had lain in bed for a long time, thinking through what she needed to do. When she finally got up, she felt exhausted. She ran a hot bath and dressed and then walked slowly down to the dining room for breakfast. He was already there and looked up sharply as she came in. She wished him good morning, sat down, poured herself some tea and, taking a deep breath, started to lay out what she had decided.

"I've been thinking – I know you don't think they'll need me at the trial, but I feel it's important for me to speak on this issue. I also think Sarah should appear as well, since she found the note in the first place. I'd like –"

Johnson cut across her. "I really don't think that's necessary. Look, if it helps, I'll speak again to the lawyer, tell him what you think, and we can then let him make the final decision."

"That's very kind of you but you've had one long and tiring ride to Sligo – I'll take a carriage and go myself with Sarah. Give me the lawyer's name and where he resides – we'll go first thing tomorrow morning."

Johnson felt growing alarm. He had ridden to Sligo but only to make sure everything was in readiness for the trial. He had also wanted to find out what the gossip was on the ground and to seek reassurance that Foley's identity was still unknown. The wretched man would have to appear as the key witness during the trial, but it was important no-one found out who he was before then.

"Look – I said you weren't needed. You don't need to go –"

"Well, I'm afraid I disagree –"

Johnson gave her an icy stare; she was aware he was struggling to suppress his anger.

"May I remind you of our arrangement. I said you don't need to go – that's an end to it. Don't provoke me – I'm warning you."

She glared back at him.

"So, you would rather McGuiness hang then? Because that is what will happen if I don't explain where the note came from and what my suspicions are – they'll argue it's a forgery, trumped up by his cronies to try and get him off."

"You're not going – "

"Oh, but I am. I've thought it through – you might have what you would describe as evidence against me, but it relies on you persuading Sarah to give me up. She can't do that without implicating herself, which means she would also hang. So, do your worst – produce your evidence and let's see if you can find anyone to believe you. I was Clifton's wife and I'm still a force in this county; you're nothing, a jumped-up little prick of a man."

He no longer bothered to hide his anger. "You're playing a dangerous game – you've no idea what evidence I've got on you; it doesn't matter whether Sarah gives you up or not. And you were happy enough to let me fuck you, weren't you? To come crawling into my bed. You're pathetic." He stood up. "I'm leaving now. When you come to your senses, come and find me. Have a care though – I'm not a patient man. If I find your carriage gone tomorrow, I'll…"

"You'll what? You think I'm frightened of you? You're dismissed – find yourself other employment. Get out. And if you're not gone by this evening, I'll have you evicted."

He slammed the door as he left. A moment later, she heard the heavy oak front door slam shut as well.

She went to the window and stared out, watched him stride across the gravel and then disappear through the trees.

What have I done? she thought. I don't really know what evidence he has – perhaps he does have enough to hang me. Well, it's done now – God help me if I'm wrong.

At that moment, Sarah came into the room. "Is everything alright?" she said anxiously. "I saw Mr Johnson leave –"

Emma looked at her. "We need to talk Sarah – you'd better sit down."

CHAPTER FORTY-FIVE

Emma was alarmed. On arriving in Sligo, she had been directed to Smethwick's offices in Finisklin Road close to the docks. His clerk had told him a Mrs Clifton had come to see him and he was immediately intrigued as to why this might be. His initial conclusion was that perhaps she had some fresh evidence tying Michael to Clifton's murder but if this was the case, why had she come to him?

Smethwick ushered her to a seat.

"You've come a long way – I trust the journey wasn't too tiring. Can I first offer my condolences on your husband's unfortunate –"

Emma cut across him.

"Thank you – you're most gracious. It's been a very difficult time, as you might imagine."

"Yes, I most certainly can – he was much admired, your husband."

"Thank you – that's very kind of you. I miss him dearly."

She bowed her head as though about to cry and carefully wiped under her eyes with a finger.

"I'm very sorry – can I offer a handkerchief?"

"No, thank you. I have one, should I need it."

Again, she bowed her head. This is hard work, she thought. I don't think I can keep up this nonsense much longer. Still, I think I've shed more tears stubbing my toe than I have over my bastard husband.

Smethwick coughed politely to get her attention.

"What can I do for you Mrs Clifton?"

"I've come to discuss the note with you."

"Note, what note?" he asked in puzzlement.

Emma stared at him.

"Why, the note my land agent, Johnson, brought, of course. I would like –"

It was Smethwick's turn to interrupt.

"I'm afraid I haven't received a note – and nor have I met Mr Johnson either. Why –"

"But you must have met him – he told me he had seen you, had given you the note."

"I'm sorry, but I'm confused – perhaps you can explain?"

"Well, not as confused as I am. Sarah, my housekeeper, found the original note supposedly delivered – if you can describe a rock hurled through your window as delivered – by McGuinness. The note given by my husband to the sheriff was a forgery. The handwriting on the original is completely different."

"Sorry, I'm struggling to understand –"

"Look, I saw a copy of the note which was given to the sheriff. The script is very different. My husband told me that the lettering was virtually identical with that in the documents taken from McGuinness's house. The note Sarah found is different – the handwriting is much cruder."

"And you think the note Sarah found is the real note?"

"Yes, I'm convinced of it. Why else was it hidden?"

"But that means –"

"Someone was trying to lay the blame with McGuinness –"

"My God, if this is true, it blows a hole clean through their evidence. But why do you think I've got it?"

"Because Johnson told me he had given it to you."

"Well, I'm afraid he didn't."

"So, what's happened to it?"

"I've no idea – all I know is that Johnson has never visited me, and nor have I been given a note. He told you he had seen me, did he?"

"Yes."

"Then we have a real problem – without that note I have nothing to present to the court."

"Johnson's lied to me, damn him to Hell. And if he's lied, then I bet he's destroyed the note as well. What do we do now? There must be a way – would it help if Sarah and I testified at the trial, told the court what had happened?"

"It might – but without the note…"

"But this is terrible – McGuinness is innocent. We have to find a way of helping him."

"Well, the two of you testifying would be quite powerful on its own." Smethwick thought for a moment. "Perhaps we could call Johnson as a hostile witness – if he denies everything, he runs the risk of perjuring himself which is very serious and could land him a gaol sentence. If I could make him understand the risk he's running – remind him he's under oath – then perhaps we might have a chance. What's your relationship with him like – putting aside for the moment the fact that he's deceived you?"

"Not good – I had to dismiss him. He's a very arrogant man and I never forgave him for his role in the evictions at Tyrone."

"Well, that's probably all to the good. Are you sure Sarah will testify? It can be quite an ordeal and both of you will have to face cross examination by the prosecuting barrister."

"Sarah's a strong woman – I'm sure she'll be fine, and I'll manage as well, believe me."

"Then we have a way forward. Let's hope it works."

CHAPTER FORTY-SIX

Michael stared at the jury; they had been selected locally and he knew none of them. All twelve were men. Smethwick had told him that two of them were landlords and therefore unlikely to be sympathetic. Several of the jury members looked uncomfortable but not these two. They regarded him with a mixture of fear and hatred. Michael's lawyer had arranged for new clothes and had also bribed the guards to allow a large pot of water to be brought into the cell so that Michael could wash and shave. Michael was now dressed in a fresh blue linen shirt, grey britches and white woollen stockings. Smethwick had even managed to find a fine pair of polished brogue shoes for him. It was important his appearance made him look like a respectable citizen; turning up in the rags he had worn in his cell, unshaven and unwashed, would not make a good impression on either the judge or the jury.

He looked at the gallery above the courtroom, searching for Sorcha. He was dismayed when he couldn't see her. Mary was there though, alongside Simon, and she smiled encouragingly at him. He tried to smile back but he knew it was more a nervous grimace than a real smile.

Smethwick sat at the front of the courtroom, a pile of papers in front of him. He was side on to Michael and was looking up at the judge. The prosecution's barrister, Adams, sat at the front of a row of benches to Smethwick's left and the new sheriff Anderson sat directly behind. Scanning the seats around him, Michael was surprised to see Emma Clifton and her housekeeper Sarah. Were they to appear as witnesses for the prosecution, he wondered? Near the back of the court he could also see Johnson – well, he would certainly be a part of the prosecution.

Michael's thoughts were interrupted by the sudden appearance of the judge who entered through a door to one side of the long bench which sat above and in front of the seated areas, dominating the courtroom. The judge was a man in his fifties, Michael guessed, with a large beak of a nose which gave him the appearance of a bird of prey. A clerk had entered with him and it was clear that he would be responsible for providing a transcript of the testimony given. The judge was known as a hard but fair man and Smethwick had told Michael he was both relieved and pleased with his appointment. There were far worse judges and Smethwick suspected some of them were also corrupt and easily bribed.

The court rose to its feet and the judge then asked everyone to be seated. He gestured to the prosecution lawyer who stood up and began to outline the case against him. Smethwick scarcely glanced across; he sat, one hand placed against his forehead and made a series of notes in an elegant copperplate. A small pot of ink sat in front of him and he dipped his nibbed pen in this every few seconds to reload it. As Smethwick had expected, the evidence presented centred on the note delivered to Clifton, the attempted murder by Gerard and the alleged final murder itself by McGuinness, acting either on his own or with others. The charges were those of sedition and murder; both serious enough to hang Michael.

Once the prosecution barrister had finished his opening remarks, Smethwick was beckoned forward by the Judge to present the case for the defence. He knew the preliminary arguments were part of the ritual of court proceedings and the real substance of the trial, with the presentation of witnesses and their cross examination by both sides, would be where the trial was lost or won. Nonetheless, he was careful to address his remarks both to the judge and to the members of the jury; the prosecution lawyer had given a supercilious summary of the case against Michael and had scarcely glanced at the jury members, preferring to address all of his opening speech solely to the judge. Smethwick knew this was a mistake; it was important to get the jury on your side at the earliest possible opportunity. Ignoring them completely was a very poor opening gambit.

The judge gestured to the prosecuting barrister.

"Mr Adams," the judge said. "Perhaps you could call your first witness."

"Thank you, m'lud. As you might imagine, I am in some difficulty; the key witness, Mr Clifton, has been murdered – which, of course, is germane to this trial – and the former sheriff, Mr Flynn, has also been murdered. Such are the times we live in. I therefore call on Captain Sanders."

A tall thin man, who still appeared to be in his thirties, walked up to the witness box. He had dark hair cropped short and swept back, a roman nose, and a thin mean mouth. He was also dressed in full uniform, a red tunic fastened with gold buttons, a white band around the tunic itself and black trousers with a red seam running down the outside leg.

"For the benefit of the court, can you state your name and occupation?"

"My name is Martin Sanders and I'm a Captain in the Grenadiers. Our regiment is currently stationed at Westport."

Adams peered down at his notes. "I believe you were present when Mr McGuiness was arrested – is that correct?"

"I was – the sheriff had asked us to assist them in the arrest, so I'd brought a small detachment of men with me."

"And what did you observe?"

"There was a copy of *The Nation* there which one of the women tried to hide."

"So, there was seditious material. In your opinion, do you agree it was a meeting to foment rebellion and to target the landlords?"

Smethwick rose to his feet. "Objection m'lud. The prosecution is attempting to lead the witness."

"I agree with you," said the judge. "Proceed with care, Mr Adams."

"I withdraw the question. The sheriff in post at the time, Mr Flynn, believed it was McGuiness who had been reading aloud from *The Nation* because no-one else in that room could read or write."

"I'm afraid I don't know what his belief was because he never shared it with me. A copy of *The Nation* was found in the house though."

"The publication was also smuggled under the shift of one of the women in an attempt to hide it. Is that correct?"

"Yes, that is correct."

"Is it also the case that the sheriff discovered the newspaper and kept it as evidence of sedition?"

"Yes."

Adams turned away. "I have nothing further for this witness."

The judge fixed his gaze on Smethwick.

"Mr Smethwick – do you wish to cross examine the witness?"

Smethwick again rose to his feet. "No, m'lud."

"Very well. You may proceed with the next witness, Mr Adams."

"I would like call Mr Derek Johnson to the stand.

"You can proceed."

Johnson was also sworn in.

"For the benefit of the court, can you state your name and occupation?"

"My name is Derek Johnson and I was the land agent for the now deceased Mr Charles Clifton."

"Thank you. A note wrapped around a rock was thrown through one of the upstairs bedroom windows of Mr Clifton's mansion. When the message was unwrapped, it was shown to contain the following message which, for the benefit of the court, I will now read: 'You've destroyed Mullangar and now we'll destroy you'. It's signed the Molly Maguires and underneath the signature is a crude drawing of a coffin. If Mr Smethwick agrees, I would like the jury to see a copy of the message."

"I have no objection, m'lud."

"Very well," said the judge. "I understand the note has been supplied as evidence to this court; can the clerk now pass this round amongst the jury members?"

The clerk laid down his pen and nervously searched the papers on his desk, finally unearthing the note. He got to his feet and walked over to the jury. The note was then passed from juror to juror, as though they were handling a fragment from the Book of Kells, and carefully read by each of them. It was then handed back to the clerk who returned to his seat.

Adams waited patiently while this was done. He spoke again, making sure he directly addressed the jury and only occasionally turning to face the judge and Johnson.

"As the court is aware, the Molly Maguires are a notorious gang responsible for the murder of both landlords and their agents. The message which you have all now seen was therefore intended as a warning by this gang and subsequently, as we well know, an attempt was then made to assassinate Clifton. Although injured, Clifton survived the attempt. His dog killed his assailant. The Molly Maguires didn't give up though and staged a further attack on Clifton which, this time, was successful. Clifton was beaten to death in a most savage attack and left for dead within his own grounds. Now Mr Johnson – how did you become aware of this note?"

"Mr Clifton showed it to me. He was naturally very alarmed by it and asked me to deliver it to the former sheriff, Mr Flynn. I agreed with Mr Clifton that very few people could have written it because there are only a handful of people in the district who can read and write. McGuinness had the most to benefit from the note because he knew the tenants in his own village were to be evicted. He was also the only person in his village who could read and write and knew his numbers."

"And which village was this?"

"Tyrone, barely three furlongs from Mullangar."

"Surely there were others in his village who could read and write – his own sister and wife for example? After all, if he knew his letters, he might have taught them himself."

"I believe that's possible but it's very unlikely that either would have had the nerve to write such a message and deliver it via a rock through a window. It was also late at night, with heavy snow on the ground. Clifton saw his attacker flee on a horse and was convinced this must have been a man. Very few women have that sort of horsemanship and, even if they did, it would have taken a hell of a nerve to do it."

"Thank you. I have no further questions."

Mr Smethwick, do you wish to cross examine the witness?

"I do m'lud. Thank you."

He rose, glanced briefly at the jury, and walked to the front of the Court so he was standing no more than a yard from Johnson.

"Mr Johnson, have we met before today?"

Johnson shifted nervously in his seat. "No, we haven't."

"Are you sure? Mrs Clifton will testify that she specifically asked you to seek a meeting with me prior to this trial. What have you to say to that? I must confess I have no memory of meeting you either, in which case it appears you ignored Mrs Clifton's request. Is this the case? Did you promise her that you would meet me and then deliberately choose not to?"

"I have no recollection of her making such a request. It's possible she did ask me and because I was distracted by other affairs, I failed to hear what she said."

At this a ripple of laughter spread through the court.

"Is forgetfulness a regular habit of yours, Mr Johnson, or is it that your hearing is not – what shall we say – as acute as it once was?"

"To repeat, I was distracted. There is nothing wrong with my hearing."

"Except perhaps when Mrs Clifton is speaking. A most singular infliction, I'm sure you would agree."

Adams jumped to his feet. "Objection – I fail to see what

relevance this has or where this line of questioning is supposed to lead."

"Well, Mr Smethwick" said the judge. "What have you to say to that?"

"M'lud, these questions are indeed relevant as I will very shortly show."

"Very well. I'll give you some latitude, but you should be aware, Mr Smethwick, that my patience is wearing thin. This is not a stage for lawyers to peacock around in; this is a trial where the defendant is facing very serious charges which, if proven, may well result in a sentence to hang him."

"I apologise m'lud. I will try and wrap this up as quickly as possible. I also assure you it's not my intention to indulge in grandstanding."

The judge continued to frown, giving a very good impression, Smethwick said later, of a bulldog eating thistles.

"Mr Johnson, I promise I shall not detain you any longer than is absolutely necessary. Please accept my apologies if I have managed to offend you. So, to sum up where we left off, you say you did not seek a meeting with me after promising Mrs Clifton that you would do just that. Why, though, did Mrs Clifton ask you to meet me in the first place?"

Johnson was feeling cornered. He was also starting to feel uncomfortably hot, with beads of sweat running freely down his back. He struggled to maintain his composure. Out of the corner of his eye he could see several members of the jury leaning forward with keen interest in hearing what he might say.

"As I've already said, I have no recollection of her asking me to see him or what the purpose of such a meeting might have been."

"Well, let me see if I can be of assistance in filling in the blanks in your memory. Mrs Clifton has told me that Sarah, her housekeeper, had found a second copy of the note that was hurled through the window. The content was the same for each note, but the handwriting was remarkably different. The note given to the sheriff and presented in evidence to this court is a fair facsimile of Mr McGuiness's handwriting. The handwriting in the second note, though, was completely different – much cruder, and nothing like my client's handwriting.

"So, what are we to make of this? Well, the conclusion reached both by Mrs Clifton and her housekeeper was that the note they had found – and which had been buried amongst a heap of papers in Mr Clifton's bureau – was the genuine one, whilst the note given to the sheriff was a fake. Someone, it seems, went to a lot of trouble first to suppress the genuine note, and then to draw up a fake second note in my client's handwriting. Now why should someone do that? Well, the only conclusion to be reached is that somebody was trying to frame my client, to forge a note in his hand so he would then be blamed and arrested. Both Mrs Clifton and her housekeeper will be testifying precisely to this effect. Given this, Mr Johnson – and again to help you fill in the blanks in your decidedly poor recollection of events – why did you not seek to meet me to hand over the new note, evidence which was of crucial importance to this trial?"

"I repeat that I have no memory of either the alleged conversation with Mrs Clifton, or of a so-called second note."

"Have a care, Mr Johnson – if you perjure yourself, having sworn to tell the truth, the possible penalties are severe. Two people can testify that the second note was placed in your hands and that you agreed to give it to me."

Johnson could not contain his anger. Flushed in the face, he was virtually shouting.

"I did not have a conversation on this and nor am I aware of a second note. You may think you're being clever in trying to trap me into admitting something I have no knowledge of, but that's all that you have – verbal gymnastics, which may impress your client but certainly not me or members of the jury. If, as you claim, a second note exists, then why have you failed to produce it in evidence? Is it perhaps because no such note exists?"

"Perhaps, but there is a second possibility, which is knowing what it might reveal, you deliberately destroyed it."

Adams again stood. "M'lud, I must object in the strongest of terms – this is pure speculation on the part of Mr Smethwick and since the so-called second note has not been produced for the court – and I doubt it ever existed in the first place – then none of this has any basis in fact and must be struck out."

"It is not for you to demand this, Mr Adams," said the judge, "and my view of the matter is that this should be allowed to stand, at least until both Mrs Clifton and her housekeeper have given their testimony. Mr Johnson, I do not care for people shouting in my courtroom. If your behaviour does not improve, I shall hold you in contempt and put you in gaol for the night. Do I make myself clear?"

"I apologise your Honour," said Johnson.

The judge turned to Adams. "Do you wish to question the witness again Mr Adams?"

"Yes, thank you m'lud – I would indeed." Adams turned to Johnson. "Mr Johnson, you have testified that Mrs Clifton did not make you aware of a second note and nor did she ask you to seek a meeting with Mr Smethwick in order to hand this over to him. Is that correct?"

"Yes, that is correct."

"You were Mr Clifton's land agent but when her husband died, she then dismissed you. Is that also correct?"

"Yes, that is correct."

"When did this happen?"

"After we'd had a row about this supposed second note. She was angry and dismissed me on the spot."

"Is it possible she invented this second note to find an excuse to get rid of you?"

"Yes, that is certainly possible. She made no secret of her dislike for me when I was employed by her husband and I'd always thought she would get rid of me as soon as she had found a suitable excuse."

"Of course, some might say she didn't need an excuse; she could have simply dismissed you because she didn't like the cut of your jib or the way you slurped your tea. Is that not the case?"

"Yes, it's true she could have simply dismissed me. But that's not what happened – I mean, she did have her reasons for getting rid of me, but they had nothing to do with some trumped-up note."

"So, what did happen then?"

Smethwick leaned forward in his chair. He suspected something had been concocted between Johnson and his lawyer and this was obviously now about to be revealed.

"I had an affair with her. She threw herself at me within days of her husband's death. Apparently – or so she told me – he was rather a disappointment…in a number of areas. Then our relationship soured somewhat; she was a woman who found fault with everything and I tired of her tirades. She was particularly difficult when she was drunk, and I now understand why her husband used to hide himself away when she was in her cups. Prior to his unfortunate death, he told me that he often slept at night in another bedroom just to get some peace. After the end of our…time together, she therefore needed an excuse to not only get rid of me as her former lover, but to ensure I would no longer trouble her with my presence as a land agent as well. To put it bluntly, this was a personal matter for her, and she wanted revenge for me spurning her. She also wanted not only to punish me by removing me from my job, but to invent something that might get me arrested and thrown in gaol. It's true what they say – Hell hath no fury like a woman scorned and she was a vicious and unpleasant woman to start with."

As one, the jury looked at Mrs Clifton, who was struggling to contain her own anger. She was aware of their eyes upon her but ignored them, her face a blank canvas. Beneath the bench, and unseen by anyone, she clenched her fist and imagined herself punching Johnson very hard in the face.

"So, she came up with the idea of a second note which you then failed to deliver as a way of trying to have you arrested for suppressing evidence. Is that correct?"

"Exactly."

"Thank you, Mr Johnson. I have no further questions for this witness."

Smethwick stood up. "M'lud, if I may, I do have some further questions for the witness."

"You may proceed."

"Thank you m'lud."

"Mr Johnson – you say Mrs Clifton invented the note as a way of getting you arrested. My question to you is very simple – why would she invent such an elaborate scheme, particularly given that it would potentially undermine the case against the very man who had allegedly murdered her husband? Why on earth would she do that? Surely it would have been much simpler to accuse you of stealing and have her housekeeper act as a witness to the theft?"

Johnson again looked uncomfortable. "I have no idea what passes through the woman's mind; most of the time I thought she was insane and she was even worse when she was drunk. In fact, I seldom saw her sober."

"And it was her insanity was it that let her to construct such an elaborate stratagem? Forgive me if I have trouble believing you. Frankly none of what you've said makes any sense – I think the insanity lies with you Mr Johnson and the incredible fictions you weave."

Johnson started to speak but Smethwick cut him short. "I have no further questions, m'lud."

"Mr Johnson, you may therefore stand down" directed the judge. "This court is now adjourned. The trial will resume in the morning. Jurors, I must ask you to ensure you do not discuss this case with anyone, including other jury members. If I find out one of you has done so, I will not only remove them as a juror in this trial, but I will hold them in contempt, and you all know what that means. It won't be just one night in gaol either. You're dismissed."

*

"So, what do you think?" said Mary. 'Do you think the jury believed us?"

Smethwick sighed. They were huddled together in a pub roughly ten minutes' walk from his home. Mary had suggested they retire to a pub immediately they had left the courthouse, but Smethwick had thought they should put at least some distance between themselves and the court in case some of the jurors or others connected with the case were there as well. It was very important they weren't overhead and the pub he finally chose was almost empty. A turf fire burned in the grate of a large, blackened, stone fireplace almost directly opposite the bar and they had retired to the cracked and worn leather settees facing it. The warmth of the fire was a welcoming sight after what proved to be an unpleasant walk through narrow rain-swept streets where they had to dodge around both horse shit and what were already deep puddles. Horse drawn carriages and heavy carts hauled by donkeys rattled past them, oblivious to the water splashed up onto people's clothes by their wheels and the hooves of the animals. The donkey carts were slower and therefore less likely to splash them, but they had to duck into doorways several times to avoid being drenched by carriages, some of the larger and grander ones drawn by as many as six horses. Some of the horse shit had been carried into the pub on the shoes of other drinkers and it mingled unpleasantly with the hop heavy smell of beer.

"I'm not sure," Smethwick said. "I think I managed to inflict some damage, but Adams was clever in leading the jury to believe that no second note existed, and that Mrs Clifton had trumped the whole thing up as an act of revenge against Johnson. He's very quick on his feet, Adams, and therefore a formidable –"

"But at least some of them must have believed us," interrupted Emma.

'The trouble is all of this is very thin stuff. We haven't got the second note to present as evidence and even if we had been able to produce it, Adams would then have argued it was the second note which was the forgery, not the first. And to be frank, that would sound not at all unreasonable. After all, we're fighting to save Michael's life and might be expected to go to extraordinary lengths to prevent him being hanged."

"I saw the gallows being erected in the town square last night when we arrived," said Sarah quietly. She spoke so softly it was almost as though she was talking to herself. She stared into the fire as she said this, reluctant to look any of them in the eye.

"That's not just for Michael," said Simon. "Three others are expected to join him. All of them were involved in the riot at Tyrone, two men and a woman. They're still hunting for the others. So, four drops are being set up."

He glanced anxiously at Mary who was sitting alongside him. Her hand rested on her lap and he covered it gently with his own.

"May God have mercy on their souls," said Mary.

Smethwick had attended a hanging in the past. It wasn't a spectacle he enjoyed, and he had sworn never to attend another. He had watched two men being hung. One, a burly fellow, had died almost immediately, his neck snapping with an audible crack. The second was a thin little man who babbled and cried even before the rope had been put around his neck. The drop failed to break his neck and it was several long minutes, his legs jerking horribly, before he finally suffocated and was still. He knew that if Michael was convicted, Mary wouldn't be able to bring herself to attend the hanging, and he would do his utmost to dissuade Emma and Sarah from attending as well. He didn't share this with them, but he was also worried the government intended to make an example of McGuinness; that they were determined to hang him no matter what evidence was offered by the defence. He knew that there were rumours Adams had in previous cases colluded with the authorities in suborning jury members. There was also the issue of the jury packing which had taken place; it was the responsibility of the local sheriff to empanel the jury and he knew it was no accident that, as a result of this, the majority of the jurors in this case were Protestant. He had had the right of peremptory challenge to get rid of at least some of the more obviously tainted jurors but he also knew that even if he had exercised this, the sheriff would simply have replaced them with perhaps an even worse set.

There was a long silence which Smethwick finally broke by offering to get them all some more beer. "I think it's whiskey we need," said Emma. "I, for one, need something to blot out this world, if only for few moments."

"I don't think I can drink," Mary said. "I'm too upset, and I think I would choke on it anyway. My throat is dry, and I can't even catch my breath."

"Try to breathe slowly and deeply," said Emma. "Focus on each breath, it'll help calm you. Daniel, would you be so kind as to fetch some water?"

"I'll fetch it now and I'll bring some whiskey as well."

He hurried over to the bar. The barman was serving someone else and was talking in a low voice to them. He seemed in no hurry to move across to serve Smethwick.

"My good man," said Smethwick, a little waspishly. "My friend is ill and needs some water."

The barman glared at him. "I'll have to get it from the kitchen. There's not a lot of call for water in these parts," he said contemptuously.

Smethwick didn't rise to the bait. The barman came back with a large tumbler of water, which he couldn't fail to notice was dirty, the outside of the glass smeared with fingerprints.

"Thank you," Smethwick said curtly. "And perhaps you would be so kind as to bring us four glasses of whiskey as well."

When the barman came to the table, he held a bottle of whiskey in one hand with four tumblers clasped in the fat yellow stained fingers of the other. He sloped the whiskey into the glasses and looked down at Smethwick.

"That will be one and sixpence, including tuppence for the glass of water."

Smethwick counted out some coins and placed them on the table where they were scooped up by the barman.

"Will ye be wanting me to leave the bottle."

"No," said Smethwick. "If we want any more, I'll come up to the bar."

"Fine so."

Mary drank the water first which seemed to calm her. The others threw back their whiskies.

Emma looked at Smethwick.

"I think I might need some more," she said.

"Me too, I'm afraid. Perhaps we'll need the bottle after all."

CHAPTER FORTY-SEVEN

Emma had slept badly, turning over and over in her head what might come out in the trial and the risks she was running. She was terrified the truth might come out – that she was the one who had murdered her husband. Rather than save Michael, she thought, I may have just put the noose around my own neck. Worse still, I can't share any of this with Smethwick. At the moment, he doesn't know it was me who killed Clifton; if he found out, then he himself would be obliged to assist Adams in seeing me hanged. Michael was his client, not me. Even if I manage to survive the questions thrown at me, Sarah might well crack under the pressure and confess. Then they were both damned.

The only thing she could cling on to was that if Johnson had voiced his suspicions to the sheriff or to Adams, then both she and Sarah would have been called in for questioning; the trial would not have been allowed to go ahead until the allegation had been fully investigated. None of this had happened, which meant her secret must be safe – for the moment at least. Johnson must have decided not to run the risk; even if both Emma and Sarah had been interrogated, he couldn't be sure Sarah would have confessed. And why would she, since it would mean she would hang as well? No, he couldn't be certain so he must have bitten down on his own need for revenge and decided to go along with the original plan to see McGuinness convicted. At least, that was what Emma hoped he had decided. She couldn't be sure. Perhaps there was something she'd missed? Perhaps Johnson had revealed what he knew to Adams and he was planning to ambush her when she gave evidence? No, she thought. That didn't make any sense. And yet perhaps Johnson had hit on a way to implicate both McGuinness and her in Clifton's murder? Her thoughts circled round and round. She would convince herself she was safe and in the next instant she was certain a trap was being set. And when she did finally fall into a fretful sleep, her dreams were haunted with the same questions, where they took on an even more nightmarish hue.

It was therefore unsurprising that when she was called to give evidence the following morning, she struggled to control the trembling in her hands and had to hide them below the level of the polished bench in front of her.

She looked at Smethwick, who gave a brief smile of encouragement.

Smethwick started by asking her about the circumstances in which the second note had been found and then led her through the subsequent conversations she had had about this with Johnson.

"Johnson says he has no memory of you supposedly finding a second note and then asking you to pass it on to me."

"So, he claims, yes."

"There is some doubt in your voice."

"He knows full well the truth of what happened. He destroyed the note rather than give it to you as I'd asked, although for what reason I've no idea."

"You say you don't understand why he acted as he did, but can you think of anything that might explain his behaviour?"

"I've no idea. Don't think I haven't lain awake on many nights trying to fathom it out, but I'm still baffled."

"Well, let me help you out, if I can. Clifton wanted McGuinness out of the way before he carried out his evictions at Tyrone. The note certainly frightened him – as was intended – but although he suspected Michael's involvement, he didn't have enough evidence to prove it. That's where Mr Johnson stepped in. The first note had been written in a way which was intended to disguise the author's handwriting and thereby his identity. Clifton knew there were very few people in Tyrone who had their letters and could therefore have written it. To get a conviction, it therefore made sense to produce a new copy which mirrored Michael's hand exactly; that, coupled with his clandestine and seditious meeting at Tyrone, was all that was needed for sufficient cause to arrest him. Then, of course, poor Mr Clifton was murdered – by persons unknown because I believe the real killer has yet to be found – and murder could then be safely added to the charges being made here today against my client."

Adams stood again. "M'lud, I have tried to exercise patience, but is there a question in all of this? This is pure speculation on Mr Smethwick's part. No new facts have been introduced and there is no evidence to support the fantastical story he has now invented. I don't think I've read better in Dickens."

There was a murmur of laughter in the courtroom.

"I'm afraid I must agree with Mr Adams," the judge said. "What Mr Smethwick has just said is to be struck from the record and the jury is to disregard it. I've already warned you once, Mr Smethwick. If you stray in this way again then I will hold you in contempt. What you said just now looked more fitting for a summing up speech than the questioning of a witness. Do you have any more questions, bearing in mind my most fervent wish at the moment is for you to stop talking and retire to your seat?"

This time the laughter was even louder, and even the judge permitted himself a smile, much to the obvious discomfort of Smethwick, who flushed a little. He tried to regain his composure by pretending to look at his notes. He decided it might be a good idea after all to retire from the field of battle.

"I have no more questions for this witness, m'lud."

There was an audible sigh of relief from the judge.

"Very well – this court is now in recess until 2 o'clock."

Emma risked a glance across at Johnson. He was staring at her with cold glittering eyes. Her cross examination by Adams would take place after lunch. She rose, but her legs were trembling so much she sank down again immediately.

"Are you alright, Emma?" asked Smethwick.

"I'm fine – felt a bit dizzy is all. You go and I'll join you all in a minute."

She waited until the courtroom had emptied and then gingerly got up again. The trembling had vanished. No doubt it would return again though, she thought ruefully, the moment Adams stands to question me.

*

"Mrs Clifton. Thank you first for your testimony this morning. It was most enlightening," said Adams smoothly.

He gave a conspiratorial smile to the jury members. "Do you hate Mr Johnson, Mrs Clifton?"

Emma looked startled. "No – no of course I don't. He was just…an employee – why would I hate him?"

"Oh, but he was much more than an employee, wasn't he? In fact, he was your paramour, someone you welcomed into your bed."

"That's, that's not true – how dare you, sir. I won't even dignify that with a response."

"Really – oh but I think you must. Bear in mind first though, before you answer, that I could also call your housekeeper as a witness and, if I do, then I will certainly ask her about this… issue…as well. So, was he your lover – yes or no?"

Emma knew she was trapped. If she said no, then she was guilty of perjury. This wouldn't perhaps have mattered but she also knew Sarah would be unable to deny this when she herself was questioned, would be far too frightened to do anything else."

"Yes," she said softly.

"Sorry – for the benefit of the court, could you speak a little more loudly."

"Yes."

"Yes, he was your lover or yes, you had toast for breakfast this morning – you need to be a lot clearer than that, I'm afraid."

"Yes…he was my lover."

"At last we seem to be getting somewhere. And were you angry when he then spurned your affection?"

"He didn't – he didn't spurn me. I spurned him – and yes, I was angry but not for the reason you suggest. I was angry because he didn't want me to testify at this trial. He even went further – he said he forbade me to go."

"Indeed, he did. And why did he do that? I think he forbade you to go to save you the embarrassment of being made a fool of in this courtroom. I submit he could see how ridiculous you were being and wanted to protect your reputation…a reputation which, I'm afraid, is now sadly damaged."

He gave a mock show of sympathy and then out of sight of the judge, inclined his head towards the jury and gave a smirk.

"That's not true – none of this is true."

Adams paused and looked at the judge.

"No more questions, m'lud."

"Mr Smethwick," said the judge. "Do you wish to cross examine the witness?"

Smethwick stood up. "If I may, m'lud. Mrs Clifton, Mr Adams has suggested Mr Johnson forbade your attendance as a witness to protect your reputation. Can you think perhaps of another reason why he didn't want you to attend?"

"Yes, yes I can. He had lied to me and said he had delivered the real note to you. He knew once I met you, the truth would come out – that's why he didn't want me to testify, he was worried I would find out."

"Thank you – no further questions."

"Do you have any other witnesses you wish to call Mr Smethwick?"

"Yes, m'lud – I would like to call Mrs Sarah Peterson."

Sarah looked terrified. Emma, too, was pale with fear. This was the moment of greatest peril she thought; if Johnson had set a trap, then this is when it would be employed.

"Sarah," said Smethwick gently. "You must find these surroundings very intimidating – I confess I sometimes feel that way myself. You just need to tell the truth as you see it – hold to that, that's all we're asking of you. Mrs Clifton has testified that you found the original note – is that correct?"

"Yes…sir…yes, I found it in a chest of drawers underneath some shirts."

"And what did you then do with it?'

"I brought it to Mrs Clifton."

"And were you aware that Mrs Clifton had asked Mr

Johnson to deliver it to me as Michael's lawyer?"

"Yes, I was – Mrs Clifton had told me of her suspicions that this must have been the real note and that the note given to the sheriff was a forgery."

"And did you agree with her suspicions?"

Sarah blushed. "It's not for someone such as I to say, sir."

"I quite understand – I have no further questions."

"Mr Adams – do you wish to examine the witness?" asked the judge.

"Yes, m'lud, but I promise you I will keep it brief."

"That will make a pleasant change, Mr Adams."

Adams gave the Judge a brief, mirthless smile.

"Mrs Peterson, you're employed as a housekeeper by Mrs Clifton – is that correct?"

"Yes sir, that's correct."

"And you have your accommodation in the Manor – is that right?"

"I do sir, yes."

"And if Mrs Clifton were to dismiss you what would happen to you?"

"I'm not sure, sir. My parents are both dead, Lord have mercy on their souls. I have a cousin in Dublin, but he has a large family – it's years since I saw him last."

"So, in short you would be homeless and without any means of supporting yourself – is that right?"

Sarah looked anxiously across at Emma. She didn't understand why Adams was asking these questions and she was hoping to see something in Emma's expression which might help. Emma stared back but she looked perhaps even more anxious than Sarah.

"I suppose so, sir," Sarah said weakly.

"So, given this, your mistress can ask you to spin whatever tale she fancies and, if she chooses, ask you to tell the most outrageous lies. Because if you don't do what she says, then at a click of her fingers you would end your days in a ditch. Given this – given this, why should we believe a word you say? I have no further questions."

He turned contemptuously away. Tears ran down Sarah's cheeks. How dare he dismiss her like this, she thought.

"I'm not a liar – I'm telling the truth."

"That's enough, Mrs Peterson," said the judge wearily. "Mr Smethwick, do you have any further questions for this witness?"

"I do m'lud."

Smethwick rose to his feet but stayed where he was, making no attempt to walk to the front of the courtroom as he would normally do.

"Mrs Peterson – are you aware of the penalties for perjury?"

"I am sir. Indeed I am."

"Thank you – I have no further questions."

"That then completes the case for the Defence," said the judge. "Does the Prosecution have any further witnesses it wishes to bring forward?"

"We do have one last witness."

"And are they here in this courtroom?"

"No, m'lud," said Adams. "The witness had family matters to attend to – they will, I'm told, ride across to Sligo tonight but won't be able to testify until the morning."

"That's disappointing, Mr Adams. I was hoping to conclude everything this afternoon – your witness is not the only one who has matters to attend to."

"I apologise m'lud."

"Very well – court is adjourned until ten tomorrow morning."

CHAPTER FORTY-EIGHT

"Mr Adams, you've told us you had one last witness to present. Is this person in court today?" asked the judge.

"He is indeed, m'lud, and I would like to call him now."

Adams turned to his side and gestured to the witness to walk up to the witness box.

"Can you state your name for the court?"

"Liam Foley – sorry, Mr Liam Foley."

Michael stared coldly across at him. Liam had been a close friend; how could he betray him like this, especially knowing what a conviction might mean? He had known Liam since they were both children. His sons had played with Liam's children and they were in and out of each other's houses all the time. In the gallery, Mary looked down at Foley with an intense hatred. Foley himself was careful to keep his face bowed, refusing to look anyone in the eye. Someone had gone to a lot of trouble to make him look respectable, buying him new clothes including grey cotton britches, calf length stockings, and stout brogues.

The shoulder-length grey hair and unkempt beard he had previously sported was gone. Now he was clean shaven, and his hair was closely cropped.

"And what relationship are you to the defendant?"

Foley shifted uneasily. "He's a neighbour of mine, we both lived in Tyrone, like."

"And would you describe yourselves as friends?"

"We were once."

"Testimony has been given that on the night Mr McGuinness was arrested he had called people to his house to listen to seditious literature. Were you there that night, Mr Foley?"

"I was, yeah."

"And what did you observe?"

"Michael – Mr McGuinness – read out bits from *The Nation* newspaper. He was the only one of us who could read, like, apart from his sister and wife. He often read to us and helped us with our letters as well, what with letters from family in America and England and rent demands and God knows what else, you know."

"And did he talk about the Young Ireland movement?"

"He did."

"I'm sorry, Mr Foley, I couldn't quite hear that – could you repeat what you just said a little more loudly so the court can hear?"

Foley coughed nervously. "He did."

"And did he incite people who attended these meetings to rise up against the authorities, to take arms against them."

"He did so."

"And were you aware he was plotting to murder a local landlord, poor Mr Clifton, now deceased?"

"Yeah, yeah, I was."

There was a gasp from the crowd.

"And were you present – in the room – when this was being planned?"

"I was yeah."

"And what happened? Who else was in the room with you?"

Foley hesitated. He had been carefully coached through the answers he should give by Adams. He had agreed only to implicate Michael and Gerard Lynch. He was terrified of inadvertently naming others who, if arrested, would then certainly hang or who, if they stayed at large, would then just as certainly murder him.

"There was just the three of us like – Michael, young Gerard, God rest his soul, and me."

"And can you confirm that Mr McGuinness and Gerard Lynch used the meeting to discuss how they might murder Mr Clifton?"

Foley again hesitated. His mouth was dry, and he knew this was the moment which would damn his soul forever, the conviction of an innocent man, the betrayal of a friend and his family. He stared at the polished lip of the witness box, but his eyes were unseeing.

"Can you answer the question, Mr Foley? Did McGuinness and Lynch conspire to murder Mr Clifton and were you a witness to this?"

"Yeah."

"I'm sorry, Mr Foley – you're barely audible. For the benefit of the court, can you repeat your answer."

"Sorry, yeah, yeah, he did."

"And how was this to be done?"

"Gerard, young Lynch, like, was to go on to Clifton's estate and shoot him."

"Just so I understand you correctly, Mr Foley – you have stated that McGuinness and Gerard Lynch plotted together to murder Mr Clifton and agreed Lynch should carry this out by shooting Mr Clifton – is that correct?"

"Yeah"

Adams nodded and turned to address the jurors. "Now as we all know, Lynch's attempt to murder Mr Clifton failed – in fact, it resulted in Mr Lynch's own death. There was then a second attempt on Mr Clifton's life which this time was successful." He turned back to address Foley. "So, the first murder attempt failed. Was Mr McGuinness involved in the second attempt on Clifton's life?"

"No, no, I don't think so…sure he was in prison."

"But what if other conspirators of his, members of the Molly Maguires, knowing what he wanted, went on to murder Clifton? Is that not possible?"

"I don't know – I can't answer that."

But it's possible?"

"Well…maybe…yeah maybe."

"And following Clifton's murder what then did you do?"

"I went to see the sheriff, Mr Flynn, to tell him what I knew."

"Mr Flynn, the former sheriff, now himself dead, is that right?"

"Yeah, that's about the height of it."

"One final question Mr Foley, if I may. The threatening note which was thrown through one of Mr Clifton's bedroom windows. Did that come from Mr McGuinness?"

"It did – I saw him write it."

There was another gasp from the crowd.

"And did you see what was written in the note?"

"Yeah, I did like enough."

"Another note has allegedly been written and is purported to be the real note. We have been asked to believe the note which has been presented in evidence to the court is a forgery." He walked back to the bench where he had been sitting and brought back a copy of the note. He handed it to Foley.

"This is the note handed to Mr Flynn by Mr Johnson – who is also present today and who has already testified as to its authenticity. Mr Foley, is this note the one that Mr McGuinness wrote?"

"Yeah, it is yeah."

Adams moved closer to the witness box and pointed at the note which Foley was still holding.

"And is the lettering that of Mr McGuinness? Is this his hand?"

"Yeah, it is so."

"Thank you, Mr Foley. I have no further questions."

"Mr Smethwick, do you wish to cross examine the witness?"

"Yes, m'lud. If I may."

"Would you describe yourself as a good friend of Mr McGuinness?"

"Arra, I thought I was at one time sure enough."

"And now?"

Foley flushed red. "No, not now I suppose…"

"And what you've told Mr Adams is the truth is it?"

"Well yeah…"

"The truth being that Mr McGuinness conspired with a Mr Gerard Lynch to murder Mr Clifton?"

Foley stared back at Smethwick. He started to open his mouth but then closed it again.

"That is what you believe to be the truth isn't it – that your friend – although friend no longer it seems – conspired to murder Mr Clifton? This is what you've told us, under oath – is that not right?"

"Well, yeah…"

"And not only was he behind the first attempt on his life but was responsible for his final murder as well?"

Foley looked uneasy. He sensed he was being led into a trap but couldn't see where the snare might lie.

"Yeah…he was."

"And the three people in the room who plotted his murder were you, Gerard Lynch, and Michael McGuinness?"

"Yeah…yeah, that's right."

"So, if it was just the three of you, and Gerard was killed

during the first attempt on Clifton's life, who were the conspirators Mr Adams said were responsible for the second attempt?"

"Sure, I don't know…I don't know what you mean" stammered Foley.

"Well, let me help you. McGuinness was in prison and Gerard was dead, which leaves just you does it not? So, are we to believe that you murdered Mr Clifton, that it was you who savagely beat the poor man to death?"

"No, no – that's not right – you're twisting my words."

"Well who murdered him then, if not you?"

"Sure, I can't say, I don't know but it wasn't me, I had nothing to do with it. I'm not up to that sort of violence… I'm a peaceable man."

"Are you Mr Foley, are you indeed? Well, if that's the case why did you not go to the police immediately after the meeting with McGuinness and Lynch? And if you didn't do it then, why did you not go after the first attempt on Clifton's life. Why, in fact, did you wait until Clifton had finally been murdered before you went to the sheriff?"

Foley looked frantically across at Adams. His lawyer started to rise to his feet to object but realising he had no grounds for this slowly sank down again.

"I…I'm a simple man…I did what I thought was right… that's all, that's all I did. I did nothing wrong sure. I did nothing wrong."

"Really? You did nothing wrong? You sat in a meeting

where there was a conspiracy to murder someone and yet you did nothing. There was then an attempt to kill poor Mr Clifton and still you did nothing. But you did nothing wrong, did you? And then, when he had been murdered, only then did you do something; only then did you go to the sheriff. But you did nothing wrong. It seems to me if Mr McGuinness is to face a charge of conspiracy to murder, then so should you, so should you, Mr Foley."

Smethwick turned away as though to sit down, but then whirled round again. "One final thing, Mr Foley. Has Mr Adams explained to you the serious penalties for lying, for committing perjury?"

Foley looked anxiously across at Adams who stared grimly back at him. Nothing had been said about the penalties for perjury.

"He didn't, no. No-one said anything to me about this perjury something, is it?'

"Let me make it easy for you, Mr Foley. Have you lied to this court?"

There was a long pause. Foley looked at Adams hoping for some sort of signal as to how he should answer. He was becoming increasingly worried and confused as to what he should say. Adams had his head down staring at his papers.

"I repeat, Mr Foley, have you lied to this court?"

"No, no, I haven't sure."

"And no-one has tried to bribe or threaten you to say the things you've given in evidence?"

"No, no."

"Be very careful, Mr Foley. Remember you're under oath. Did anyone attempt to influence the evidence you've given today? Are any of those people in the courtroom today?"

Smethwick gestured with a sweep of his arm, taking in the people behind him including Adams and those who sat in the gallery.

"No, no-one said anything. I'm my own man so."

"Your own man – is that right? Are you really your own man, I wonder, or have you been bought? I have no further questions for this witness."

"Mr Adams, do you wish to cross examine the witness?"

"I do m'lud."

Adams rose. Foley was looking both shaken and terrified and was desperately looking at Adams to now save him, to loosen the snare pinched tight against his throat.

"Mr Foley, Mr Smethwick has claimed that you yourself might have been part of the conspiracy to murder Mr Clifton. Yet, I submit there is a simpler explanation for the fact that you didn't go to the police following the meeting with McGuinness and Lynch or indeed after the first attempt on his life. You were frightened, were you not? Terrified of what might happen to you if you betrayed your co-conspirators. Is that not the case, Mr Foley?"

"Objection, your Honour," cried Smethwick. "Mr Adams is leading the witness."

"I agree, Mr Smethwick. Have a care Mr Adams," said the judge.

"I apologise, your Honour – I was simply trying to get at the truth of what happened."

"So, Mr Foley, why did you not go the police following the meeting with McGuinness and Lynch?"

"I was frightened – sure, I was terrified. McGuinness is a fierce man. God knows what might have happened."

"But once he was in prison, and Mr Lynch was dead, you felt it was then safe to do your duty as a citizen and reveal what you knew?"

"I did, yeah. I had to, see – I was sick to my stomach with disgust at it all. I wasn't sleeping – "

"That's fine, Mr Foley," said Adams. "We understand all too well how frightened you must have been. Mr Smethwick has also said there were only three conspirators involved; yourself, Mr Lynch, and Mr McGuinness. But there could have been others, members of the Molly Maguires, people you were unaware of who McGuinness was involved with, who finally murdered poor Mr Clifton?"

"There may have been – yeah, I'm sure there were."

"Thank you, Mr Foley, and thank you as well for your courage in appearing as a witness in this court."

He turned to the judge.

"No further questions, m'lud."

"You may step down Mr Foley" said the judge. "The court is now adjourned until tomorrow morning."

*

"Foley's evidence did us a lot of damage but at the same time, I think I may have done enough to undermine it," Smethwick said. "He certainly didn't come across as an honest man and there were members of the jury who clearly didn't believe a word he said. But we're not yet in the clear – we don't know how many jurors have been bought and how that might affect what now happens."

They had gathered in a small room adjoining the courtroom. Immediately after leaving the judge's chambers, Smethwick had sought out Emma and Sarah and also asked Mary and Simon to join them.

"He must have been bribed or threatened," said Mary. "I've known Foley since we were children together; he's a quiet man, and there's no more harm in him than a lamb in the fields. I think he'll have been threatened or perhaps his family were; he has a sick wife and five children, all under the age of ten. He was driven off the land when the soldiers raided Tyrone."

"I've heard tales Reith is going to offer him a fine new stone house on his land with twenty acres to farm," said Emma.

"I thought Reith was clearing all of his lands, offering the tenants passage to Liverpool or the States?" said Mary.

"He is," said Emma grimly, "but for some reason he seems to be making an exception with Foley."

"Is he, indeed?" said Smethwick. "Well, that looks like our answer. It's what we do with it is the problem."

*

"Mr Adams, as prosecuting Counsel in this trial, can you now address the jury?"

"Thank you, m'lud.

Adams rose to his feet. He stood directly in front of the jury box, so close he could have reached out and touched the juror immediately in front of him.

"Gentlemen of the jury. You have heard all of the evidence and must surely now agree that this man," he pointed to Michael without turning his head, still looking directly at the jury, "is guilty of rebellion and sedition, a heinous crime which, if allowed to go unpunished, will only spark further rebellion by its citizens. It will light a fire which could destroy this country and the rule of law. We have already seen what the violence of the mob can unleash; the murder of innocent citizens, the destruction of property, the theft of goods on which the prosperity of this land depends. It cannot be allowed. This man –," again he pointed at Michael, but this time turned to face him "– this man, is also responsible for the murder of one of the most respected landlords in this county; the note hurled through one of Clifton's windows proves it. It is in his handwriting. And not only did he make one attempt on Clifton's life – using one of his poor dupes – no, he was part of the conspiracy which was successful at the second attempt. Clifton, still suffering from the injuries incurred in the first attack, was savagely beaten to death. It wasn't a single shot to the head which killed him – which at least would have been mercifully quick – no, he was beaten, stabbed, and kicked to death. And which of you can imagine the horrible agonies he suffered until he finally succumbed and died. Worse still, the perpetrators, having beaten him to within an inch of his life, left him to die in pain and agony for long unendurable minutes which then stretched to hours. Imagine that, imagine yourselves lying there in the freezing cold darkness, racked with pain, until at last mercifully released from your suffering by death.

"The jury are aware of the facts of this case – it is for them now to reach a verdict and that verdict must be that Mr McGuinness is guilty and should be dealt with by the law in the harshest of terms. Only then can we hope to staunch the wound which is destroying this country."

Adams gave one last baleful look at Michael and returned to his seat.

"Mr Smethwick," the judge said, "can you please now give your summing up for the Defence. It's already been a long day and some of us have beds to go to, so please keep it short."

Smethwick rose. Like Adams, he too moved closer to the jury. He paused for a moment and looked at each one of them in turn. Some looked directly back at him with what seemed to him to be a show of defiance, others simply looked uncomfortable. Three of the jurors seemed to be sympathetic to Michael's plight, and he decided it was these he would attempt to influence most.

"Gentlemen of the jury, you have to perform a very serious task, one which you will all remember for the rest of your lives, some of you with satisfaction that you have made the correct decision, but others who will feel the weight and guilt of what they have done in condemning an innocent man, at best, to transportation to the colonies, and at worst, to the gallows, to an awful death.

"So, your burden is a heavy one, one where you must find my client not guilty if you have even the smallest doubt, because if you do convict him, then you have condemned not just this man but his family, his wife and children, his sister who sits in the gallery above you, and the many friends who love him. I have spent long hours with this man, and I know he is innocent. If you convict him, I will give up the law, because I will have lost faith in the judicial system in this country and can no longer bear to be a part of it.

"And why do I feel he is innocent? Because there is no real evidence against him. The note produced by the prosecution purports to be in Michael's handwriting. But there was a second note, destroyed by that man." He pointed across at Johnson. "Clifton's own wife has testified to that effect, that the second note uncovered by her housekeeper was the real note thrown through that window by persons unseen, not the trumped-up forgery presented to this court. And why should she do such a thing – a woman who loved her husband dearly – unless she was convinced the note she had been given by her housemaid was the real one. It was from a sense of injustice that an innocent man might be convicted that she has appeared before the court. What possible reason could she have to do this unless she was convinced of my client's innocence?

"And what of Mr Adams's so-called key witness, our Mr Foley? He claims he was once a friend of Michael's. Do friends betray each other in this way? Would someone betray his friend knowing what he said would send that man to the gallows? Would he betray him too, knowing the suffering he would inflict on his family and friends? No, either this man lied and was not a genuine friend or there is something else going on here. He's said he did nothing wrong – nothing wrong, although he failed to go to the police immediately he knew of the conspiracy to murder Mr Clifton. Nothing wrong, although it is evident he may – as one of the only three conspirators – himself be said to have played a major role in Clifton's death. Mr Adams has said there may have been other conspirators but failed to produce any proof of their existence. So why should we believe Mr Foley – the man who did nothing wrong, the man allegedly too frightened to go to the police until Mr Clifton lay dead, the same man who was, however, prepared to give testimony to this court. He found the courage to appear here, but it apparently deserted him when he most needed it. Still, he did nothing wrong.

"And what is the reason for his newfound courage, the man who did nothing wrong? Well, I think we all know the answer – the answer, gentlemen of the jury, is that he has been bribed, that he has been paid handsomely to lie to the court. Mr Foley, I'm afraid – and we must all pray for his soul because he is surely damned – has committed perjury, has lied to this court and if you believe that lie, then it will send Mr McGuinness to the gallows. Your duty, your duty, therefore as members of the jury, is to find my client innocent, to see through the monstrous lies presented to this court.

"Let me ask you finally, supposing you were to find him guilty, how you could reconcile such a verdict with the gaols, gibbets, and murders we hear of every day in the streets and see every day in this country? Merciful God. What is the state of Ireland, and where shall you find the wretched inhabitant of this land?

"You may find him perhaps in a gaol; the only place of security. If you do not find him there you may find him flying with his family from the flames of his own dwelling — lighted to his dungeon by the burning of his own hovel. Or you may find his bones bleaching on the green fields of this country. Or you may find him tossing on the surface of the ocean, driven to a returnless distance from his family and his home by desperation, by hunger and disease.

"Have I misrepresented the situation, or do you recognise the truth of what I've said? You are called upon in this trial to convict an innocent man, to make him yet another victim of the remorseless terror which grips this country and drives its prosecutors to condemn innocent men and women, to see them hanged or transported when they have already suffered enough. A guilty verdict in this trial would be a defiance of shame, of honour, of truth, which flatters the persecution, which tramples you all under foot. You must find my client innocent of the charges laid against him. This, at least, would be one step in righting the wrongs which afflict this country, the tiniest of steps, but from small beginnings can justice at last begin to grow and thrive in this land. Gentlemen of the jury, it is for you to decide; it is for each of you to decide how this verdict will go down in history. An awful weight has been placed upon your shoulders and I trust you will do your duty."

The court was silent for a moment and then the judge spoke.

"Gentlemen of the jury, the defendant has been accused of two very serious crimes, one of fomenting rebellion and sedition and a second of a conspiracy to murder of one of our most respected citizens. Tomorrow morning you will be sequestered to consider your verdict on both counts. Yours is a heavy responsibility and I trust you will consider matters fully before making your determination."

The Judge banged his gavel.

"The court is now adjourned."

CHAPTER FORTY-NINE

There was a murmur of excitement in the courtroom as the foreman of the jury rose to deliver the verdict. Michael gripped the rail in front of him. His knuckles were white, and he was struggling to maintain his composure. He glanced up towards the gallery. Mary was looking anxiously down at him. She tried to smile but it died on her lips almost immediately.

The judge spoke. "Have you reached a determination and are you ready to deliver your verdict?"

"We have, m'lud. On the charge of fomenting rebellion and sedition we consider the defendant…guilty. On the charge of conspiring to murder Mr Clifton, we find the defendant… guilty."

There was a palpable gasp in the courtroom. Michael slumped against the rail.

Mary screamed. "No!" she cried and fainted.

The judge looked up. "Someone take that woman from the courtroom," he said.

Simon bent down and lifted Mary up into his arms. She was still unconscious. He took her out, the other spectators moving away to allow him passage.

"Michael McGuinness, you have been found guilty of sedition against the Crown and a conspiracy to murder an eminent local landowner. It is my solemn duty to now pronounce sentence on you. Do you have anything to say before I pass sentence?"

"I am an innocent man, falsely accused. I have nothing to say to this court."

"Very well," said the judge. "Given the seriousness of these crimes, the only sentence I can give is that you should be hanged. May God have mercy on your soul."

Emma and Sarah were in tears. So too, was Smethwick. He had feared this outcome but even though he had prepared himself for it, he was still shocked. He looked at the jury and noticed that several of them were also crying.

The judge, though, was unmoved. He turned towards the jury.

"I thank you all for the service you have rendered. You are dismissed."

Adams fought to suppress a smile, looking across at Smethwick and giving him a curt nod. He hadn't been overly impressed with Smethwick's overblown speech at the end; he thought it was better suited to the theatre rather than a court of law. The man was a windy fool, he thought, even more so because he clearly thought he had had a chance of winning. In a few days' time, McGuinness would hang along with the rest of the rabble who had been arrested and convicted.

*

Smethwick arranged for a carriage to take Simon and Mary back to his house. She was still in shock. Smethwick whispered to Simon that once they got there, she should be given brandy and then put to bed immediately. He said he would return as soon as he was able. He then asked Emma and Sarah to join him in a drink at a nearby hotel.

"What can we do? There must be something? Can we appeal the sentence?" asked Emma anxiously.

Smethwick was depressed. He thought their cause was hopeless, but he needed to put on a brave face for Emma and Sarah. He sighed.

"Yes, we will certainly lodge an appeal. We can make an appeal to Labouchere – he's the Chief Secretary for Ireland. I'm afraid I don't know much about him; he's only been in post since last July so I've no idea as to whether an appeal for clemency would find favour with him – still, we have to try. We also need something to base the appeal on. I think some of the jurors will have been suborned and if we can persuade them to swear depositions to this effect, we can lodge these with him. We also need to see if we can persuade Mr Foley to retract his evidence. If we can, and he is prepared to swear an affidavit to this effect before a magistrate, then their case collapses and Labouchere must surely set him free or, at the very least, commute the sentence to transportation."

"He sounds French," said Emma.

"Well, his ancestors were – much more I don't know."

"Is there anything we can do?" asked Emma. "I can't bear the thought that poor Mr McGuinness might be hanged. We will both," she looked at Sarah, "do whatever is needed to try and free him."

"I know you will. We really need to get to Foley."

He thought for a moment.

"I think Mary is the person to do this – Michael is her brother, and both of them grew up with Foley. They considered him to be a friend. No, Mary is our best hope. Once she's up and well again then I'll talk to her."

*

They could smell the gangrene as Simon pushed open the door. Flies rose in a cloud around their heads. Mary reeled back, feeling the bile rise in her throat. She almost vomited but managed to hold it down. The hovel was dark inside, and it took a few moments for their eyes to adjust. Against the far wall was the slumped body of a woman and as they moved nearer, they could also see the corpses of three children – a girl and two boys. They were both silent for a moment and then left, Michael pushing the door shut behind them.

"Should we bury them?" Mary whispered.

"No, you've seen the bodies littering the roads and fields as we travelled. None of them were buried. No, it's best to leave the bodies where they are."

"You're right, of course. It's just that –"

She left the sentence unfinished. They had seen so many horrible sights on their journey to Cathlar, one of the villages owned by Reith and where they had been told Foley was now living. They had seen dogs in packs tearing flesh from corpses, crows squatting on bodies, picking casually at empty eye sockets. It was a vision of Hell which once seen could not be unseen.

"I think we should leave the horses here – we can make our way up to Foley's house on foot. We don't want to give him any warning of our approach," said Simon.

Mary nodded. She suddenly felt overwhelmed with fatigue, felt that if Simon wasn't with her, she would drop to the ground and sleep where she fell.

Most of the houses in the village had been abandoned. Some stood roofless, open to the elements, others looked intact, but their doors stood open and they could see with a glance that they were no longer occupied. Foley's house stood on a small rise at the end of the village. Emma had been right; the house was much larger than the hovels they had passed walking up. It had been built with limestone blocks and had a slate roof and mullioned windows. A brick chimney stood proud above the house, thin ribbons of smoke drifting lazily into the air.

A woman walked out in front of them as they neared the house. She was dressed in rags, her feet bare, and was shivering in the cold. Mary judged her to be around thirty but with her sunken features and grey pallor she could have passed for a woman in her sixties, if not older. She held a bundle against her chest which Mary initially thought must be clothing.

"Will ye have pity on a poor woman?"

"We have no food, I'm afraid," said Simon, "but I have some coins perhaps."

"It's not food I want, sir – I need money to bury my child. It's for the coffin you see."

She held out the small bundle in front of her and Simon and Mary noticed to their horror that it contained the corpse of a baby, one which was barely a week or two old. Simon hastily pushed a handful of pennies into her hand.

"God go with you," he said.

"And with you, sir, and with you."

As they got closer to the house, the door suddenly opened, and Foley now stood in front of them. He had been careful to pull the door closed behind him and obviously didn't want them to go inside. Mary thought he must have been watching their approach through one of the windows.

"What do you want?" he said gruffly.

"We want to speak to you," said Simon. "You know Michael is to be hanged, don't you? Do you not feel any guilt about that? Are you not ashamed?"

Foley stared defiantly at them.

"Why should I be ashamed? They would have convicted him anyway, whether I gave witness or not. I have five childer and a wife to feed; should I let them perish when I have a chance to save them? Look around – what do you see? Half this village is dead from hunger or fever, the rest wandering the roads. Is that what I want for my own family? You can't judge me – you have a well-fed belly, money in your pocket. What would you know of our lives and how we suffer?"

"Liam," said Mary gently, "Michael was your friend – you've known him half a lifetime. I know how it is – God knows I do – but this is not the way. You cannot do this and live with yourself, condemning an innocent man, my brother to –"

She couldn't finish, tears springing to her eyes.

Foley stared at the ground. "Go – you're not wanted here," he said angrily. "Go, for the love of God, leave me alone." His face full of anguish, he turned and went back inside.

Mary and Simon stared at the closed door. Then Simon gently took Mary's elbow, pulling her away.

"It's no use, Mary. We're wasting our time."

"No, he can't – we must try again."

She banged on the door. The house was silent. She fell to her knees, careless of the mud, and wept.

"Please, please – I can't bear it."

Simon hesitated and then pulled her to her feet.

"Come on my love, let's get you home. Foley is dead to us, but Smethwick will think of something. He won't let us down, I'm sure of it. Please – we need to go."

He led her away. Rain was now falling steadily but Mary was oblivious to it. If she had been on her own, she would have thrown herself to the ground, given up and wished only for death. But Simon held her up and together they made their way back to the horses. He made sure she was safe to ride, and they left.

CHAPTER FIFTY

Smethwick had fared better. He had managed to track down two of the jurors. Both confessed they had been bribed. They had been badly affected by how the trial had ended and were only to eager to sign depositions. Smethwick had then gathered together Mary, Simon, and the others and told them he intended to take a carriage to Dublin Castle the following morning. Mary had asked whether she might accompany him, but he had explained it was better if he sought an audience with Labouchere alone. He was unlikely to be swayed by a grieving relative; hard facts and evidence would be the only things which might persuade him.

The original plan by the authorities had been to hang Michael alongside the other villagers they had arrested, but it had since been decided it would make more of a spectacle if he was hanged on his own. They also wanted to use a short drop. Where a long drop was used, the criminal's spinal cord was usually severed, and they died almost immediately. With a short drop, the convicted man or woman would endure a slow, agonised strangling which might last twenty minutes or more. Relatives had been known in such circumstances to mount the gallows and, hugging the accused around their knees, use their full weight to drag them down so their neck might break and release them from their suffering.

Smethwick had explained what was intended to an appalled Emma and Sarah.

"Even with a short drop," he said, "the condemned will sometimes lose consciousness within mere seconds – we can only hope this is true for Michael."

"When is this to happen – the hanging, I mean?" said Emma.

"Saturday week – there will be a market that day and the authorities are therefore hoping there'll be a good number in attendance."

"And when will you travel to see Labouchere?" asked Sarah.

"I leave tomorrow."

Emma hesitated. "Might I travel with you?" she asked.

Smethwick looked anxiously at her. "Normally I would be delighted to have your company. It will be a hard journey though – even by carriage – and the roads are very dangerous now. People have been shot dead, mobs have besieged carriages, turning the occupants out on to the road and seizing the horses; whether to sell or eat, I don't know."

"Still...I would like to go – if you'll allow me. I might be of some help in Dublin. Sometimes a woman can be more persuasive than a man..."

Smethwick looked at her. Emma was a very attractive

woman. Yes, he thought grimly, there was a class of men who might be sufficiently beguiled by her, would be susceptible to her charms. It was worth trying at least. The journey itself would also be dull and he couldn't pretend he wasn't attracted to her himself. She had spirit and a fierce intelligence, and he always loved women like that. His own mother was from the same mould. His father had abandoned the family before he had reached his fifth birthday. She had been left alone to bring up him and his younger brother. Despite being poor, she had been determined both should have a good education, make something of themselves. She had died of cancer of the bowel two years previously, after a long and horrible illness. There wasn't a day since that he had not thought of her.

"Yes, yes, perhaps you could be of some assistance. I can't pretend that having someone to converse with won't make the journey pass both more quickly and pleasantly either."

Emma looked at him. She was smiling and there was a glint in her eye. Did she know, he thought, that I might be attracted to her? Yes, probably, there was very little women missed, particularly in terms of their effect on men. He smiled back.

"It's agreed then. You'll both stay again with me tonight and we'll leave tomorrow at first light."

*

"What's that you're looking at, Charles?"

Trevelyan looked up from the papers spread out on the desk in front of him.

"Oh, nothing you might be interested in – just some old Irish ballads and poems I've been collecting."

Labouchere raised his eyebrows in surprise.

"Really – you never cease to amaze me."

"Why?"

"Well, Irish ballads – why might you be interested in those?"

"Because some of the airs and melodies are quite wonderful – they're also full of emotion. There's often a terrible sadness which runs through them."

"And that would appeal why?"

Trevelyan looked embarrassed. "I can't say – it just does. How might I help you?"

Labouchere laughed. "I don't need your help, Charles – I simply popped in to see how you are. My clerk tells me you've been working very hard lately – in fact he says you work such long hours, he's surprised you bother to go home at all."

"Well, even I need to sleep sometimes," said Trevelyan grimly.

"Well, I don't know how your poor wife puts up with it. Mine wouldn't, I know, although spending less time with her does sometimes seem a very attractive proposition."

"She knows my work is important to me."

"No doubt, no doubt," said Labouchere. "I have a difficult case I need to pronounce on today – some lawyer is coming to see me about this wretched McGuinness affair. You've heard of it, I'm sure."

"Half the country's heard of it. He's to be hanged for sedition and a conspiracy to murder a local landowner I believe."

"Yes, and this lawyer wants clemency – claims some of the jurors were suborned."

"Well, if that's true, then that's a very serious matter and perhaps his appeal has some merit."

"It might well have merit," said Labouchere, "but this is a political matter – I'm told he's to be made an example of to deter others from pursuing a similar course."

"I understand the politics, but the fair administration of justice is surely more important."

"Perhaps, perhaps. But justice is a slippery concept – what is more just? The clemency given to one man or the suppression of a rebellion which might otherwise cost many more lives?"

"Well, you must do what you feel is right," said Trevelyan.

Trevelyan was annoyed but he was careful to hide it – I don't need a lecture on moral philosophy from a fool like you, he thought. "Look, if that's all, I have a lot of work to get through today and I must really make a start," he said.

"No, no I quite understand." Labouchere replied. "We all have work to do. Perhaps a spot of brandy this evening if you've time. I can tell you how it all went."

"'Yes, why not – is seven alright?"

"That means I will have to work late myself. Still, as long as I don't make a habit of it."

"No indeed – that would be most unfortunate for you."

*

"So, how did it go?" asked Mary anxiously.

Smethwick looked at Emma. They'd had a long conversation about the meeting during the carriage ride back to Sligo. Neither of them was sure as to what the likely outcome would be. Emma had thought Labouchere unsympathetic and cold. Smethwick was more hopeful. Now they were in Smethwick's living room, comfortably settled in armchairs and a long settee in front of a log fire.

"I honestly don't know," said Smethwick. "He said the final decision would have to be made by London, by Russell himself, apparently, although why, I simply cannot understand."

"I think I know," said Simon. "It's a political decision and therefore not one Labouchere can make on his own."

"Yes, you're probably right," said Smethwick thoughtfully. Simon was clearly far sharper than he had at first appeared. "I had hoped he had the power to make the decision himself but clearly he's reluctant to do this."

"Did he say how long it would take?" said Mary. "It's only two days until…" She left the sentence unfinished.

Simon clasped her hand in his and gently squeezed. Emma glanced at Smethwick, her look a warning to him not to say anything which might alarm Mary.

"I'm sure we'll hear before then. Labouchere knows the date, is aware of the urgency."

"It will be alright, Mary," Simon said, his voice scarcely more than a whisper.

"Will it?" said Mary. "Why should this be alright when everything else, everything, is so fucking awful?"

She burst into tears. The room was silent. No-one spoke.

CHAPTER FIFTY-ONE

Smethwick attended the hanging on his own. None of the others had wanted to be there. He felt depressed, as if he had let everyone down. Nothing had been heard from Dublin Castle. He had thought about travelling again to Dublin to press their case, but he knew it was useless. It would have taken the best part of a day to travel there and getting back in time would have been an issue. There had been rumours that people would quit the town as a protest rather than have to witness what was about to unfold and he could now see that this was indeed true. The streets had been eerily quiet during the short walk from his house to the town square. He had been greeted by a small troop of soldiers on horseback together with a handful of policemen when he entered but none of the townspeople were there. The gallows stood at the far end of the square. The soldiers were a contingent of the 8th Dragoons, an Irish unit, intimidating in their foot-high brown bearskin caps.

Smethwick's last hope lay with the arrival of the mail coach from Dublin; if there was to be a reprieve, it would be amongst the Dublin newspapers and packets of letters delivered that morning. The official responsible for overseeing the execution, Sir Anthony Felton, had delayed it at Smethwick's request. It had been agreed that Michael should remain in his cell until after the coach's arrival and an hour had already passed beyond the time it should have arrived.

Shortly before noon, the coach suddenly appeared, stirring up a cloud of dust as it rattled into the square. Smethwick ran towards it. The coachman was unaware of the importance of his arrival and wearily stepped down to the ground, his bones aching after the long journey.

"I need to see the mail," said Smethwick.

"Really – and who might you be?"

"Look, this is important – a man's life –"

Felton, who had now walked over, cut across him.

"Let's see the mail. Now."

The coachman stared for a second. Then he turned and started to tip out the packets of mail and bound bundles of newspapers on to the ground. Impatiently, Smethwick knelt. Pushing the newspapers aside, he quickly sifted through the mail packets. He saw it at once, a letter addressed to Felton, sealed with the government's red crest. He picked it up and handed it to him. Felton nodded and, breaking the seal, tore open the letter. He scanned the contents and then smiled down at Smethwick.

"Can I see it?"

"Certainly, you can. Congratulations. It seems your client has a reprieve after all."

Smethwick stood up and took the letter. He read it carefully, hardly daring to believe that it was true. The last paragraph, though, brought him up short. Michael had been spared a hanging but because of the alleged seriousness of his crimes he was to be transported to the colonies for a term of seven years. Still, he thought, as awful as the sentence was, it was far better than the alternative.

*

Smethwick had hurried across to the prison to let Michael know what had happened. He had been relieved, but this quickly turned to dismay as he realised his sentence would separate him from his wife and children.

"All is not lost, Michael – the sentence is for a term of seven years. After that, you'll be a free man. You don't need to come back – you can make a new life for yourself in Australia. You may not be parted from Sorcha and the boys either – they could choose to join you."

Michael looked at him, a spark of hope in his eyes. It quickly disappeared.

"And where would I find the money to bring them out – sure, I have nothing. What poor savings we had went long ago. Even if she did come, would they even allow her to see me?"

"I don't know Michael – but I know this, Sorcha would

move heaven and earth to join you. If it comes to it, I'll lend her the money myself."

"I'm grateful, Smethwick, but you've done enough for us already – I couldn't allow you to do this."

"Michael, this is no time for false pride – if need be, I'll give her the money and there's an end to it."

Michael stared at the ground for a moment and then slowly raised his eyes.

"No. I really don't want to put this on you."

"It's done, Michael. Now, no more foolish pride. Mary has seen Sorcha and told her what's happened – she's bringing her here tomorrow to see you."

Tears sprang in Michael's eyes and he used the heel of his hand to wipe them away.

"I'm sorry, Smethwick, it's just that it's been so hard."

His voice cracked with emotion and Smethwick grasped his shoulder.

"I know, Michael, I know, but now there's hope."

*

Mary and Simon walked towards the prison. They had agreed that Smethwick would meet them there and bring Sorcha with him. Together with Rian, she had stayed with the lawyer the previous night. Mary and Simon had taken an adjoining room.

Sorcha had remained silent. When they had first arrived and entered the dimly lit bedroom, she had been lying in her bed with her back to them and she had made no effort to turn to face them, or to acknowledge their presence.

Mary told her what had happened but still she stayed motionless. Mary wondered if Sorcha had even tried to understand what she had just told her, whether her hearing had shut down with her speech. Were people's words now a meaningless babble, muffled sounds behind a wall of glass Sorcha had herself erected and had no interest in breaking.

Mary and Simon's walk slowed as they neared the prison.

"We can't tell him about Declan – it would break his heart and he's suffered enough."

"When would we tell him then? He's got to know at some point."

"He does but not now – I'll find a way of telling him later. It will be too much for him and seeing poor Sorcha in her current state is already upsetting enough."

"Yes, alright – he's your brother and if anyone should know how best to handle this, then it's you."

As they rounded a corner, they saw their lawyer standing next to the entrance of the prison. Sorcha stood beside him and she looked at them dully as they approached.

Smethwick drew to one side to whisper to Mary.

"He doesn't know about what's happened to Sorcha, so this is going to be difficult, a terrible shock for the poor man, and he's suffered enough already. Will you tell him as well about Declan?"

"No, that can wait – this is hard enough as it is."

"Yes, I know, I'm sure it will be – well we'd better go in."

*

Michael hurriedly got to his feet as he heard the sound of visitors approaching. There was a rattle of keys, the heavy iron door to his cell swinging slowly open as the gaoler led everyone in. Smethwick came behind him, gently holding Sorcha by the arm.

Michael hurried towards her and hugged her tightly. Taken by surprise, Sorcha allowed herself to be held but made no attempt to hug him back, her arms remaining stiffly at her side.

Michael's eyes were full of tears. He pulled away a little and, still holding her, started to stroke her hair. Very slowly, Sorcha raised her arms and put them around him.

"Sorcha, my love, I've missed you so much."

His voice cracked with emotion.

Sorcha looked up at him. There was a hesitancy in her eyes. Her voice, when it came, was hoarse and faint, scarcely more than a strangled whisper. She uttered a single word, tears sliding slowly down her cheeks.

"Michael."

CHAPTER FIFTY-TWO

The two men were waiting for them as they made their unsteady way down the gangplank of the ship onto the dock. The men's clothes were stained with grease and they both wore battered black hats, pushed so low on their heads that their eyes were virtually hidden. The taller of the two addressed them and gave a mock bow.

"Welcome to Liverpool, the finest city in this fair land. So, where next for you, if I may be so bold? Is it New York you're headed for?"

Mary tried to ignore him, placing an arm around Sorcha's waist to move her ahead and motioning for Rian to join them. Simon was intrigued by the two men, curious as to what they were up to.

"What's it to you?" he asked.

"Why, we can take you to the best ship broker in the city, a man able to book you on the finest ships to New York, or Canada, or indeed anywhere else you need, and all at the best prices too."

"We already have on onward passage booked. But thank you for your kind offer."

"Well there's lodgings too; there's some terrible slums here. You'll be needing somewhere to stay whilst you wait for your passage and we can take you to some great accommodation less than a ten-minute stroll from here. We can arrange a porter to take your belongings too – those chests look a fair weight."

Mary could see Simon was hesitating – their ship did not sale for another two days and it was true they would need somewhere to stay.

"Simon, we don't need their help – we're fine as we are."

Simon smiled ruefully at them. "Well, thank you again but we can manage ourselves."

The man seized Simon's arm in a tight, almost painful grip, and gazed intently at him. He leaned in close and Simon recoiled from his foul breath. There was barely a tooth in the man's head, Simon noted with disgust, despite the fact he must be only in his mid-twenties.

"You're sure now? This city's full of the most terrible thieves, robbers, and murderers who would slit your throats for a penny piece and leave you to die in the gutter. We can protect you, but can you protect yourselves, if you get my meaning?"

Mary stepped forward and roughly pushed the man away. He staggered and almost fell and looked furiously round at a group of men who had stopped to watch the fun and were now openly laughing at him.

"It's you who'll need protection if you don't leave us alone, you gobshite – now fuck off out of it or I'll fetch the police."

"Watch your mouth, lady, and while you're here, you'd better watch your back too."

He drew a knife from a leather scabbard attached to his belt, pulling it out just enough to make sure she got a good look at it, and then pushed it down into the scabbard again with a leer. He gestured to the other man, who had struggled not to laugh when he saw his mate pushed backwards. They walked away, the taller man attempting a swagger which again prompted laughter from the cluster of men behind them.

"She's a fierce one," muttered the smaller of the two once they thought they were out of earshot. "I wouldn't mind riding her, I can tell you."

"If you want to ride her, you'll have to wait until I've warmed her up first with a knife – no bitch gets to do what she did and live."

A small group of men had watched the encounter and one of them came across.

"You did well there – those men prey on passengers as they leave the boats. They get a commission from the ship brokers for every emigrant and sometimes they'll sell you a cancelled ticket themselves, or perhaps a child's ticket for an adult. They're full of tricks and many's the poor soul has found themselves cheated out of their money before they've even walked off the gangplank. If you need accommodation, I can take you somewhere – it won't be the finest you've ever stayed at, but the prices are fair and the landlady honest."

Mary looked at him. He was well groomed and looked to be in his early thirties. She felt an instinctive trust in him.

"That's very kind of you. I'm Mary, this is my...friend, Simon, and this is my sister-in-law, Sorcha. And this little fella is Rian. And you would be?"

"Lawrence Wheeler. For my sins I'm a physician. My role is to assess the health of those passengers alighting from some of the poorer vessels, the cattle boats. It's those that have the greater concentration of disease, both typhus and dysentery. I don't have time to look at all the ships coming in, I'm afraid – not in this lifetime anyway."

"Is there much disease here, Mr Wheeler?"

"Yes, I'm afraid so – we've had to establish a quarantine station here. Sometimes there is so much contagion on a ship, the Port authorities order the ship turned around and sent straight back to Ireland, the poor souls on board never setting foot here at all."

"I can't believe how bad our crossing was," said Mary. "I, for one, would certainly not wish to be turned around and sent straight back. I thought I would die, I was so sick, and shortly after that I hoped I would die just to escape the misery."

"I don't think there was a man, woman, or child who wasn't sick on that boat," said Simon. "The waves must have been thirty feet high – I still don't know how the ship managed to stay afloat. One lad was killed by a barrel sliding across the deck, another poor woman lost overboard. It was awful and to think we've still got the voyage to Australia ahead of us."

Wheeler looked sharply at him. "Australia is it? Why would you go there?"

Sorcha, who had been walking alongside, nudged Mary's elbow with her own. Mary took its meaning immediately.

"We have family there" she said.

Wheeler knew there was more to the story but decided not to pursue it.

"It's an awful long journey," he said. "Four months if you're lucky and a lot worse if you're not."

"We know what we're facing, Mr Wheeler," said Mary.

I wonder if you do, thought Wheeler. If that were really true, you would have remained at home because only fools and the reckless chose Australia over the States or Canada. The only people he knew who travelled to Australia were convicts and they had no say in the matter.

Sorcha suddenly stopped. "Rian – where's Rian?" she cried.

Mary spun round in alarm. She saw him – he was standing a little way back, gazing transfixed at a juggler spinning brightly coloured balls into the air, catching them and immediately releasing them again, throwing them higher and higher each time. A small crowd had gathered to watch. Sorcha had seen him in the same instant and she darted back, pulling him away.

"Rian – leave it, will ye. You must stay with us; you gave me an awful fright."

"But Ma," Rian squealed.

"Don't Ma me, come away out of that."

The juggler stopped, gathering the balls with ease back into his hands. He winked broadly at Rian who, delighted he should honour him in this way, grinned back. After that, Sorcha held him grimly by the hand, virtually dragging him along the streets, Rian's head spinning like a leaf in a whirlpool as new wonders presented themselves. Men with strange slanted eyes and ponytails sauntered in front of them, other men strode past wearing frock coats and black top hats. A few men sat on the ground with begging bowls in front of them, their arms raised aloft in supplication, red-rimmed eyes flicking nervously from side to side.

"Forgive me, but to get to the boarding house we have to first go through some of the more unsavoury parts of Liverpool," said Wheeler.

"Don't worry on our account," said Sorcha. "Sure, we'll have seen much worse at home."

It was the stench they noticed first as Wheeler turned into a narrow alleyway. The centre of the lane was an open sewer, clogged with shit and foul-smelling stagnant water. The smell was so bad they could taste it on their tongues. They crept down the side of the lane to avoid it but ragged children around them splashed carelessly through it in bare feet, calling to each other and laughing. The end of the lane though opened on a large square surrounded by imposing terraced houses linked by an ornate colonnade. Mary marvelled that such squalor should be so close to such an extravagant display of wealth.

"You don't mean for us to stay here, do you?" said Sorcha.

"No," laughed Wheeler. "There's some lodgings not far from

here – we need to cut through a lane at the far end of the square and then it's a little way down."

The alley they now turned into was much broader than the one they had emerged from. It was cobbled and neat houses bordered it, jostling for room with merchant and tradesmen's shops. There were blacksmiths and leather makers, shops selling fine lace and linen, their wares displayed on benches outside. People scurried to and fro, women with wicker baskets of fruit and vegetables, others with loaves of bread and pastries. Couples dressed in fine clothes idled before the shops, tradesmen shouldered their way roughly through the crowds carrying timber and buckets of mortar. Both Mary and Sorcha felt ashamed of their rough clothing and hugged the sides of the alley, their eyes downcast. Suddenly Wheeler stopped.

"This is it," he said, standing before a large terraced house. "Journey's end."

Mary stared. A placard was hung in one of the windows fronting the street.

"Boarders welcome. No Irish."

"The sign," she said timidly.

"Don't worry about that. I know the landlady and I'll vouch for you."

"Are you sure?"

"Would I have brought you here if I wasn't? Come – let's go in."

*

Emma had given them the money for their passage. Now they stood on the dock, shivering against the cold. A watery sun had just risen but it was still obscured by fog. What seemed to be dozens of masts loomed through the mist and the hulls of ships appeared and then vanished as the fog swirled around them. Immediately in front of them, stood their own ship, people waiting patiently to board, their belongings on the ground around them. A man stood checking their tickets and as he waved them through, they could see men dragging heavy wooden chests up the gangplank, whilst their wives and children followed on. They either carried their remaining belongings in heavy canvas bags or simply clutched them to their chests.

Mary looked at Sorcha and Simon. Rian held Sorcha's hand and stared in awe at the vast ship.

"Well," said Mary, "this is it. A new start for all of us."

"Yes," said Sorcha bitterly. "A new start but little hope."

"Hope is enough," said Mary. "Hope and God will see us through."

And with that she turned towards the gangplank.

CHAPTER FIFTY-THREE

The last time Michael had been allowed to see his wife and sister had been in prison in Sligo. From there, he had been transported with a small group of eight other convicts in two carts to another prison on Spike Island, a low fortified rock which sat within Cobh harbour.

There, the convicts were made to change into prison clothes of drab, brown canvas. They transferred to their ship, the barque Parmelia, the following day. Michael first caught sight of his family and his sister as he ascended the gang plank. Sorcha had screamed his name and he had glanced round, immediately spotting her, Rian, and Mary in the crowd. He called back to them and for a moment stood still, half turned around. He was pushed roughly in the back by one of the soldiers.

"Keep moving."

Michael glared at him. He gave one last despairing glance back, and resumed his reluctant progress upwards. Once on deck, and despite their heavy chains, the prisoners rushed to the rails to try and get one final glimpse of their loved ones but were soon beaten back with blows and shouts from the soldiers. They were forced down below deck and the ship made ready to depart. From below, they could hear the heavy rasp of canvas as the sails were lifted into position and the grinding roar of the anchor chain. When they were finally allowed back on deck, the ship was already some distance from the shore.

It was a dank November day, the grey sky almost indistinguishable from the roiling sea beneath it but it was just possible for the convicts to make out the shapes of their grieving families and friends still standing on the dock. Their faint moans carried across the waves, a low bass line against the shrieking treble of the seagulls. Some of the men stood with tears in their eyes, others swore quietly to themselves, whilst others affected not to care, laughing loudly with their companions. Michael stood watching for a long time, even after many of the others had turned away. He had told himself he would never leave and yet here he stood, wrenched away from the land of his birth by dark forces beyond his control, torn from everything he loved most in the world.

Would he ever see his family and Mary again, he wondered? They had promised to come out after him but what they were going to was so far beyond all of their imaginations that it was impossible to conceive of a time when they might all be together again. He gave an involuntary shiver against the cold and looked up at the sky; it had been mainly overcast but for a brief while, the sun had emerged and blessed him with its warmth. Now it had vanished. Darkness fell.

ACKNOWLEDGEMENTS

I'd like to thank my Mum for all the tales she's told about growing up on a farm in Ireland, many of which I've used both in this novel and my previous one, *The Faces That You Meet*.

I'd also like to thank Susan Cahill my editor (susancahill. co.uk). Her advice has been invaluable in helping me to shape the novel and to improve on my very poor first draft.

Thanks as well to Jackie Vernau (jacquelinevernau.com) who has done a brilliant job proofing the book, and to Mark Thomas (coverness.com) for his design and typesetting skills and guiding me through the grim process of getting this novel published.

I relied on a number of historical sources in researching the novel Including, *The Graves are Walking* by John Kelly, *The Famine Plot* by Tim Pat Coogan, *The Great Irish Famine: A History in Four Lives* by Enda Delaney, and *Famine Echoes* by Cathall Poirteir. Of these, I particularly admired and enjoyed John Kelly's book.

I also spent time In Ireland, visiting the National

Famine Museum in Strokestown, County Roscommon (strokestownpark.ie), and EPIC, the Irish Emigration Museum in Dublin (epicchq.com). I can also recommend a recording by Declan O'Rourke, *Chronicles of the Great Irish Famine*, which I stumbled across in my visit to the National Famine Museum (declanorourke.com). This is a stunningly beautiful collection of songs, all of them original compositions.

Remarkably few novels have been written about the famine but of the ones which have been published the best is *The Killing Snows* by Charles Egan. This novel also forms part of a trilogy.

Many of the incidents in this novel are based on real events. The anathema or excommunication near the start of the novel is a real incident but the circumstances have been altered; the real "Mary Hogan" sent her children to a Protestant school but she was pregnant at the time and the priest did curse everything about her including "everything that would spring from her."

The trial at the end of the novel is a conflation of two incidents: the trial and conviction of William Orr in 1797, a member of the United Irishmen who was executed in what was widely believed at the time to be "judicial murder" and the trial and hanging of a landless labourer, Brian Serry. I'm indebted to Pat Orr, William Orr's ancestor, for drawing my attention to his trial. In real life he was hanged but I decided to have his sentence commuted to transportation to the colonies. The speech in the novel by his defending lawyer may seem overblown but is very closely based on the real speech by his lawyer John Curran.

Charles Trevelyan remains a deeply controversial figure

even to this day. Having studied most of what has been written by him I wonder myself whether he might have been autistic or perhaps had Asperger's, but this is purely speculation. Others may well reach the conclusion that he was a high achieving psychopath. What is not in doubt though is that he demonstrated an extraordinary lack of empathy with the sufferings of the Irish people who were the victims of his belief in laissez faire economics and the importance of a free market. Trevelyan wrote to Lord Monteagle of Brandon, a former Chancellor of the Exchequer, that the famine was an "effective mechanism for reducing surplus population" and was "the judgement of God". He went on to write that "The real evil with which we have to contend is not the physical evil of the Famine, but the moral evil of the selfish, perverse and turbulent character of the people."

I'm tempted to draw parallels with Margaret Thatcher's free market ideology and the imposition of that ideology on the British people. This was the woman, of course, who observed that there is no such thing as Society.

Trevelyan, along with Sir Stafford Northcote, was instrumental in the creation of the modern Civil Service. You can draw your own conclusions as to the value of that.

There are also fascinating parallels with the United Kingdom's Brexit crisis and the repeal of the Corn Laws which brought down a government.

Prime Minister Theresa May's repeated attempts to gain parliamentary approval for the European Withdrawal Bill echo those of the Liberal Whig Charles Villers' proposed motions for repeal in the House of Commons every year from 1837 to 1845. In 1842, the majority against repeal was 303; by 1845 this had fallen to 132.

The resulting split within the Conservative Party led to the formation of the Liberal Party which drew its membership from disaffected members of both the Conservatives and Whigs. The controversy over the repeal of the Corn Laws led directly to the creation of the modern Conservative Party.

Patrick MacDonald, Cambridge, August 2020

ABOUT THE AUTHOR

Patrick MacDonald is married with two sons and lives near Cambridge.

He has published two novels, *The Faces That You Meet* and *Darkness Falling*. Both are available in Kindle and paperback editions on Amazon.

You can stay in contact with Patrick via his website:

www.patrickmacdonald.online.

Or via the following social media:

www.facebook.com/patrickmacdonaldwrites
www.instagram.com/patrickmacdonaldwrites
www.twitter.com/patrickmacdonaldwrites

Made in the USA
Coppell, TX
16 May 2022

77837356R10225